Cyber Case

Cyber Case

Nikki Rashan

www.urbanbooks.net

Urban Books, LLC
78 East Industry Court
Deer Park, NY 11729

ISBN 13: 978-1-60162-278-5
ISBN 10: 1-60162-278-3

First Printing August 2010
Printed in the United States of America

10 9 8 7 6 5 4 3 2 1

Distributed by Kensington Publishing Corp.
Submit Wholesale Orders to:
Kensington Publishing Corp.
C/O Penguin Group (USA) Inc.
Attention: Order Processing
405 Murray Hill Parkway
East Rutherford, NJ 07073-2316

For my sweet Twinkie

Acknowledgments

As always, I'm grateful for the opportunity to share another creation with you. This book has been a blast to bring to life and I pray that you, the reader, enjoy the story even more than I loved writing it.

A special thanks to my MySpace and Facebook friends; I appreciate all of your support and I thank you for the connections we've made.

I am fortunate to say that my circle of friends remains consistent and I'm thankful for each of you.

To B . . . 7-14-02 . . . is a day I'll always cherish. Our journey has been one of the greatest gifts of my life and with each continued step I am ever by your side.

Dawn, Bernell, Shenay, Pam, Alta, Monique, Valerie and Bo: Love and appreciate you all.

My JJ & CooCoo: You shouldn't be reading this until you're eighteen. However, thank you both for your patience all those days and nights you (somewhat) granted me the quiet needed to work. Always love my little chicas.

A final thanks to my greatest inspiration, E. Lynn Harris. This one is for you.

Prologue

Two nights ago I dreamt I was choked to death by a snake. In the dream I was in my car singing to a song on the radio and headed home after work. When I slowed to approach a stoplight and lifted my right foot from the gas to the brake, I felt a light tingle around my ankle underneath the cuff of my pant leg. A smooth, slippery movement crept around my calf and up my thigh. Its grip tightened, latching around my skin. My heart pounded in panic as I began to slap at the bulging motion under my slacks. Just as the light turned green, a petrifying shiny black snake with deep gray eyes bolted from beneath the belt that circled my waist. A horrified scream escaped my mouth as the intimidating snake thrashed its slinky tongue and hissed in my face. I reached for the steering wheel, intent on moving forward. However, within a second it had wrapped its body around my neck, and forced my head backward. My arms flailed in fear as I felt myself losing the ability to breathe. Blaring car horns became faint, and my body weakened. My last vision was of my girlfriend, Melanie. She appeared at the driver side door, struggling to open it, her hands pounding wildly on the window. The snake peered in her direction, became silent, and clenched its body around my neck one final time.

In bed I sat upright and reached for my collarbone. I exhaled, grateful to realize that I had been dreaming. Through the darkness of the room I looked to my side. Melanie slept soundly, peacefully. I snuggled into the silhouette of her body and placed her hand against my breast. She stirred and instinctively hugged it with her palm.

"Are you okay?" she mumbled. Her warm breath against my neck soothed some of the tension that remained from the pressure felt in my dream.

"I'm fine. Go back to sleep," I whispered.

She wasted no time and was back asleep in just a moment. I closed my eyes, wrapped her arm around me tighter, and tried to erase the memory of the snake's intimidating gray eyes that flashed in my mind.

Chapter One

"What time is it?" I mumbled, startled by a loud bang coming from the kitchen. That meant that the broken screen door had slammed shut, a sign that Melanie hadn't caught hold of it before it whammed closed against the wooden frame. I stretched my body and reached for my cell phone on the floor. It was 11:35 P.M.

My feet throbbed. I kicked off the black patent leather pumps I was still wearing while I slept on the couch after a twelve hour working day. My skirt had crept up my thighs and rested around my waist like a cushioned floatation device. It seemed that although I hadn't completed the task, I had begun the process of undressing as the top three buttons of my silk blouse were open to reveal damp, sweaty skin from sleeping in my clothes. It was an unexpected mid-June eighty degree night and I hadn't turned on the air conditioning. I sat up and released the clip that held up my curly hair. It fell against my back and rested stiffly. I ran my right hand through the strands to loosen the curls that had hardened from the mousse I used in the morning before heading to the mortgage office my brother, Ronan, and I owned.

A light crept through the entryway to the living room when Melanie opened the refrigerator. I could hear her rumbling about, moving aluminum cans and tossing aside packaged lunch meat, undoubtedly searching for the chocolate pudding I had forgotten to pick up for her after work.

"Jo," she groaned softly.

Melanie loved chocolate pudding. She'd eat two or three small containers a day, often substituting spoonfuls of creamy chocolate for a bowl of cereal, or slurping on her favorite snack upon late night arrivals like tonight. I appreciated her craving most when she'd lick my skin after spreading the tasty treat on various parts of my body.

"Jo," Melanie repeated, just as she entered the room.

I leaned my head backward and looked at her upside down. She bent to kiss my lips. "You forgot my pudding," she stated, disappointed, with a rumple to my hair.

"I'm sorry, I forgot, Mel. It was late when I left the office and it slipped my mind," I explained.

"What am I going to eat now?" she asked.

I smiled slyly.

Melanie and I had been a couple for four years, though we had known each other for five. We met one morning in the Cook County courthouse after I had spent an hour waiting to see the judge and five minutes before him pleading my case as to why I was speeding through a construction zone. I was headed to my grandmother's house on South Halsted on an early Sunday morning. It didn't matter to the judge that the new driver of the church van had inadvertently bypassed my grandmother's house that morning so she had called me at my north side Chicago duplex to take her to service. I was racing across town to assist my grandmother on the two-mile trip to the Catholic Church she had attended for forty years when I was pulled over by Officer Hamilton. He was a cocky young new-badge wearing fellow who was impressed by his authority. I asked him to overlook what would be my first speeding offense. How was I to know that construction workers were doing overtime that Sunday morning as I sped through orange cones and construction signs? They surely must have been taking a full-crew break as I didn't recall seeing one orange-vested person. He merely smiled smugly at my explanation, and took twenty minutes running my plates and driving record before handing me my ticket. My six-year clean driving record was smeared.

As I headed toward the rear of the small courtroom saving thirty dollars off my fine and a two point recovery on my license, I caught sight of a woman wearing an off white business suit with a black V-neck blouse underneath. She sat near the back, briefcase open and papers strewn about her lap. She bit gently on a pen before sliding it behind her ear and opening a folder. Her eyes lifted briefly as I approached and then passed by. A minute later, while I stood in the hallway viewing the enclosed courtroom map, she appeared behind me.

"Need some help?" she asked.

I didn't turn around, but could feel her five feet nine inch frame towering close behind my five feet four inch body. After a few moments without a response, she turned sideways and leaned her right forearm on the glass. She turned a set of chestnut brown eyes to me. In response I returned her gaze, wondering why she was so close in my space.

"Just trying to find directions to the room where I can pay my fine," I finally answered, holding her stare.

"I know exactly where that is," she said, and took hold of my hand, guiding my first finger and placing it on a small square on the map. "Go down one level to your right."

"Thank you," I said, eyeing her suspiciously and tugging my hand from her grasp.

"Most welcome," she smiled confidently, rising back to her full stance and peering at me.

We held eyes for a moment before I turned around and walked a few feet away to the elevators. After I pressed the down arrow I couldn't help but look back toward the courtroom. There she stood holding the door handle, staring back at me. She laughed arrogantly, as if saying I knew you would, and re-entered the courtroom. Cocky, I thought. Cute too. Physically, she was just the kind of woman I found attractive.

Ironically, several weeks later I was meeting a client for lunch at a bistro two blocks away from the courthouse. After we were seated, Ms. Cocky breezed through the entrance with two gentlemen. She had a briefcase in her hand and was sporting a dark blue pantsuit, white blouse, and comfortable, but fashionable heels. Though her femininity shined through the suit, I caught glimpses of a slight tomboy demeanor. Particularly the athletic spring in her step and the way she tugged at her pants when she sat down at a booth three rows kitty corner from mine. She leaned back comfortably in her seat, knees parted, sitting similar to a woman bench side at a basketball game. While I examined Ms. Cocky I found myself temporarily inattentive to my client who was discussing her poor credit rating. Ms. Cocky was pretty in a sweet handsome way. She wore her hair combed back into a short flip at the top of her neck. Her skin was an unbelievably smooth and vibrant umber brown. Her large brown eyes drooped slightly at the outside corners below perfectly arched eyebrows. Her smile was wide as she exchanged conversation with her friends. She studied the menu before the waitress stopped to introduce herself to them.

Just as I was ready to encourage my client that I could still find her a decent interest rate despite her previous bankruptcy, Ms. Cocky excused herself and headed toward the back of the restaurant, past where I sat. Her eyes rested on mine for a moment, though she continued to walk by. For some reason I felt slighted, having spent two minutes fully engaged in her every movement only to be ignored upon her noticing me. I turned around and watched her enter the restroom. Temptation to follow her rose inside, though my client's pleading eyes hindered my departure. When Ms. Cocky returned to her seat, she never looked my way again.

Once I informed my new client that our next meeting should occur at my office, I left the tip and got up from my seat. Unexpectedly, Ms. Cocky's full attention was directed at me. She held up a finger to her lunch partners and stood to greet me as I was about to pass her by. Again, she crowded my space and spoke a mere few inches from my face.

"No more speeding tickets for you, right?" she joked.

Inside I blushed, strangely grateful that she had apparently ignored me intentionally.

"I'm obeying the law," I responded with a small smile.

"Melanie." She extended her hand. I took hold of her firm grip.

"Jovanna."

"Nice to meet you. Hey, I'm a lawyer. If you find yourself in need again, call me." She reached for a business card held in a small clip that was in her pocket. "For anything," she added.

Sideways I glanced at my client whose helpless mood seemed suddenly intrigued.

"I will. Thank you." I attempted to end the conversation for business reasons. Apparently Melanie had no problem shamelessly flirting with another woman in front of her friends, however, my client and I did not know each other on a personal level and I preferred to keep it that way. My experience had taught me that most lesbians were more discreet and a bit more conservative in their flirtations, particularly around straight individuals and especially when unsure if the object of interest was same-sex loving or not.

"Do you have a card?" she asked before I could walk away.

I lowered my head and exhaled, then peered at her through the curl that had fallen over my right eye. I handed her a card from my wallet which was still in my hand.

"J&R Financial," she read, then placed the card in her clip. "Let's connect soon."

"Yes, okay," I quickly agreed, then shuffled my bewildered client toward the door.

I chose not to call Melanie. While she was certainly attractive and charming, she was a bit more aggressive than I preferred. In high school I had intimately befriended one guy, Philip, to whom I lost my virginity. Since graduation, I had only dated two women. My immediate assumption about Melanie was that someone as forward as she was likely the womanizing type that I had managed to steer clear of since my first girlfriend at eighteen. We dated four years until age twenty-one when my then girlfriend decided she wanted to spread her wings and explore opportunities with other women. A year later I found myself in my next relationship with a woman nine years my senior whom I had thought would have been beyond the exploration phase. It turned out she was indeed past the exploration phase, yet had entered the maternal phase. At twenty-four and still in the process of completing my Master's degree, I was not yet ready for parenting. Therefore, our relationship ended. For a year I occasionally went on a few dates, however, I am the settling down type and many of the women I encountered were not. I even considered dating a man and had lunch with the cousin of one of my brother's friends. I immediately shunned that idea. The simple sight of chest hair creeping through the buttons of his shirt grossed me out. After Philip and the way he grunted, groaned, and slid his slim teenage body over mine, I knew that a heterosexual woman I was not. It wasn't that he turned me gay; I don't believe a person has the power to do that. He did, however, confirm what I had internally suspected: my gay versus straight balance scale weighed heavily toward women. Philip was the only man I had been with sexually, and the one-hour lunch encounter with the cousin of my brother's friend was the closest I had been to the opposite sex since.

For three months Melanie left weekly voice mail messages on my work phone. Diligently, every Monday she'd call and ask if I were free for lunch anytime that week. The final message that caved me was when she reminded me that my card contained my work address and if I didn't call her back, she'd just have to show up the following Monday to be sure I was all right. I laughed at the message, as stalker-ish as it sounded, and returned her call the next day. We met for drinks that Friday evening after work.

Melanie was working her second mojito by the time I arrived at the energetic bar. An extended late-afternoon closing had delayed my arrival to meet her.

"I apologize," I offered when I joined her at a tall, circular wooden table and sat on a red-colored stool.

"I'm patient," she smiled. "You must know that by now."

"Yes, I see that," I answered just before I stopped a red-headed waitress passing by and asked for a glass of white wine.

"Sure, I'll let your server, Bonnie, know," she responded cheerily.

"And why is it that you're so persistent?" I asked. "If you go around picking up all women you see in the courthouse I can't imagine you'd be hurting this bad for a date," I joked.

Melanie laughed and twisted the mint leaves in her small glass. She wore gray slacks and a long-sleeved button down shirt. The top three buttons were undone revealing a small, but decent sized cleavage. Unlike our previous two encounters, that evening I noticed a small and extremely sexy beauty mark mole just above the left side of her lip. My eyes were magnetized toward it. I briefly imagined planting a sweet kiss on it, but I was getting way ahead of myself.

"I don't pick up all the women I see," Melanie said. "Just the cute ones like you."

"How could you even have known I'd be interested?" I asked. "Most people wouldn't guess that about me."

"I know. I thought I'd take a chance though. I'm sure it came off as aggressive, but I'm harmless." She grinned.

"We'll find out," I said as I accepted my glass of wine from Bonnie.

Melanie's eyes danced around the large black curls on my head and the thick baby hairs around my temples.

"What are you?"

"A woman," I answered with a smirk.

"Funny." She chuckled. "You got this Dorothy Dandrige look to you. The hair, your skin color . . . what ethnicity are you, if you don't mind my asking?"

I chuckled on the inside, reminiscent of the many times my grandmother told me that I resembled the famous actress. We both shared the same full round face, straight nose, pouted lips and shy dark eyes.

"Well, you already asked if you didn't notice," I said before I took my first sip. The wine was delicious with a surprising sweet twist. "I'm Puerto Rican and black," I told her when I lowered my glass to the table.

Melanie nodded. "Are you from Chicago?"

"Yes, lived here my whole life. I grew up with my grandmother on the west side of town. And you?"

"Originally from Gary, Indiana. My parents moved us here when I was five, me and my brother, Ferris. Everyone still lives here."

"Is your brother older or younger?"

"He's younger by three years, but he's already married with two kids."

"My brother is the opposite. He's older by six years and looks like he has no plans on settling down anytime soon."

"And what about you?" Melanie asked.

"What about me what?" I asked, unclear what she was asking.

"Are you settled down?" she wanted to know.

"If I were I wouldn't be here, would I? Well, I shouldn't be at least," I added.

Melanie was quiet for a moment. I sensed the pause in her response was for good reason. I waited a few more seconds yet she didn't say anything. Surely I wasn't out having drinks and entertaining conversation with an attached woman.

"Are you settled down Melanie? You have a girlfriend?"

She took a sip of her mojito. "No, I don't have a girlfriend. I'm single. I wouldn't be out with another woman if I were settled down."

I sighed with relief. "Good."

"But," she began then stopped when Bonnie dropped by and asked Melanie if she wanted another drink. Melanie responded with a quick *please*.

"But what?" I asked impatiently.

"My ex and I broke up about five months ago, but we still live together."

Her admission wasn't surprising as I was familiar with ex's continuing to live together until one was able to move out, sell the house, or whatever the situation may be. Although I understood her predicament, I had no wish to become a third party to their affair. I finished my wine in three swift swallows.

"Melanie, it's been nice meeting you." I took hold of my purse, pulled out a ten and left it on the table.

"Wait, where are you going so fast?" Melanie asked and lightly reached for my elbow when I stood up.

"I appreciate you being honest with me so quickly, I really do. And I understand your situation. But until you're completely free from any ex attachments, we don't need to talk. Call me when one of you moves out," I said as kindly as possible, and left the bar.

Six months later she called. A month later we went on a date. Two months afterward we were an official couple. During our courtship I first learned that Melanie had never dated or so much as kissed a man. Her ex, Samantha, the one she had been living with, had been over her head in credit card and student loan debt and needed a year minimum to pay off some bills before being able to afford living on her own again. Melanie obliged, though they lived very separate lives during the time with both eagerly anticipating their final separation. Melanie assured me that any emotional connections to Samantha had dissolved long before our meeting in the courthouse. By the time we united for our second date, her heart was completely healed and she was ready to move forward with someone else.

With each day that we got to know each other better, I found Melanie increasingly intriguing and complex in a way that took some adjustment. When Melanie was engrossed in a case, as she examined documents and researched information for her client she could ignore my presence like I simply didn't exist. At other times she was the complete opposite, requiring incessant attention by way of a rub to her shoulders while she sat at her laptop, or pleading with me to cuddle next to her while she read from a manual. I easily learned how to read which mood she was in. If I stopped by her townhome after work and she didn't hear me enter, I would head on back out. However, if I stopped by and was greeted with the sweet call of my name before I had one foot in the door, she needed me that night.

Both of our schedules were fairly busy, though Melanie made time to stop by my office for lunch when able. I returned the favor once every couple of weeks as well. We spent most weekends together, attending shows in the theatre district, shopping at some of the city's best malls and boutiques, and expanding our palates by exploring various restaurants. The first time we made love Melanie was as fully engaged into satisfying my desires as I was determined to please her. Unfortunately I soon learned that Melanie's love making pattern was just as intricate and intense as her attention span when she worked. Either she was all about sex, being creative, spontaneous and passionate, or she was disconnected, her mind too distracted by whatever case in which she was involved. Though I was a lover of intimacy, a nymphomaniac I was not, so I adapted to Melanie's patterns and settled into a comfortable groove of sex multiple times one week, and possibly none the next.

When we moved in together two years ago, we each left our individual places and found a two-bedroom, two bath condo in Boystown, a spirited large community populated with Lesbian, Gay, Bisexual and Transgendered (LGBT) individuals. We adored the colorful environment, the restaurants and coffeehouses, and the feeling of togetherness as we grocery shopped, danced at local clubs into the early morning hours, or simply walked the neighborhood hand in hand on warm summer nights.

At this point in time we had developed a relaxed and satisfying relationship, each of us thankful for the open communication we shared, delighted by the smiles we could place on the other's face, and appreciative of the strong future we were building together. I could honestly say that at age twenty-nine I was feeling more secure and serene than I had in my adulthood thus far. The mortgage lending company Ronan and I ran was bringing in a steady flow of clients, helping first-time buyers realize their dreams while assisting others through a refinance and in some cases, prevention of foreclosure. Melanie, now thirty-three, had flourished into a competent lawyer, no longer distracted by skirts and heels in the courtroom, but focused on her work and protecting the interests of the defendants she represented.

"What would you like to eat, love?" I asked.

From behind Melanie ran her hands down the front of my blouse, using her fingertips to circle over my nipples through the delicate fabric. She then unclasped the remaining buttons and leaned far forward to kiss around my shiny belly button ring.

"You're going to fall over, Mel," I laughed, though I enjoyed the tenderness of her kisses on my skin.

Melanie stood, removed her jacket, and tossed it on the loveseat to my side. She walked in front of me and lifted me by both hands.

"Let's get you out of the rest of these clothes," she suggested, and reached under my skirt, slipping me out of my panties first and then releasing the zipper to my skirt. She removed my blouse and then bra until I stood naked, sweaty and already ready for her. In return I removed Melanie's blouse and slacks, then her black boy shorts and cotton bra. She laid me on the couch and began a slow grind between my legs. Our bodies moved together fluently. An hour later I nestled my head between her breasts. Just as we began to fall asleep she mumbled.

"Don't forget the chocolate pudding tomorrow, Jo."

Chapter Two

The following afternoon I was nestled under an oversized pillow in the corner of our beige chenille sofa, comfortable in shorts and a tank top. Melanie was out for a run by the lakefront while I chilled out with my friend, Alinandra; we called her Ali for short. Ali and I had met about five years prior through Olivia, a woman I had gone on a couple of dates with during the six month time frame preceding Melanie's final phone call that brought us together. It quickly became apparent that Olivia was not interested in a relationship while I was steadfast in my desire to have one. In light of this fact, Olivia introduced me to her friend Ali, a woman hung up on another woman who refused to settle down with Ali, even though that was Ali's wish. Olivia thought we might connect with our common craving for companionship. That didn't happen as I immediately became Ali's much needed support cushion and friend.

During our first meeting Ali talked about Noni, her ever elusive obsession, for nearly an hour. I learned that they met and became best friends during their junior year of high school. The friendship escalated to lovers after Noni had several too many shots of vodka while celebrating her twenty-first birthday. Before that encounter Ali had only experienced being with a woman on three other occasions, all of them with a volleyball teammate in college. After the unexpected rendezvous with Noni, Ali's affection shifted overnight from a warm fondness for Noni to falling in love; or least she believed she felt that way. Though Noni was surprisingly sexually gratified by the experience, she had only dated men. She had no desire to make a commitment to Ali, nor exclude men from her life. So they remained friends and part-time lovers to Noni's delight and Ali's acquiescence. That was nearly seven years ago and nothing had changed.

Ali had just finished making freshly squeezed lemonade and had brought two glasses into the living room before she took a seat on the rug atop the hardwood floor. That was so Ali. She was one of the gentlest, sweetest, most humble women I had ever met. Her demeanor was delicate, her voice light. She had a Bohemian quality about her and spoke highly of the universe and our need to love all elements of the earth. Whether others considered them alive or not, Ali believed that the tiniest ant had a life spirit and that the trees breathed energy into our world each day. She was a vegan, rarely drove the hybrid car she owned, and would open her wallet to any homeless person that asked for her assistance. She was an amazing spirit. I had yet to understand why she settled for a less than gratifying relationship with Noni.

"Tonight she's going out with Curtis," Ali told me after she took a sip of lemonade and started toying with the frayed bottoms of her jeans.

I took a sip as well. "Your lemonade is delicious as usual," I commented.

"Did you hear what I said?" Ali asked.

"I heard you, Ali. What do you want me to say?"

"Ask me how she met Curtis."

How Noni met Curtis didn't matter to me at all, but I asked anyway to appease Ali. "How did she meet Curtis?"

"Through one of her clients."

Noni was a hairstylist at a downtown Chicago salon in which she had the opportunity to meet clientele of various backgrounds and social status. Even though Noni only shared half of her heart with my friend, I still liked Noni as a person. I respected how honest she was with Ali and how she had chosen not to enter into a monogamous relationship in which she would not be fulfilled. Noni knew this would hurt Ali even further. Ironically, Ali admired this same quality in Noni and not once blamed Noni for her own disappointments. For some reason she had surrendered to the ongoing lesson she felt the universe was teaching her.

"He's a former NBA player whose career never took off. After two years he was cut," she continued. "This client thought they might hit it off."

"And what does Noni think?"

"You know Noni, she's all about socializing and having a good time. If it sounds like fun, she's up to it."

"So what are you going to do tonight while your girlfriend is out on a date with a man?" I asked.

"I'm not sure," she responded.

"Well, I'd hate to see you unoccupied with your mind wandering about what Noni may be up to. Mel and I are going to Murmur tonight if you want to join us," I proposed. "You know it's always a good time."

"I'll think about it," Ali answered. "Is everyone else going?"

Everyone else included three other couples that made up my and Mel's circle of friends. There was Prestin and Jaye, an astonishingly gorgeous power couple who cocked heads wherever they went. Prestin was a Chicago club promoter who hosted well-attended third Saturday of the month girl parties at Murmur, a funky nightspot reminiscent of the 1970s disco era with dark walls and brightly colored strobe lights that flashed across the lighted dance floor. The club closed on Mondays and Tuesdays, and allowed promoters to host specialty nights every Wednesday through Sunday. Prestin's events bring in the largest crowd, many who venture out just to see her. Her silky straight, dark brown chin-length bob and modelesque features landed her on the cover of many local newspapers and magazines as one of Chi-town's most beautiful and powerful professionals. Aside from events held at Murmur, Prestin was highly sought after by organizers of other events seeking her promotional expertise, her assistance on how to attract the Lesbian, Gay, Bisexual and Transgendered community to their particular affair, or simply wanting to use her name as a sponsor. At thirty-five, Prestin had established herself as a stand-out face among Chicago's "who's who."

Prestin was also famous for rocking amazing stilettos to her Murmur parties. Patrons couldn't wait to see what designer shoe Prestin would be wearing. Fashionable stores and boutiques often sent stilettos to Prestin with hopes that she would wear the pair to an event and provide free advertising for their store. Her partner, Jaye, often teased about the fun they would have in Prestin's stilettos after the parties.

Jaye was the ex-wife of an Oakland Raiders NFL player and was a California girl at heart. She was, by stereotypical definition, athlete wife pretty. She was tall and lean, with a small waist, curvy hips and an enviable firm ass. She sported an undetectable weave that hung in flowing layers down her back. However, Jaye was atypical when it came to playing the role of wife to a famed athlete. Instead of spending her days at the gym and spa, one year into her marriage Jaye obtained her master's degree and afterward, a Ph.D. in Psychology. Shortly thereafter she and her husband divorced when he traded her in for a younger woman who was more interested in catering to his needs than fulfilling her own dreams.

Jaye heard about Prestin four years ago while Jaye was in town visiting a friend, Marcie, during the annual summer Taste of Chicago festival. Prestin, a party to organizing some of the entertainment, was all over the grounds on the particular day that Jaye attended the event. The two caught eyes and shared a smile while Jaye and Marcie stood sideline to a concert stage in which Prestin was introducing a local artist. Marcie, a bit awestruck, noted Prestin as a big-time promoter, rattled off Prestin's impressive resume, and ended the spiel with *and she really is gay!* Jaye merely nodded her head, acknowledged the announcement and made a mental note to Google Prestin when she returned to California. And that's what she did.

Jaye found Prestin's website and promptly clicked the e-mail link to contact Prestin and introduce herself. Although Jaye had never been with a woman before, for some reason she found herself instantly intrigued and wanted to get to know Prestin better. Prestin, recipient of a large number of e-mails from a variety of individuals, including straight women, took caution in responding, expressing appreciation that Jaye contacted her and that she had enjoyed her time at the Taste. Follow-up e-mails from Jaye every few days maintained a friendly exchange. Soon Prestin found herself looking forward to Jaye's conversation. Their discussion upgraded to the phone, video chat, and then frequent trips between California and Chicago as their fondness for one another increased. We all fell for Jaye's charm when she attended her first Murmur event a year later. Six months afterward Jaye relocated to Chicago, joined a small clinic as a therapist to abused women, and became known as the woman that finally tied down the notoriously "single and loving it" Prestin. Surely Ali knew that both Jaye and Prestin would be in attendance as hostesses of the evening's affair.

It was likely that Landon would be at the party as her girlfriend, Christina, was a bartender at all of Prestin's events. Christina was a spunky woman in her mid-twenties whose only desire in life was to become a singer. It was all she thought about, talked about, and focused her energy upon when she wasn't putting together tasty drinks for thirsty women. She constantly collected business cards from anyone who might have a connection of some sort to a music producer or to anyone who may help to launch her career.

Christina had been in the studio on a few occasions by way of contacts through Prestin, however, to her disappointment she had not yet had the opportunity to lay down a single that epitomized the kind of music she wanted to represent. Christina's voice was soft and light. She preferred to sing lyrics of love's beautiful beginnings, painful ups and downs, and survival through time. She refused to touch a song that spoke of shaking her ass in the club or about playing second to a cheating man. Christina wanted to swim waters few artists had and openly release an R&B CD about same sex female love. Until that break manifested, her yearning was all we heard about.

Landon, Christina's partner, lived to cater to Christina's every need. She was a stud, with an amazing smile, and glowing tan skin with long blond dreadlocks she most often wore down in a contrasting feminine manner. Women in the lesbian community came as diverse as faces around the world, with the most common distinction being with the femme versus stud identity. Femmes were, for the most part, the feminine complement to a stud in a relationship in which one woman identified with her femininity while the other identified with her masculinity. Christina adored every aspect of a stud, especially their manly style of dress. Landon was usually seen sporting the brown uniform required by her work as a delivery driver, except for Murmur nights when she'd typically wear baggy slacks and an oversized button down shirt. After we all joined together for a charity run a couple summers prior, we'd often taunt Landon about the means in which she'd conceal her body. We all were speechless at the sight of Landon in spandex. We had no idea her body was tight and right in all a woman's desired places. We gave her flirtatious hell the entire race as we commented on her ass while running behind her. I'm not sure if she's forgiven us yet.

Finally, Ivy and Donna completed our friendship ensemble. By far they were the shakiest couple between all of us, even surpassing Ali and Noni's uncommon companionship. At least in Ali and Noni's case there was an understanding of the status of their relationship: they were intimate best friends in an open relationship, both having the freedom to date outside, even though Noni was the only one who took advantage of the opportunities. Ivy and Donna present an entirely different scenario. Most of us were perplexed by their relationship. Why would two opposites insist upon trying to sustain a relationship and connection that had died shortly after their meeting?

Without a doubt, Ivy was the sexiest white woman any of us knew. We each had to admit that we held mild crushes on her when Donna, her partner, first introduced us to her. She was an incredible beauty, with a dark mane of layered hair, powerful blue eyes, and lips that were always lusciously glossed into a provocative smile. She wore daring high heels, tight skirts and low cut tops at all times. Ivy was boldly aware of the strong sexual aura that surrounded her and relished in sassy behavior with any woman in which she was inclined. It was not unusual to find Ivy doing body shots with a woman she had just met, licking salt off of each other's skin after downing an ounce of Tequila. Later the two could be found grinding against one another in the corner of the club. All the while Donna watched it unfurl.

It wasn't that Donna was so in love with Ivy that she'd allow Ivy to do whatever she pleased just to keep her near. In fact, it was the opposite. Donna was still in love with the "one who got away." Donna has remained hopelessly and desperately in love with Beverly even since the day their friendship forever changed nearly seven years ago. Beverly and Donna were friends who had never quite figured out how to turn their friendship into something more, even though they both were lesbians with similar passions and desires. By the time Donna had mustered up the courage to ask Beverly if she wanted to give a relationship a shot, Beverly had met and fallen in love with someone else. An underlying discomfort and sadness engulfed their once close bond and within months their friendship evaporated to rare interactions.

By nature Donna was conservative and quiet. A writer in her late thirties, she was often lost in her own thoughts. However, we all knew when she had been in contact with Beverly, which was once, twice a year maximum. Sometimes we'd catch her blushing at her BlackBerry and knew that Beverly had responded to one of Donna's e-mails. Or she'd hastily rush one of us off the phone at the clicking of her other line. Only Beverly caused such reactions. Otherwise, Donna remained in a monotone state, complacent with her freelance writing career and blasé about her unconventional girlfriend.

"I haven't talked to anyone else, but I'm sure they'll be there," I told Ali. "You know we always have to support Prestin."

Ali fingered the dangling bracelets that hung from her wrist. "Okay, I suppose I can hang out tonight," she decided.

"Good," I said, and finished my lemonade. "Hey, walk with me to the store, will you? I need to pick up some pudding."

Ali took our glasses to the kitchen while I grabbed my wallet. We headed out into the warm air and lively streets of Chicago.

Chapter Three

"What are you up to?" I asked Melanie over the phone when I took a break during work the following Monday.

"Taking a look at some paperwork I just received about a new case we're taking on," Melanie said. "This one sounds quite interesting."

"Why is that?"

"It looks like this will be my first lesbian client." Through the phone I could hear her flipping papers.

"Is that so?" My interest peaked as well. "What happened?"

"Client confidentiality, Jo, you know that," she responded.

"That hasn't stopped you from telling me whack stories from some of your other clients, has it?" I retorted.

"Relax." She laughed. "If there's anything exciting to share about this case, I'll tell you."

"Okay, I'm holding you to that."

"I know you won't let me forget."

Melanie knew that a strong memory was one of my greatest assets. Mentally I could maintain at least a twenty item grocery list, could recite lines from a number of movies on cue, and could remember the details of any story Melanie or my previous girlfriends had told me. If Melanie told me she worked through lunch on Monday and at some point in time mistakenly told me she had worked through lunch on Tuesday, I'd remind her of the previous statement she made. It wasn't that I distrusted her or quizzed her unnecessarily because a skeptical woman I was not. I simply had the ability to maintain detailed information that came in useful whether I was studying for an exam or recalling facts of a possible lie I may have been told.

"What's going on with the parade this year?" Melanie asked, referring to Chicago's annual Gay Pride parade that generally attracted over 400,000 to Boystown for the afternoon event. 2010 represented the parade's forty-first run through the East Lakeview neighborhood.

"I think Prestin has secured a spot for us on someone's balcony. She's not in the parade this year so this time she can chill back with us and enjoy it."

"That's cool. Okay, I have to go and finish this reading. We have a meeting about this new case in a few hours."

"All right, when should I expect you tonight?"

"Usual, around 6:30."

"See you later, sweets. Love you."

"*Te amo*," she responded, which was the extent of her Spanish-speaking abilities and how she often chose to say "I love you." I appreciated her effort and took extra pleasure in her words when she'd whisper them in my ear in between kisses to my neck.

Honestly, I loved Melanie more than I ever thought I would, considering my initial wariness toward her. She had proven herself unfaltering in her love for me, especially when she passed a case on to a colleague as she comforted me through grief-stricken nights after my grandmother died a year ago. It was my grandmother who had raised me and my brother. She tamed my unruly curls into smooth pigtails when I was a little girl. She taught me how to cook all the delicious Spanish dishes I had mastered as a teenager. She listened to my frustrations about her daughter, my mother. Now that I am an adult my mother wants to initiate a relationship with me, but I refuse to yield to her advances.

My mother had always preferred the company of men over

the company of her children. My grandmother took over the care of my brother when he was three months old and it was my grandmother who took me home from the hospital. Although disheartened by my mother's unwillingness to own up to her responsibilities, my grandmother never spoke a harsh word to me about my mother. It was only late nights as a child that I'd heard her vent aggravated disappointments in Spanish to my grandfather.

Despite the estranged relationship my brother and I shared with our mother, several years ago we financed the purchase of her first home and paid the mortgage ourselves. It wasn't long after the closing that a male friend moved in with her. Surprised we were not, as we expected nothing more from her.

Melanie would sometimes suggest that we invite my mother over for dinner and usually I would decline. However, after my grandmother's passing I caved, and Ronan and I planned what was to be an enjoyable evening sharing a traditional Puerto Rican meal at my and Mel's condo. Unfortunately, an intake of too much rum by my mother soon turned the occasion sour as she began spewing words of anguish and regret for not being more active in our lives.

"You two are the best kids a woman could ask for," she had told us, her words muddled over her thick tongue. We all sat at the table and listened while my mother flared her napkin in the air with each dramatic gesture of sorrow.

"Jovanna, I missed your first dance recital," she cried and reached to hold my stiffened hand. "Ronan, I wasn't there for your first soccer game. I'm so sorry," she apologized.

Ronan and I may have been more receptive to the sudden outpouring of affection had it not been preceded by accounts of the places she had traveled and exciting life she had lived. Surely the recounts were what brought about the onset of remorse, but by that time it fell upon deaf ears. We sent dessert home with her by way of a plate and saran wrap. Although we spoke every few weeks, our relationship was anything but close and Melanie had resigned to accepting that truth.

That afternoon I began the preliminary stages of planning the surprise birthday party I was jazzed to throw for Melanie in August. I planned to utilize Prestin's skills to throw Melanie an unforgettable thirty-fourth birthday celebration. The guest list would include our friends, her family and colleagues, many of our acquaintances: neighbors she served volunteer duties with and even our favorite salesperson at the specialty shop where Melanie purchased most of her business suits. I wanted to show her just how much she was loved and adored, not only by me, but by all those she encountered. I picked up my cell phone and dialed Prestin's office number.

"Prestin speaking," she answered, her voice graceful and professional and just as classy as her appearance.

"Hey, Prestin, it's Jovanna. How are you?"

"Hey, Jovanna, I'm well. Working on some special entertainment for July's Murmur party. What's going on, hun?"

"Well, I'm calling for some help. I want to throw Melanie a surprise birthday party in August and I want to know if you can help me out. Help me put it together into something really special for her."

"Are you kidding? Of course I will," she happily agreed. "Just tell me what you're looking to accomplish and I'll do all I can."

"I was hoping for her birthday on August thirteenth. It should be easy to get her to meet me some place for happy hour."

"True. How many guests are you expecting?"

"I haven't yet jotted a list down, but throwing some numbers together in my head I'm thinking maybe forty."

"Okay, well I'll start thinking of some potential places to host the party. I don't think we need to buy out a place for forty folks so a lounge or restaurant with a separate private section would do. What do you think?"

"I agree. You're the expert so I'll trust you on whatever you suggest. Why don't we connect again in a couple of weeks and by then I should have the invite list together. We can talk about locations, food and how to plan this without Melanie finding out."

"That's the thing. I mean, she's a lawyer so she knows to look for the unsaid."

"Yeah, I'll have to pretend that I have something else planned instead. Hopefully she won't suspect anything."

"All right, Jovanna, I got you."

"Thanks, I appreciate it. By the way, Murmur was hot last weekend! Everybody must have been waiting for the weather to break so they could get in. It was crazy packed."

"I know. I love Murmur, especially because of their support all these years. But if attendance keeps growing, we may need to look for another venue."

"You're right. Well, I know women will follow you wherever you go," I teased. Even though it was known that Prestin was in a committed relationship, it did little to deter fascinated admirers from throwing themselves at her everywhere she went.

"Funny. Anyway, let me go. See you at the parade Sunday."

"Okay, talk to you soon."

I disconnected the call and smiled as I leaned back in my chair, grateful for such good friends and for the incredible woman I had in my life.

When I got home from work around five, I was still elated and filled with anticipation of planning Melanie's party. Melanie was big into her birthday, and had shared with me the stories of how, while she slept, her parents would decorate the house in streamers and balloons on the eve of her special day. She woke up on her tenth birthday with her luggage packed and a surprise trip to Disneyworld. So thanks to Melanie's parents, she grew up with full expectation that her birthday, August thirteenth, was a day meant for her honor.

Growing up, Ronan and I were treated to quieter birthdays that most often consisted of a home-cooked meal by our grandmother, one special gift, and usually a call from our mother with explanation of why she hadn't been able to see us. While I was still made to feel honored on my festive day, it was far from the red carpet rollout Melanie had experienced, and still wanted to receive, on an annual basis.

Inside our master bedroom I slid out of the casual cotton dress I had worn to work and entered the attached bathroom. I opened the glass door of the shower stall, stepped inside, and turned on the hot water. The water flowed over my head and ran in fast streams down my body. I closed my eyes and visualized Melanie coming home early from work, stepping inside the shower with me, and allowing me to lather and caress her skin under the steamy water. The thought brought a smile to my lips.

Afterward I put on comfy boy shorts, a fitted tank top, and slid on one of my many pairs of slipper socks. I inserted a Sergio Mendez CD into the player attached just below a kitchen cabinet above the dishwasher and hummed to the music as I began gathering ingredients to make mojitos. From our first meeting at the bar five years earlier, and subsequent dates a year later, I quickly observed that Melanie's drink of choice was a mojito. Since then I had made it a point to learn how to make the cool cocktail. I always maintained a stash of all the necessary items to put together a drink for Melanie and myself whenever we were in the mood. Tonight I was in the mood. I hoped that she was too.

An hour later I was halfway through my first mojito. I was lying on the chaise with my laptop checking my online social networking accounts. Socializing on the internet had begun innocently enough. Actually, it was just prior to meeting Melanie at the courthouse. Ronan and I were visiting relatives in Milwaukee. During the stay our cousin Leandra showed us her online account and suggested we maintain better contact using the internet. Her profile provided basic information about herself including her ethnicity, height and weight, if she had children and her relationship status. She had also included a short bio about herself, speaking about her recent college graduation, how she couldn't wait to find the right man, and that she loved cats and hated dogs. Leandra had adorned her page with photos of herself partying on the weekends with friends, hugged up with various men in affectionate poses and with women making kiss faces into the camera.

After spending a few minutes browsing pictures of different women, Ronan was ready to create his profile right away. We spent the following Monday creating our individual profiles while in the office. At Leandra's suggestion we had picked out photos that we felt best represented us. I had selected five pictures. My profile picture was a professional black and white photo that I used on business cards at the time. The photo was a bit conservative with my curly hair smoothed into a bun. However, Ronan had chosen the photo stating it accentuated my features by focusing on my eyes and smile.

I had also selected one of Ronan and me at a White Sox game, one of myself sitting at my desk in the office, and two candid shots that had been taken by my ex. One was of me trying to put together an entertainment center we had purchased. She had managed to catch a confused and exasperated expression on my face as I tried to piece the portions of the unit together. The second was a shot of me laughing with a group of friends while out bar hopping.

Ronan, on the other hand, opted to exploit himself. My brother was fine and he knew it. He selected mostly professional shots he had from photo sessions he had participated in. He had photos of himself wearing trendy suits, shirtless in jeans with bare feet. He even had some where he was wearing nothing other than boxers or fitted briefs. Ronan saw online network-ing as yet another means to expand his growing Rolodex with new names and phone numbers of women.

My bio was short and to the point. It stated that I was new to meeting people online and hoped to use the network to stay in touch with family and maybe gain a new friend or two. I talked about my degrees, our mortgage company, and that I was an out lesbian who enjoyed long-term relationships. I also added that I loved theme parks, dancing, and roller skating along the lakefront.

Leandra also told us to add at least one song to our profile and informed us that it could be updated with more music at any time. The song I chose was "Pon de Replay" by Rihanna because it was my then favorite dance song with its thumping beat and island feel. Ronan had dipped back to the nineties and elected to add "I Wanna to Sex You Up" by Color Me Badd.

Ronan and I became each other's "friends" when we publish-ed our profiles, each of us placing the other in the number one spot which, according to Leandra, was the prime place for someone special. I remained in Ronan's top spot for about two weeks until he traded me in for the first of a string of new ladies that captured his attention. He never moved me far. I held a steady place at number two while every few weeks he would spotlight a new beauty as his number one.

At the start I was amazed by the ease in reconnecting with high school and even elementary school classmates. It was interesting to discover the different roads our lives had taken us, with some attending universities out of state, others who had joined the armed forces, and even more who had already settled down and were married with children.

Because I identified myself as a lesbian on my profile, it didn't take long to build an online network of lesbian friends in the Chicago area. Prestin and I became friends through her promotions page and from there I "met" a slew of women I had seen out in clubs or had casually met through acquaintances. It seemed most lesbians congregated toward one another and soon I became friends of their friends. Before long I became both fascinated and confused by the flirtatious world of online networking.

Bethany, a woman who lived in Chicago and one of my first friends, sent me an e-mail within an hour of our becoming friends. "I like your profile," she had told me. "We should meet offline. Call me." She left her phone number.

A little naïve I was in the beginning, and I called her the next day.

"Bethany?"

"Who's this calling?" The woman's voice was soft and quiet.

"This is Jovanna. We met online yesterday."

The other line was silent, and I could hear rapid tapping against a keyboard. "Oh yes, the Latina."

I scrunched my face at the phone and then replaced it to my ear. "Well, half Latina," I explained.

"Whatever you are, you're hot. You're sexy, mami." She giggled lusciously into the phone like I had dialed a 900 number.

"Thank you."

"So you want to get together or what?"

"Get together and do what?" I asked back.

"I like all kinds of stuff. And I think I like you."

"You don't even know me."

"I like what I see and I want to know you if you know what I mean." Again, she giggled.

"That's all right, I'll pass," I told her, realizing she wanted something from me that I had no intention of giving.

"You don't find me sexy too?"

"I have to go." I hung up the phone and prayed she wouldn't save my number.

Although my reason for being online stated that I was seeking friendship only, I found that many women, like Bethany, chose not to honor my position. After a friendship invitation I would often receive an e-mail with request for more personal information about myself than I had disclosed on my profile. *What do you like to do in your spare time? Where do you like to hang out? Why are you single?* Initially I found myself cordially responding to each e-mail with hopes of maintaining positive connections with the strangers I was allowing into my space with the possibility of a slow-building friendship. I wasn't prepared for the aggressiveness of some women who became persistent in pressuring me to develop a deeper friendship with them instantly; those attempting to innocently learn all they could about me with a blatant silent motive to change my relationship status from "single" to "in a relationship." There were a couple of women with attractive photos and solid careers that I found intriguing, although their pushiness was a turnoff. Eventually I ignored most of them.

Though I thoroughly enjoyed consistent e-mail contact with a couple of friendly, non-invasive women, by the time Melanie and I reconnected and the promise of a relationship emerged, I was relieved to have a solid reason to maintain only casual interaction with many of the other women I had encountered. I was particularly thrilled that Carina, one of my ex's that I had befriended online, would hopefully stop her attempts at sending subliminal messages to me via the quirky comments she often left on my profile. Melanie got a kick out of some of the communications I shared with her when I'd check my profile account in her presence. Sometimes she'd recognize women who I was friends with, sharing stories of women she knew they had dated or details she had heard about their lives.

When the moment arrived that I was ready to change my status to "in a relationship" Melanie and I created a profile for her. Ronan was at last moved to the number two spot that he still holds. Melanie's profile displayed a fun mix of both the professional and light sides of her personality and life. In her bio she talked about her passion for the law and desire to uphold the rights of all. She boasted about her firm's commitment to defend its clients to the best of its ability. She discussed her love of family, the joy and relaxation she found in running, and her weakness for chocolate pudding. Finally she spoke of us reuniting and the love that had soon materialized between us. She posted several pictures of us varying from posed pictures we had taken while out with friends to some of her favorite photos of me alone. Her particular beloved shot was a black and white photo Ali had taken of me. We had been sitting on the patio of an outdoor café and Ali was in the midst of a Noni rant while toying with a new camera she had just purchased for an upcoming photography class she was taking. My elbow was on the table, my hand against the side of my face with my head tilted slightly back. Ali suddenly snapped a shot, catching me with a direct stare into the camera, no smile and no expression. However, Melanie said the photo captured me in my most natural state. She favored the shot over all of my posed photographs.

In turn, I added pictures of us to my online photo album and included my favorite of her, a cropped photo in which she was grinning sweetly, looking sideways with a sparkle in her eyes. The photo reminded me of the way she looked at me the day we met in the courthouse as I viewed the courthouse map. However, in the photo she was really smiling at something amusing on the television, hence the reason I altered the photograph to a close up. Like her feelings toward my photo, I favored the gentle essence of her natural state that the picture captured.

Melanie also connected with several old friends and made

a few new ones of her own. Soon the majority of my friends became hers as well and in no time we were all looped into one online family of intertwined women connected by sincere friendships, casual associations, and innocuous flirtatious banter.

About a year into our relationship, one individual had raised Melanie's eyebrows in question about my online activities. She and I had grown accustomed to the normalcy in complimentary exchanges, often receiving comments in which we were called "sweetie" or "babe" and "beautiful" or "sexy." However, after a woman out of Seattle left one too many flattering remarks on my profile in conjunction with persistent e-mail correspondences, Melanie asked me how I was responding to the woman's advances. She had never come off as the jealous type, although I understood her curiosity.

"Who's this Debbie woman leaving all these comments on your profile?" she had inquired one day while browsing the site.

"What woman?"

"This one," she answered, and turned her laptop to face me. On my profile I saw that within two weeks I had approved four comments from Debbie in which Debbie had applauded my appearance and praised my accomplishments. I recalled that the comments seemed extreme, though it hadn't occurred to me that Melanie would find them troublesome.

"I don't even know her," I told Melanie.

"Does she e-mail you too?" She quickly inquired.

"She has."

"About what?" Melanie was then irritated. It showed in the way her eyes latched onto my every move like I was a squeamish witness on the stand attempting to evade an answer.

"I think it was more of the same. Just compliments," I testified.

"Did you respond?"

"I did."

"What did you say?" She studied my mouth and searched for a stutter, a flinch, something to signify I was going to trip over my words.

"I only thanked her, that's it." She didn't say anything. "Would you like me to show you the e-mails?"

Melanie shook her head sideways and gave me a silent no.

"You don't look like you're being honest," I told her after observing her continued pinched stare in my direction.

"You said that's all it was so that's fine."

I didn't like feeling that Melanie may have had any thoughts of mistrust toward me so I took a business card from my wallet and wrote down my user name and password to the online site.

"You're welcome to read anything on there." I handed the information to her.

She eyed the card a moment, then willingly accepted it within seconds and checked my account the next day. Pleased she found that I had responded with cordial "thank-you's" only and had completely ignored the last three e-mails the woman had sent. In time, the woman gradually disappeared. I later found her leaving the same stalker messages on someone else's profile as she had left on mine. Then, Melanie and I could only laugh.

Melanie had also provided me her account information one day when she needed access to an old friend's phone number. The internet on her phone was temporarily not operating and she had no access to a computer. I wrote the information down on a Post-it note, logged on, looked up the e-mail she requested, and then logged off. I kept the sticky note in my wallet in case she ever needed my help again. To my knowledge, Melanie had never logged on to my account since the Seattle woman incident and I hadn't logged on to hers again either.

Just as I was about to leave a message on Ronan's page—a funny remark to be on time to work the next day—Melanie waltzed through the door seemingly upbeat and whistling softly. When she entered the living room, I smiled at her and moved the laptop to my side. She took off her jacket and tossed it on the loveseat, just as she did every night. She returned the smile just before she bent over to kiss my lips.

"Mmm, mojito," she said with a smack of her lips.

"Yes," I replied. "Let me get yours for you." I said as I began to rise.

Melanie glanced at my computer screen and laughed. "So who thinks my lady is beautiful today?" she inquired.

"Just you Mel," I answered with a quick kiss to her cheek.

She followed me into the kitchen and headed straight to the refrigerator for pudding while I put together her drink.

"How was your day love?" she asked.

"It was busy. We have a lot of people in the position to buy a home again so business is picking back up," I said, grateful for the upswing in the market. Even during the down time Melanie and I were never worried or at a financial strain. Her salary covered our expenses on its own.

"That's good to hear, I'm glad." She then fell silent and only when I turned to give her the finished drink did I see she was standing, smirking at me while licking the last bits of chocolate off of her spoon.

"What, sweetie?" I asked.

"I'm waiting."

"For what?"

"For you to ask me about my case," she answered.

"Well, you said you'd tell me anything interesting that came up so I guess something has come up already."

Melanie took the drink and we headed back to the living room. Before sitting down on the couch, she unbuttoned her shirt all the way and allowed it to hang open, exposing her bra and solid abdomen. Melanie knew how sexy I found her in that stance. On many nights we would be talking to one another from across the living room and I wouldn't be able to contain my thrill of her in that visual position. I'd often choose to cuddle next to her and stroke the skin around her belly button as we continued our conversation.

"It's a case involving two female ex-lovers. The guys couldn't wait to get my take on the case."

"What happened?"

"My client has been accused of violating the restraining order her ex-girlfriend placed on her."

I raised my eyebrows. "Seriously?"

"Yeah, well we learned that the order was put in place by the ex because she stated that my client was harassing her after their breakup. She moved out of the apartment that they shared, but would call at all hours and show up at the apartment building trying to get in. Guess she went up to the woman's job when she didn't get a response."

"How can she prove it?"

"Hopefully she can't, but that's what we have to find out. The order prohibits all contact to the plaintiff, and absolutely no in person contact."

"That's crazy. I mean, I know it's your job, but sometimes I wonder how you can handle defending some of these people that are in the wrong."

Melanie took a few swigs of her mojito. "We've had this conversation before. You know I respect your feelings but I love what I do. I believe people make mistakes and deserve second chances. And don't forget that sometimes the people we defend turn out to be innocent. They need us."

"Okay. But how would you feel if some woman was harassing you? Bothering you when all you want to do is move on away from her?"

"Don't try to trip me up." She wagged a finger at me playfully.

"You know you can't answer the question honestly without contradicting yourself," I teased.

She didn't answer. Instead she quickly removed her shoes by using the toes on one foot against the heel of the other to slide off her pumps. She readjusted her body into a lying position and then chuckled lightly.

"What?" I asked.

"You told me about that girl you used to do drive by's on."

"Melanie, I was not stalking that girl, I only did that once," I corrected her, but still found the memory funny.

"Well, tell me again what happened," she laughed.

"You are so funny," I giggled, slightly buzzed from the mojito. "She told me she was going to bed because she wasn't feeling well so we couldn't go to this party we had planned to go to. But earlier that day she was just fine and I remembered that she had casually mentioned that her ex-girlfriend was going to be at the party. I just got suspicious. Something inside me said she wasn't being truthful so I went by her house around ten. I was going to play it off that I wanted to surprise and take care of her, but of course she wasn't home."

I paused to see if Melanie actually wanted me to continue. When she motioned her hand as if saying "go on" I finished the story.

"Soooo, I parked at the end of her block and waited for her to come home. I sat in the car a good two hours before she got there. When she pulled up, I hurried up and pulled up behind her. She was shocked to see me there, startled as hell. I asked her what was going on and she tried to lie. She said something about having to go check on something for a family member. But I smelled alcohol and cigarette smoke on her. At first she was trying to explain herself. Then I guess the drunken side took over and she started yelling and acting all belligerent. I went right along with it so there we were, about midnight, outside arguing, acting like fools." I shook my head.

"I can't even picture it, Jo," Mel commented, then retracted. "Wait, that's not true. I know you have some hot blood in you. Just glad I haven't seen it."

"You haven't given me reason." I smiled. I finished my mojito then knelt in front of her feet. I took one in my hand and began pressing my thumbs in a circular motion at the arch of her foot. She leaned back and relaxed her head against the cushion.

We were silent while I massaged her feet. Melanie's feet were less than pretty, though that did nothing to prevent me from treating her to massages, foot soaks and home pedicures. Because of her love for running, her toenails suffered most and were often discolored and her heels were usually calloused. Tonight was no exception. When I momentarily stopped kneading her arch to pick at one of her big toenails, Melanie looked up.

"Leave it alone Jo," she instructed. But I couldn't help picking at the black spot, checking to see just how bad the fungus was. Finally Melanie snatched her foot away.

"Why are you messing up a good massage?" She got on the floor and playfully pinned my body underneath hers. She pecked my lips with hers and my heart smiled. I loved Melanie so much. Some days I cringed at the thought of what my life would be like had she not followed up and called me after ties were severed with her ex. I knew that Melanie loved me back, though we showed each other in different ways. I was more verbal, expressing my adoration for her at every opportunity. I told her I loved her over the phone or during late nights as we made love. I complimented her appearance, her work ethic, and the devotion she felt toward her family. I made sure she knew I appreciated the way she showed her love to me, which was more visibly articulated.

Aside from the occasional "*Te amo*" she said to me, Melanie most often displayed her affection by way of sweet gestures. She

often sent flowers to work, and left "Have a great day" notes on
the refrigerator or in the bathroom if she left for work before
I awoke. She found pleasure in taking my car for a wash and
cleaning the kitchen after I cooked a meal. And after Melanie
learned that I had a fond appreciation for hats, she would
often surprise me with a variety of headwear. My expansive
collection consisted of colorful knit caps for cold winter
months, casual newsboy caps, stylish fedoras, baseball caps,
and wide brim hats for sunny days at the beach. Many days I'd
arrive home to a box that contained a new hat that Melanie
wished to see me adorn.

Suddenly, Melanie let out a soft groan.

"What's wrong?" I asked.

"I need to look something up online."

"Use my laptop," I suggested. "Do you want another mojito?"

"I do," she said, and lifted herself from my body. Once
standing she took hold of my hand to lift me up. I stared
into her brown eyes and immediately saw distraction behind
them. When Melanie's mind shifted attention, it showed
clearly. I could see that her thoughts were already absorbed by
whatever she needed to research. I left her with my laptop and
went into the kitchen to prepare a second round of drinks.

"Jo!" she called a few minutes later.

"Yes?" I yelled back.

"Who's SexyC73?"

What was she talking about? "Who?"

"You just got an instant message from SexyC73."

"Well, just ignore it. I'll be there in a minute," I responded,
and tried to figure out whom that was. Generally I sent messages with only close friends and family members and should be
able to recognize their contact information. After I finished
making the drinks, I went back to Melanie and my laptop. By
that time she was immersed in a website and took her drink

from me without saying anything further about the instant message.

"Thanks," she said, with a brief glance at me.

"You're welcome."

I took the throw from the couch and wrapped it around my body before taking a seat. Then I turned on the television, searched through the guide, and settled on a *Girlfriends* rerun. I kept the volume low, just enough to hear the dramatic antics of the four women who constantly expressed disappointment about the men in their lives. A couple of hours later Melanie rubbed my shoulder. She had on cotton underwear, a tank top and I could see that her face was freshly washed. The TV was off and my laptop was closed.

"Come to bed," she said.

She held my hand and led me into the room where she had pulled down the sheets on my side of the bed. I laid down and got comfortable with my pillow. She pulled the sheet over my body and kissed my forehead before getting in bed beside me and wrapping her arm around my waist. "So who is this Sexy person?" she asked into my ear.

"Nobody," I murmured.

"She's somebody if she's sending you instant messages."

"Mel, it happens sometimes. But I don't know her."

"Okay." Her tone was short.

"Okay what, sweetie?" I turned over to face her.

"You spend a lot of time online. I don't know what goes on there."

"There's nothing to worry about on there. And I bet if you spent more time online, the same thing would happen to you. Some of those women have no respect for relationships."

"I bet. And I have you, so what do I need them for?"

"It's mostly innocent. There are just those few," I said, and twisted my body so my back was to her again.

"Those few that what?"

"Persist."

Melanie didn't reply, and I felt her breathing slow. In the middle of the night I felt a light graze against my back as Melanie glided her fingers across my tank top.

"Mmm, Mel, that tickles." I laughed and squeezed my neck after I felt the tip of her tongue lick my earlobe. Melanie was quiet and when I reached over my shoulder to caress her face, I felt a sharp piercing to my finger.

"Ouch!" I screamed, and turned over to find my finger trapped in the mouth of the same gray-eyed snake I had dreamt about. A frightening wail escaped my lips as I swung my hand in the air in an attempt to release it.

"What's going on?" Melanie shrieked, and grabbed my arm.

My breathing was erratic and my chest heaved. I opened my eyes and saw Melanie staring at me with a concerned expression. Her hand was wrapped around my wrist. There was no snake. She leaned close and stroked my hair with her free hand.

"Are you all right?"

"Yeah, yeah, I'm okay." My pulse slowed and my body calmed.

"What's wrong?"

"Bad dream."

"Here." She prepped my pillow and laid me down.

I pressed my face into her chest and inhaled her scent.

"Do you want to talk about it?"

"No," I answered, and kissed her skin.

"Okay, close your eyes. I'm here."

"Thank you. I love you Mel."

She didn't answer and I realized, again, she was already asleep.

Chapter Four

"I love your hat!" Ali squealed when Melanie and I joined everyone for the Pride Parade the following Sunday.

I touched the brim of my cream colored floppy hat with black scarf wrapped around the bottom of the crown. It was the perfect accessory for the cotton sundress I had chosen to wear for the Sunday afternoon Pride celebration. Melanie was casual and comfortable in army green carpenter shorts, same color tee shirt and flip flops. Her eyes were behind sleek, sporty sunglasses with bronzed lenses that allowed me to still see the expression in her eyes.

"You look great too," I told her, complimenting the vintage, bohemian skirt she wore with a wife beater and lightweight, colorful scarf around her neck despite the hot summer temperature. "This is a great view," I added, admiring the perfect shot we had of the parade route below with Chicago's famous skyline just to our east.

"Yeah, Prestin hooked it up." Ali stared at the tall buildings downtown in appreciation of our view as well.

As always, Prestin and Jaye were fabulously stylish. They were both dressed in summer slacks and sleeveless blouses with open toe heels. Prestin was dressed in gray slacks and white blouse,while Jaye wore black and white pinstriped slacks with a lightweight black blouse. They complimented one another perfectly. There were a few unfamiliar faces about the loft and balcony area. Prestin and Jaye were busy networking with the group before they settled on the outdoor patio furniture for the festivities.

"Hey, Noni," both Melanie and I said at the same time. Noni had come behind Ali, wrapped her arm around Ali's waist and handed her a small plate of spinach dip and bagel chips with her other hand. She kissed Ali hard against her cheek. Ali shamelessly blushed.

Best friends they were, however, by the way that she adorned Ali with affection in the presence of other same-sex loving women, a casual observer would never know that Noni was a non-committal bisexual woman. Perhaps that was one of the reasons Ali stayed, if only to gather up the most of these treasured memories with Noni.

"Hey, pretty ladies." Noni released Ali and gave both Melanie and me a hug, with her red fingernails grazing the exposed skin on my back.

Noni wore red polish every day. No matter the season, the outfit, or the shade of her lipstick, red was her signature color. Noni cherished her hands as prized possessions. She splurged on weekly paraffin treatments and manicures to keep her slender hands delicate, groomed, and flawless, never chipped or peeled. Noni flaunted her hands and fingers like jewels. She loved to point at the most inconspicuous item, stretching her first finger outward, flashing a shiny nail in front of her.

According to Ali, Noni also flirted with her fingers, using them to entice attractive men. When she met a man, she'd purposely caress his palm when they shook hands, allowing her fingertip to softly graze his skin. This hidden gesture left men captivated by her sensuous touch. She used her fingers in a more aggressive manner with Ali. I recalled the story Ali had shared with me about their first sexual encounter. Ali had described how her scalp tingled and stung as Noni dug her fingernails through Ali's natural curls into her skin while Ali knelt before Noni and ate her out. I could only imagine all that Noni loved to do with her beloved fingernails and wondered if they continued to be as physically painful to Ali in more ways as their sexual experimentation developed.

Melanie and I excused ourselves to make plates of our

own and to find a suitable drink for the noontime party. Of
course Melanie had the bartender put together a mojito and
I went with a pineapple crush that consisted of pineapple
juice, pineapple vodka and red rum. We had returned and
were sitting comfortably in lounge chairs when Donna and
Ivy arrived. Melanie glanced at me and widened her eyes
underneath her sunglasses. I swallowed hard and tried not to
react to what Melanie had seen. Ivy was wearing a baby doll
mini dress so short that we could see her silk underwear with
every step she took.

Ivy walked her usual seductive strut in our direction and
bent to plant a firm kiss at the corner of my lips. She then did
the same to Melanie, Noni and Ali. Ivy was the only of our
friends who attempted such gestures and the only one that we
all would allow to get away with it. She was a sexual person, we
all knew it, and accepted her frisky, though innocent actions,
with us friends at least.

Donna was the opposite; she smiled quietly and said hello
to each of us with a wave.

"Sugar plum, let's get a drink," Ivy told Donna. Donna nodded and they went through the balcony doors. We all caught
peeks of Ivy's creamy ass cheeks as they walked indoors.

"That girl is something else," Melanie said with a smile.

"Who you tellin'? I couldn't have my Ali showing all her
goodies for the world to see. That's only for me, right Ali?"
Noni stroked Ali's cheek.

"Right," Ali confirmed.

"That's just how they are," I offered. "Donna must be all
right with it."

"Girl, Donna doesn't care. She's so lost in Beverly fantasies
all the time anyway," Noni commented.

"Does anybody ever hear from her?" Ali asked.

"I don't hear from her," Melanie answered. "But a friend of
mine is good friends with Bev's partner. I haven't heard from
her in a while though."

"I wish those two had gotten it together. Not to slight Ivy in any way, but I know how much Donna loves Bev. We should all be able to be with the one we love," Ali said with a brief glance at Noni.

Melanie and I took simultaneous sips of our drinks and remained silent. Although I had innumerable conversations with Ali about Noni, I never interjected when the topic arose in the presence of both. I preferred to remain Ali's one-on-one confidant.

As the sound of a thumping beat became audible, Prestin and Jaye finally made their way to join us. Only after Prestin asked us to accompany her in a group photo for the photographer that had been following her, were she and Jaye able to unwind. They sat side by side, their pinky fingers linked together, professional and composed as they always were. Even during Murmur events it was a very rare occasion in which Prestin danced or even had a drink. Although a pure pleasure to be around, she remained sharp and polished in public. Only during private gatherings would Prestin shake off her business-like demeanor and loosen up. Surprisingly, she had rhythm like some of the best booty-shaking girls in music videos and we relished those times when Prestin would delight us with her interpretations of some of the women that filled Murmur's dance floor. We all promised to keep her amusing mocking to ourselves.

An hour into the parade, Christina and Landon appeared, sporting colors of the LGBT community's symbol of diversity and inclusion, rainbow leis and carrying small rainbow flags for each of us. By this time we were all standing, cheering each float that passed by, whistling at the half-dressed men and women, and dancing to the fast-paced music. Melanie performed a slow grind against my backside while I leaned against the railing and grooved to a pulsating beat. Ali and Noni acted like the best friends and lovers that they were, laughing and enjoying the parade while sharing kisses and hugs. Although I could see that Prestin and Jaye had a cool buzz going on, they remained seated in front of the balcony railing, chatting with us and enjoying the parade from an attendee's viewpoint rather than as a participant. Donna was fairly reserved, though her eyes were low and heavy from the two shots of tequila that she and Ivy had done. Meanwhile, Ivy was on the opposite end of the balcony sipping on a margarita while one of the unfamiliar faces, a tall, butch woman with spiked blond hair, stroked Ivy's skin just under the hem of her dress. Ivy bit her bottom lip while the woman said something into her ear. Only once did I shoot Donna a questionable look; she simply shrugged her shoulders as if to say *I don't give a shit*, and went back to enjoying the parade.

When the parade ended, we were all hot, feeling light and easy, and hungry for more than the appetizers we had eaten over the three-hour timeframe. To our gratification, Prestin surprised us with an assorted delivery of foods from a nearby Thai restaurant. The unknown guests left and the ten of us took the party inside the modern loft.

"Guess what guys?" Christina asked us all once we had each added a healthy heaping of food to our plates. "I met a producer who's interested in the music I want to sing," she said excitedly.

"Really, who?" Ali wanted to know.

"Her name is Sarina. Real cool chick who has worked with a few artists out of L.A. Landon and I met her at a talent event last week. She said she liked my song."

"What did you sing?" I asked.

"My baby sang a cappella. A song she wrote herself," Landon told us proudly.

"You go, girl." Noni congratulated Christina.

"That's cool. Chris," Melanie added.

"Let us hear it," I requested.

"Yes, sing to us darling," Ivy urged.

Christina looked at Prestin, who had been quiet, her eyes dancing smiles back at Christina. Prestin looked at Jaye who looked back with a *why not* expression. In turn, Prestin nodded her approval at Christina.

"Well, it was going to be a surprise. Prestin was going to allow me to perform it at July's Murmur event," she beamed.

"The ladies will love it," Prestin finally said.

"What's it about?" I asked.

"It's a romantic song about making love to a woman for the first time," Christina answered.

"All right now," Noni laughed and she and Ali exchanged knowing glances.

"What's the title?" I asked.

Christina closed her eyes and said, "Gently."

We all positioned ourselves comfortably about the living area while Christina took the stage in the middle of the hardwood floor. She paused, closed her eyes again, and began a soft hum.

Mmmm, Mmm, baby . . .
If I had known what tonight was like
I wouldn't have waited so long
To feel your touch, to feel your kiss
You got my body gone
Got me feeling high—let me breathe you in
Baby you feel so good to me
Say my name, just one more time
Take me there—I'm about to climb . . . to the peak of your love
'Cause baby you got me gently
Rockin' side to side
Back and forth
With you
You got me flowin'
Just keep on goin'

Up and down . . . gently

Christina's soft voice intensified over the next verse, chorus and then bridge, as she sang about the way her first-time lover made her feel. By the end of the song I think we all were horny.

"Damn, girl, that was hot," Noni said as she placed long strokes with her fingernail against Ali's skirt.

"I love it, Christina," Ali added.

"All right, ladies, we have to go and take care of some business," Melanie said, joking, as she stood up and playfully reached for my hand. We all laughed before she sat back down.

Even Donna spoke up. "That's nice."

"You all really like it?" Christina asked with her eyes near tears.

All together we chimed in our positive thoughts about the song.

"Like I said before, Murmur will love it. Be sure Sarina comes that night," Prestin told Christina.

"I will," Christina giggled.

I excused myself to go to the restroom, which was through the living area past the kitchen. I smiled at the vision of Christina wooing the crowd with her sweet voice. Most women already knew of Christina's passion for singing, though I wasn't sure if they all knew just how beautiful her voice was. With Christina's performance they would finally have the chance to hear her sing and hopefully she'd win their support. When I opened the bathroom door, Prestin was waiting for me with a finger held over her mouth. I didn't say anything and stepped back into the bathroom. She followed.

"I have an idea," she whispered. "There's a new spot that I think would be perfect for Melanie's party. I know the owners and they're trying to get their name out there and are offering a cool deal if we host the party at their place. You'll love it.

It's a great restaurant and after work spot for professionals, yet relaxed enough that everyone won't be feeling uptight, you know."

"That's cool!" I had tried to whisper back, although my excitement escalated the volume of my voice.

"Get with me this week with the number of folks you're inviting, okay?"

"I will. Thanks, Prestin."

"I told you I got you." She winked before she opened the door, peeked around to make sure no one was there, and then left. Again, I smiled to myself, envisioning the shocked look on Melanie's face when she realized that the evening would be spent amongst loved ones celebrating her special day.

When I re-entered the living area, it seemed that everyone was indeed anxious to leave and get to whatever intimacies their minds had imagined since Christina's song. Prestin and Jaye stayed behind after we said our goodbyes to take care of some formalities associated with our afternoon spent at the loft. Outside, Ivy blew us kisses before she led Donna toward her sporty, Nissan two-seater. Ali and Noni headed to Noni's south side home while Melanie and I began a ten-block walk to our condo. The streets were still active and busy, with crowds of tipsy men and women hanging outdoors around the bars and restaurants. We blended in, holding hands, feeling giddy and carefree.

Inside the condo, I removed my wedge heels at the front door and Melanie kicked off her flip flops. I plopped on the couch.

"It's nice and cool in here," I said, grateful that we had left the central air on.

"Let's heat it up," Melanie grinned, and made her way to the couch beside me.

"I like that idea," I replied, and opened my arms to her.

"No, not in here."

"Where to?"

Melanie only smiled mischievously. Then I knew what she wanted. Melanie had a dangerous fetish for making love to me where we could be seen, or at least daringly close to being seen. On a vacation to Mexico we had made love three times on the balcony while below passersby walked along the ocean. Once Melanie suggested a bathroom rendezvous in a clean, elegant restaurant we had visited. That surprised me considering she was a lawyer and knew the consequences of our being caught. The thrill led me to a swift climax after she lifted my skirt, spread my legs and fingered my walls. However, she left most of our voyeuristic adventures to the inside of our condo.

I followed Melanie into the bedroom, where she opened the blinds to the balcony that overlooked the square courtyard in the center of the complex. She stood about four feet in front of me and I waited to see what she wanted. She unlatched her belt and removed it from the loops in her shorts just before she let them fall to the floor along with the belt. In one move I lifted my cotton dress over my head and onto the floor. Melanie then removed her tee shirt. I unlatched my bra to reveal my dark brown, stiffened nipples. Melanie eyed them deliciously. She removed her undergarments and stood naked, her firm body catching light from the sun that shined in between the tall blinds. Finally I removed my panties and felt the wetness that had already developed between my legs.

"Mmmm," Melanie moaned. She walked toward me and gently pushed me against the wall next to the balcony. Against the wall she took hold of my hair in one hand and a breast in the other while she kissed my lips. I closed my eyes, opened my mouth, and invited her tongue to greet mine. She accepted the invitation.

Soon Melanie bent her knees until our hips met and began

a grind against my pelvic bone. With her head lowered she ran her tongue across my neck, over my collarbone, down to my breasts. She kissed, sucked and nibbled them, all while continuing to rub against me. The heat between our bodies increased.

"I want you," I whispered.

"I want you too," she breathed back.

Melanie got on her knees and kissed my stomach, flicking her tongue across my skin. I ran my fingers through her hair while she continued to sprinkle my belly with kisses.

"Spread 'em Jo," she instructed.

I parted my legs and planted my feet in a firm position on the carpet. Melanie took hold of my lips, spread those as well, and opened my clit to her. She opened her mouth and took it inside, sucking gently, her tongue grazing back and forth.

"Damn, Mel," I exhaled. It felt so damn good. She kissed and licked, sucked and kissed, licked and sucked some more. I squeezed my own breasts, and toyed with my nipples which heightened the sensations I felt. My thighs began to shake, my stomach tightened and my heart beat faster.

"I'm about to cum," I said anxiously. And then I did.

A few moments later I looked down at Melanie. She peered up at me, desire in her eyes. She took hold of my hand and guided me to the floor.

"On your stomach," she said. This was one of Melanie's favorite positions. I laid down, my face sideways against the carpeting. Melanie straddled me from behind. She positioned herself on my ass, spread my cheeks, and placed her clit in between. With her hands at my waist, she rocked her hips back and forth against my ass. Occasionally I would squeeze, which tightened the grip around her clit.

"Cum for me, Mel," I said when I knew she was reaching orgasm. She began to grind faster and her breathing became heavy. She moaned louder and louder and her legs tensed.

Then she was temporarily quiet. She always did that just seconds before her release.

"Oh, oh, ohhhh, Jo! Fuck," she said and gripped my waist tighter. "Damn that was good," she said a few moments later. She reached for the blinds, parted them slightly, and smiled, pleased that a couple across the courtyard were sitting on their balcony enjoying the weather.

I twisted underneath her, turned my body over and laughed. "You're so nasty, Mel," I teased.

"You like it though, don't you?" she asked, though she knew my answer.

"I sure do," I answered. "I really do."

Chapter Five

"I'll be home late tonight," Melanie told me the following Wednesday afternoon while I sat in my office which was located in the Wicker Park neighborhood of Chicago. We enjoyed the buzzing energy of the community and appreciated the diverse clientele that came to visit us.

"I'm making one of your favorite dishes tonight," I baited.

"What are you making?" she asked curiously.

"Grilled fish," I told her. Melanie loved the grilled fish dish topped with sofrito sauce, plantains, sour cream and cilantro.

"You can still make it, Jo," she urged. "I'll eat when I get home."

"No problem, sweetie." I jotted the ingredients down on a piece of paper for shopping after work. Not that I would forget, but just in case. "So what's got you in the office late?" I asked.

"I'm about to meet with one of my clients," she answered.

Just then Ronan entered the office wearing a dark blue suit with a yellow and navy pinstriped tie. Ronan, who was a bit obsessive about his appearance, always wore business suits while working. Ronan believed that all first impressions were met with the eye and if a person could win someone's confidence by the visual first, then winning them over in business would be just as easy. I didn't agree completely with Ronan's theory, as I had encountered many individuals who looked the part, yet failed miserably the second they spoke a word. However Ronan, blessed with a well-articulated voice as silky as cream pie, could converse with the CEO of an organization just as easily as he could loosen up and chat with a young man whose pants were sagging low. Ronan hated that look and would startle some boys with questions about why they chose to leave their asses hanging out.

"Well, okay. I'll see you when you get in."

"Okay, Jo."

"Love you, Mel."

"I know," she laughed and we ended our call.

Ronan wasn't alone. He was accompanied by Jillian, also known as ♥♥ "J-LO" ♥♥ online. I immediate-ly recognized her from his current number one position. She was a beauty; a cream colored Latina with dyed honey blond hair, dark eyes, curvy hips and thick thighs. Not that I was checking her out. However, when I saw her profile photo in which she was wearing a two-piece swimsuit while sucking on a lollipop, I was like, *damn*! Melanie and I had a lovely time observing the photos Jillian shared in her online photo albums. We still couldn't figure out why a professional man like Ronan selected such a provocative woman to entertain.

"Hey, Jo, everything all right here?" he asked.

"Just fine," I answered, and stood to greet Jillian. "Jovanna." I extended my hand to her.

"Jillian," she said, and offered her hand back to me.

"You two should be friends," Ronan said, suggesting that she and I become online acquaintances, which he knew I didn't do with his women, even upon their request. I didn't want to have to respond to a slew of e-mails from any of them when Ronan juggled their position throughout his top friends or removed them all together. When I didn't answer, Ronan smiled smugly to himself with his backside to Jillian. Of course he wanted to make sure she knew it was me that had the problem, not him, as he had nothing to hide. He could be such an ass.

"Have a seat." He offered Jillian the client chair in front of my desk, which was opposite his. She sat and her short dress rose to reveal her juicy thighs. Both Ronan and I stared for a moment. Jillian noticed and smiled at me.

"She's mine," Ronan joked at me. I frowned back. Ronan and I were exceptionally close and I loved him passionately, but I couldn't stand to be around him and his women. Underneath his business suit and aside from his strong and admirable determination for success, he was one of the most pompous, arrogant assholes alive and loved to show out in front of his girls. I prayed for the day when he would meet a woman that didn't lick his ass after wiping just to be sure it was clean, but instead one that could ignite the more humble side of his personality and bring out the respectful qualities that I knew existed.

I wanted to remind Ronan that Jillian was all his as I wasn't into women that couldn't offer more than a pretty face. Instead, I asked Jillian what she did for a living.

"I go to school part time online and I'm a dancer at a gentlemen's club. That's where I met Ronan," she blushed. My eyebrows raised and I looked in Ronan's direction. "I served Ronan the most delicious Long Island Ice Tea, that's a specialty dance, and he gave me his business card," she continued.

I clenched my teeth to prevent my mouth from falling open. Ronan was handing out his business card with our company name in the strip club? He sensed my disapproval.

"No worries little sister," he soothed. "Jill here didn't pass my card around the club. She's actually here to talk to you about buying a house."

Jillian nodded her head eagerly and Ronan winked at me.

"You want to buy a house?" I asked, although Ronan had just said that.

"I do."

"Okay, well, let's talk about it." I retrieved a client questionnaire from my drawer.

Jillian and I began to discuss the basics in order to get to know one another. She told me she currently rented an apartment with a friend and was ready to purchase and own her own property. She told me about her job and that she had been an exotic dancer for six years, which was pretty damn good as far as length of employment history. And when Jillian told me her salary I had to work extra hard to conceal the "*are you serious*" expression that I so desperately wanted to display. Jillian must have had some exceptional talent twirling and spreading her legs around the stripper pole.

"What a beautiful photo," she commented in the midst of our interview and after Ronan had busied himself at his desk.

"Thank you," I replied, and smiled at the close-up shot of me and Melanie.

"That's your girlfriend, right? Ronan told me you're into women. I tried to look at your profile but you have it private."

"Yes, I do." That's why I had it private; I didn't want all of Chicago in my business the way that Jillian was making her way into it.

"Lots of women visit our club," Jillian went on. "Some of the dancers are into women too. I'm not. However, I do lap dances for them. It's fun. You should visit sometime," she offered.

With our tight office space and his desk only fifteen feet from mine, I knew that Ronan overheard Jillian's suggestion, even though he pretended not to.

"Thank you, Jillian, but I try not to mix business with pleasure."

"So you go to gentlemen's clubs, right?"

I sighed on the inside. Ronan had placed me in an unpleasant position to be cordial and do business with his temporary girlfriend while she pried into my private life.

"I have been, yes." I left it at that.

Only on one occasion had I been to a strip club. Melanie, on the other hand, always a lover of women, had begun visiting several in the Midwest at age twenty-one and continued to do so in most cities where she traveled. She started going with some of her male buddies while in law school. Melanie still felt it was a great place to unwind and relax with a drink in hand. During a trip to Miami, Melanie had convinced me to go with her. I can't lie. The entertainment was sexy and made me hot for Melanie once we were back in our hotel room. However, I didn't share her same desire to frequent them on a regular basis. Since we've been together, Melanie's trips had lessened to just a few times with colleagues. One time she had arrived home so horny I thought she'd suck the skin right off my body by the aggressive manner in which she gripped my nipples and thighs with her teeth. The other times she was so tired that she had fallen asleep the moment she laid in the bed.

Jillian and I finished the questionnaire and I let her know that I'd get back to her with some preliminary numbers. She appeared excited and thanked me before she traded in the chair in front of my desk for the chair in front of Ronan. Jillian leaned against the backside of the chair and seductively placed a finger between her teeth. From behind I could see her lift her dress and open her legs slightly. *Oh my God.* Ronan deliciously eyed the space between her legs and Jillian giggled. She turned her head around to look at me, licked her fingertip and smiled before she lowered her dress and turned back to Ronan. The exchange was so inappropriate I didn't know what to do with myself. Quickly I packed my briefcase and stood to leave.

"See you Ronan," I said on my way out. I left them to do

whatever it was they were about to do in the office. "Jillian, I'll be in touch soon."

Outside I walked to my car with my heels clicking hard against the concrete. It wasn't that I was a prude; hell, obviously Mel and I enjoyed semi-public displays of affection as well. However, never would I consider such behavior in front of Ronan and certainly not a business client. I simply did not agree with intermingling business with pleasure, unless there was some *"written in the stars"* type occurrence that brought true soul mates together by way of work. I guess Ronan saw it differently since he was about to get some ass and get paid on top of it.

On my way to the grocery store I wanted to call Melanie, though I knew she was busy. Instead, in an effort to brighten my mood, I called Prestin to let her know that I had completed the guest list. After our meeting in the bathroom the past Sunday, I worked diligently on the list the next day. I finalized it just this morning. I told Prestin the headcount would be forty-nine if all invitees accepted. In turn she was going to send me a link to the website for the restaurant-lounge that would be hosting the party.

Later that evening around eight o'clock I was lying on the couch watching music videos. That was something I did only when I didn't want to think about anything, just be entertained. As a shapely woman grinded her hips and shook her titties for the camera, I couldn't help but begin to wonder if I was too rigid in my personality. I had always been a straight-laced kind of girl. I always preferred a one-on-one committed relationship to dating and bed hopping. I never cheated on a test, never cheated on a woman, and had never gotten into trouble with the law (aside from my speeding ticket). No one had ever seen me loud and drunk in the club, or talking shit to someone who had stolen a parking space from me. I cursed a little, though not offensively. I dressed cute and sassy, especially with my spunky hats, though no one could ever say my dress was too short or my neckline was too low. My most risqué adventures were coaxed by Melanie and her voyeuristic tendencies. While I knew many women who lived life in a more carefree manner, I was a bit more conservative, and enjoyed the quiet, calm and stable life I had built for myself.

Melanie walked in and peered at me in my reflective disposition on the couch. She, too, seemed a bit pensive and lost in thought. She took off her shoes and blazer, and walked toward me in her slacks and sleeveless top. She lifted my feet, sat down, and placed my feet on her lap. She looked so tired.

"What's wrong?" I asked.

"Nothing, it's just been a long day, that's all," she explained. She closed her eyes and rubbed them.

"Want me to make you a plate?"

"Yes," she answered, though not nearly as eager as I thought she would have.

I went into the kitchen, warmed up a plate for Melanie, and brought it back to her. She accepted silently. I let her eat quietly. Apparently she was in one of her distracted moods. I knew it best to allow her to mellow out for a while.

I watched a couple more videos while she slowly ate the food. Once she perked up and gave me a satisfied "ok" gesture with her hand. Other than that, her demeanor remained subdued. We were each sequestered within our own thoughts.

"Jo, can you bring me a pudding?" She had finished her meal and handed her plate to me.

"Sure." I took the plate and went back to the kitchen.

After her first bite of pudding, Melanie seemed inspired to finally engage in conversation.

"How was your day?" she asked. We hadn't talked since the afternoon and I hadn't been able to tell her about our newest client.

"You won't believe this," I started. "Ronan brought online J-LO to the office today. Check this out: he met her in the strip club. I guess we should have known by those photos, right? And not only that," I said, speaking louder, "she invited us to come see her at the strip club. Can you believe it?"

Melanie grinned. "You want to go?"

"Stop, Mel," I said quickly. Then immediately questioned myself and wondered if it would really be that bad of an idea. I still thought it was.

"So she's Ronan's girl and now your client," Melanie commented. "It's all right. You can't fault her for what she does for a living. It's legal."

"I know it is. It just doesn't feel right. She was so lewd. She looked like she wanted to start riding him while I was sitting right there."

"Damn, for real?"

"Yes! And she acted like it was funny or was supposed to turn me on, I don't know which. I just left."

Now Melanie laughed. "Loosen up. That's their business. You just focus on the work side."

"Why did you tell me to loosen up?" I asked, probably a bit too sensitively.

"Because you seem all upset about it."

"You don't think it's a problem?"

"Okay, I don't necessarily think it's cool to be meeting potential clients in the strip club, no. But we can't judge that. And you already know your brother. Girl, he's a player to heart. Now is not the time to start taking his behavior personal. You do your job and let him do his thing. And by the way, do you know how much line crossing happens in business?"

"Maybe in the office between co-workers, but not with clients. At least it shouldn't."

Melanie just shook her head and finished her pudding. Suddenly I began to wonder if in my sheltered state of living I had grown to be naïve.

"So who had you in the office late?" I asked.

Melanie became still again and paused a moment before responding.

"My new client" she said casually.

"Oooh, the lesbian" I smiled, interested to hear how their meeting went.

Melanie attempted a smirk back at me but didn't say anything.

"So what happened?" I asked.

"What usually happens with my clients. We talked about her case and how we'll proceed."

"I know, Mel. I mean, does it seem like she's really a stalker? Come on, tell me what's up. This is interesting."

"I don't know, Jo. I have to find out. It doesn't matter what she did or didn't do, she's my client and I have to defend her." She offered no more. "I'm about to take a shower," she announced, lifted my feet from her lap, and stood up.

"Can I get you anything?"

Melanie bent and kissed my cheek. "No, I'm good." Then she headed to the bedroom.

I picked up Melanie's plate and pudding container and took it to the kitchen. While Melanie showered, I cleaned the kitchen. Still I made it to bed before she exited the shower. I was wrapped in the sheet and comfortable with my pillow when Melanie entered the room, naked, wearing just her shower cap.

I loved Melanie's body and its soft masculine yet alluringly feminine physique. She had long strong legs, a delicate waist, a surprising bust and muscular arms. Melanie sat on the edge of the bed and began to lotion her skin. When she finished her front side she laid on her stomach on the bed. She handed me the lotion and I rubbed it into her back, over her firm cheeks and down the back of her thighs and calves. I added a light massage as well with hopes of easing some of the tension that seemed to have built inside her. She moaned appreciatively.

"You're the best, Jo," she said when I was done.

"I know." I laughed.

Chapter Six

"What do you think?" Ali asked me on Saturday morning while we were volunteering at a food drive boxing up canned goods.

"I don't know Ali. Why would you straighten your hair after all these years of never having a relaxer? Your hair is pretty just how it is."

Ali touched the naturally soft curly twists that she wore. They were the perfect complement to her stylish, yet earthy appearance.

"I was thinking, you know, with Noni being all trendy and wearing all kinds of hairdos, that maybe that's what I need to do to keep her."

"I don't think Noni's going anywhere Ali."

"Well, maybe not," she said, and reached for the tape to seal a box. "I guess what I mean is maybe that's what I have to do to make her mine. All mine."

"Should you have to go through all of that? Really, you feel you should have to change who you are in order to make someone be with you?"

"It's just hair, Jo."

"I know it's just hair. And I'm not saying changing your hairstyle is a bad thing. People do it all the time. I'm talking about the reasoning behind it. If you want to change your look because that's what you really want to do, then go for it. But if you're doing it with hopes of Noni settling down, you might be setting yourself up. One, she might not like it, or two, what if she loves it? And then she wants you to start dressing different. What if she wants you to stop being a vegan? How much would you compromise to be with her?"

Ali walked her box outside and stacked it on top of the others in the delivery truck.

"I'll do anything to be with her," she said upon return.

"Anything? Why?"

"Because I love her. It's that simple."

I understood Ali's love and desire for Noni. What I didn't understand is the lengths Ali was now willing to take, seven years into their undercover relationship, with dreams of securing Noni's heart once and for all. This didn't make sense, especially when a woman who would appreciate Ali in all of her beauty, inside and out, might be available if only Ali would come up from under Noni's spell.

"Ali, you know I love Noni. She's one of the girls. I would just hate to see you go through all of this for no reason."

"I won't know unless I try though. Every time I'm with her I love her more and more. And I know she loves me too. I just want her to love me and only me."

"Can she do that? She even said the other day that she's not into women full-time. What does that tell you?"

I didn't want to make Ali feel badly. However, I just as equally didn't want her to spend a lifetime yearning for something she'd never have, at least not completely. In all honestly, while I loved being her support, I didn't want to spend a lifetime hearing about it either.

"It tells me that there's a chance. She loves me enough to continue loving me in her own way."

I gave up. "Okay, Ali, it's your choice. What you might need to do is start dressing like a man since men are keeping her from loving you and only you." I was joking, though I could see by Ali's expression that she took my words to heart.

"You think so?" she contemplated.

"I was just kidding."

"But you're right. I mean, maybe if I harden up I can be all the man and woman she needs."

Instead of responding, I continued to add more cans to my box. With the ever-present femme-stud role in the lesbian community, I had seen several feminine women transform to studs in an effort to catch the attention of the femmes they couldn't hook while also being femme. Ali wasn't a super femme; she didn't wear makeup or heels. However, a lovely woman she was and I couldn't picture her any other way than how I had always known her. I sealed my full box and took it outside.

"I'm going to meditate on it," Ali said when I came back in and began to fill another box.

"Okay. Tell me what Buddha says."

"That's not funny, Jo," she pouted.

I hated to poke fun at her. However, I was somewhat mad at myself for suggesting what may very well be a catastrophic event in their relationship.

"Seriously, whatever you come up with is all right with me. So long as you're happy and as long as you can deal with whatever the consequences may be."

"I'm not worried. I know I'll be led to do what's best for me and Noni." She smiled, her spirit lightened.

"Let's finish up. Mel and I are shopping for new kitchen accessories today. It's time to change it up."

"That's fun." Her face brightened.

"It is, except we haven't agreed on what color to paint the kitchen. Mel wants to change to a bright color and I want to keep a more neutral, toned down look."

"Live a little," Ali said. "Color is good. Just choose a color that represents good energy, like orange."

"I don't want a bright-ass orange kitchen," I protested.

"Mel might."

"Yeah, she might, except I do all the cooking so I'm the one who has to deal with it. What if I want a late-night snack and turn on the light to all that color?"

"It'll make you smile," she offered.

I laughed because I couldn't help it. Ali always wanted everything to be like a ray of sunshine and for people to feel happy.

"You're right, Ali, thank you. I'll talk to Mel about it," I said, though I was far from convinced that orange would be our selected color. Still, Ali seemed pleased by my response and I was at least grateful that we were no longer talking about Noni.

"All right, let's get this done so you two can go shopping," Ali said. We continued to pack boxes for another hour before we each headed in our separate directions.

Melanie and I had been inside Home Depot looking at shades of paint for over an hour and had reached the point where we had gotten on each other's nerves. While I held color cards in shades of varying beige, cream and tan, Melanie's ideas were more expansive with colors ranging from teal, yellow and green. Melanie wanted our new kitchen to pop, while I wanted it to be calming. Melanie wanted the kitchen to scream *Hey!* I wanted it to exhale a soothing *Welcome.*

"But Mel, the rest of the house isn't this vibrant," I told her.

"I know, and we can consider painting the rest of it too. You know most condos are being updated with color in each room."

She was right and I knew that very well from some of the purchases I had seen our clients make. However, I hadn't considered an update to our low-key wall color. They weren't insane asylum white. I believe the color was called Desert Sand.

The husky woman behind the paint counter, who had assisted us with a few questions between helping other customers and mixing paint, interjected in our continued debate.

"Gals, let me help you out here," she offered.

Melanie checked the woman's name tag again. "Thank you, Debbie. We need some help."

"It's obvious to me that the Mrs. here isn't fond of color overload," Debbie said to Melanie. "And she doesn't want to fall asleep every time she enters the kitchen, ya see," Debbie told me. Debbie then stood in front of the vast array of color cards and pondered like she was selecting her next permanent tattoo. Melanie and I watched Debbie squinch her eyes, reach for a card and then shake her head "no." A few minutes later Debbie smiled to herself, chose a card, and brought it to us.

"This one right here gals," she said, and pointed. "Aurora Orange."

Well, I'll be damned, I thought.

"It reminds me of the first peek of the sunrise in Mexico Mel." I stared at the small card and reminisced about our early morning awakenings to catch the sun rise over the waters.

"It sure does. And guess what, Jo? It's not beige," she said, and kissed my forehead. "Debbie, we must thank you."

Debbie crossed her arms over her chest and mumbled some objections. "Eh, just doin' my job."

"We appreciate it. I think you saved our relationship," I teased, with a quick nestle of my head into Melanie's chest. "We also need white paint," I added and we spent another few minutes choosing the proper white paint for the trim.

"You ladies look good together," Debbie said. "Real nice I tell ya. Good to see. Now let me get two cans of paint ready for ya. Walk around and come back in a bit. If you need me to pick out something else for ya, just holler," she said with a cackle.

Melanie and I roamed the store for a while before I needed to excuse myself to the restroom.

"I'll be right here." Melanie had been standing in the aisle that displayed various kitchen faucets, When I returned, Melanie was frowning at her Blackberry.

"What's wrong babe?" I asked.

She hesitated before she responded. "I was just checking my e-mails and saw that some people are requesting online friendship."

"And what's wrong with that? It happens all the time. You just don't check yours on a regular basis."

"I know, I really don't have much time for it," she said, yet continued to scrunch her face at the screen.

"Why are you looking all stern at the phone?"

"One of my clients wants to be friends."

"Oh, I see. Is that a good idea? He or she is going to know more about you on a personal level when it should be business. You know about those lines Mel, we just talked about it."

"I know, but you know what's interesting is that we just had a meeting at work about online networking. It's the way of the world right now and a lot of businesses are utilizing the services."

"Lawyers too?"

"Oh yes, even lawyers. But it was suggested that we have a business profile separate from our personal."

"Okay, well if that's the case, don't accept the request."

Melanie stared back into her phone.

"Who is it anyway?" I asked curiously.

She paused. "It's the woman. The lesbian."

"For real? Let me see," I said excitedly.

Melanie seemed uncertain before she reluctantly handed her phone to me. I squinted my eyes at the small photo and then widened them in awe.

"*This* is your client?" I asked in disbelief.

"Yes."

"Somebody has a restraining order against this beautiful woman right here?" I questioned more.

"Yes."

"Hmph, she can stalk me anytime," I remarked in fun, though Mel seemed to have found no humor in it. She ignored me and put her phone back in the case and slid it into her pocket.

"You think the paint is ready?" she asked.

I checked my watch. "We've been walking around about thirty minutes so maybe."

"Let's head back that way."

Inside I was puzzled as to why Melanie had clammed up about her client. It confused me that she seemed so distraught about the friendship request. Especially since the answer had already been given to her; if she set up a business profile, she could add her client then.

"Here ya go," Debbie said enthusiastically upon our return. She handed Melanie and I a can of paint each. "Good luck in that kitchen gals."

"Thanks Debbie," I responded. Melanie only gave a half smile in response before we headed to the checkout counter to pay for the paint.

"You all right babe?" I asked Melanie.

She looked me in the eyes and the distressed gaze she had been expressing disappeared and her attention reverted back to me.

"I'm good. Work is really busy right now, that's all," she answered.

I wanted to tell her that stressing her client's friendship request had nothing to do with work being busy. However, I refrained and was grateful that the tense moment had passed I did make a mental note that she seemed especially uptight the last two occasions that particular lesbian client came up in conversation. I didn't want to make too much of it since Melanie was easily distracted by her work and became quiet when she had clients on her mind. At the same time, this incident was different. She had not previously represented a lesbian client, nor had any previous client attempted to extend the relationship beyond the office and courtroom. I understood her apprehension, not wanting to befriend someone whose livelihood was in her hands. What if Melanie lost the case? She won many, and lost some. How would her client react if she lost the case? Would she attempt to defame Melanie online? On the other hand, if Melanie won the case, would her client praise her and increase Melanie's potential clientele? It appeared to be a risky venture the firm was considering. I was curious to find out how the firm would choose to proceed.

"Are we still going to Crate & Barrel?" I asked.

"Of course. We need new accessories to go with our new, colorful kitchen," she chuckled, like she had won the case of Melanie vs. Jovanna even though I didn't feel that I had completely acquiesced to her demand. After all, Debbie had selected the color.

Melanie and I spent most of the afternoon picking out an assortment of new items with which to decorate the kitchen. By the time we finished shopping Melanie was going to have the vibrant kitchen she had hoped for. We purchased a new tabletop runner in striped shades of a delicate orange, light brown, a faint mustard yellow and white. The new curtains, a shade of the orange, accessorized perfectly. We added to our dinnerware a sixteen-piece set in white and another in orange. We found colorful napkins and silverware that matched that of the tabletop runner.

Besides these items, I picked up a few new cooking appliances and utensils. I selected a set of new baking pans, mixing bowls and a powerful new hand mixer all in stainless steel. They were the perfect completion to the stainless steel cookware set I had purchased the year prior.

When we returned home and placed all of the purchased items in the guest bedroom, Melanie surprised me and took me in her arms. She held tightly and squeezed.

"I want you to enjoy the kitchen," she said into my ear.

"I will," I replied, genuinely excited for the change in color and fresh items we would display and utilize.

"I appreciate all that you do," she added, I assumed in reference to my doing most of the cooking for us.

Because Melanie was more action than word, I was a little taken aback by her statement. Though her words were simple enough, I fully expected the fact that she had taken care of the day's bill to suffice in my interpreting her appreciation for me. She tugged at the back of my ponytail and I looked up at her. She kissed me gently on the lips.

"Thank you Mel," I told her. She smiled back and then tapped me on the side of my hip.

"Let me do something, okay?"

"Okay. I'm going to start clearing the kitchen and getting ready to paint. Are we starting tomorrow?"

"Yeah, early, okay? No sleeping in this Sunday."

"Just this one Sunday," I agreed and headed toward the kitchen. Most Sundays I preferred to sleep as late as I possibly could, which generally was only about 10 A.M. At that time I usually prepared breakfast while Mel watched news shows, read a book or continued to rest.

In the kitchen I began to remove pictures from the wall. When I passed through the hallway to put them in the guest bedroom with the new items, I saw Melanie sprawled across the living room chaise peering intently at her laptop screen. I knew instantly what had her attention. Her expression was that of thoughtful interest mixed with uncomfortable uncertainty. A queasy knot began to form in my stomach as

I watched her review her client's profile. I didn't know what it meant nor did I want to presume that the unsettled feeling signified trouble. I did, however, recognize a red flag when one waved in my face. Melanie's client had begun to prove herself as a caution and warning in which I needed to heed.

Chapter Seven

The following morning Melanie and I had planned to get up around 7 A.M. to begin painting the kitchen. We had removed all of the items and placed them throughout the condo the night before. We had begun the masking tape process, although grew tired of the task and retired to our bedroom for a movie with delivered pizza.

When Melanie had finished her time on the laptop, her mood toward me was still tender the remainder of the evening. Nonetheless, that didn't prevent me from waking thirty minutes early to spend a little time on my own laptop.

Quietly I crept out of bed and carried my laptop into the living room. Once online I logged onto the networking site and ignored the three e-mails I had along with four requests for friendship. Instead, I went straight to Melanie's profile to view her list of friends. The number had increased slightly, though I hadn't paid all that much attention to her friends list in the past. When I clicked the option to view Melanie's most recently added friends, there she was—SunnyDay79—in a much better view than I had seen on Melanie's phone.

Her client was absolutely breathtaking. She was a combination of Prestin, Jaye, and Ivy all combined into one glorious woman who appeared to be of Domincan Republic heritage. She had a full shaped face with skin that was a lucent soft honey. Her brown hair was parted on the left side and hung into a loose, soft bang that fell into layers that landed at her collarbone. She smiled sweetly, almost shy-like, into the camera, but what captivated me most were her eyes. They were wide and a unique shade of gray that, when I squinted closely at the screen, sent a shudder through my body. She gazed directly into the camera and with the close-up head shot it felt that she was looking right at me. There was something in her eyes; a fixated, intense and powerful stare that contradicted her bashful smile.

I clicked on the photo to view her profile only to find that it was set to private. I moaned, aggravated, because I was curious to learn more about this woman to see what had Melanie so captivated. I wondered why she had chosen to go ahead and add her client to her personal profile rather than wait until she created a business page. Obviously her client was beautiful, however, surely that couldn't be the reason Melanie was so distracted. Melanie and I were around beautiful women all the time. Hell, our closest friends included a few of the most gorgeous women Chicago had to offer. Certainly Melanie wasn't simple enough to get caught up just by a pretty face. There had to be something else I was missing.

Or maybe there wasn't. It wasn't odd for Melanie to occasional-ly withdraw when she was engrossed in a case or was mentally working even though she may be present with me. I already knew that about her and had adjusted to the preoccupied states in which she would sometimes fall. However, this added personal element seemingly had nothing to do with the case and therefore, the nagging I felt in my gut remained. Why would a client want to cross the business line and in turn, why would Melanie allow it? She had never befriended any of her DUI clients or clients accused of assaulting another. Why now with such an exceptionally magnificent beauty?

I leaned my head against the cushion of the suede couch and closed my eyes. Questions flowed about my thoughts, though it was only moments before my mind quieted down and I fell back into a light sleep.

"Joooo," Melanie sang my name.

I woke with a jerk and saw Mel bent down next to me, smiling, apparently having watched me sleep for a moment or two. My eyes darted to my laptop, which remained open while it sat on my legs. Thank goodness the screensaver had activated to cover up what I had been looking at. Quickly I closed the laptop shut.

"Time to get started?" I asked.

"It is," she said, then took my laptop and moved it to the side so that she could sit next to me. She took my head and gently laid it in her lap. She rubbed her fingers through my twisted curls. I closed my eyes and focused on the feeling of her fingertips as they grazed across my scalp.

"Still sleepy, huh?" she asked.

"Yes," I murmured.

"Well what had you up before seven anyway?"

I was silent for a moment. I hated liars. I had a deep down, passionate disdain for people who couldn't speak the truth. However, I wasn't one of those people that believed a lie was a lie. I didn't feel that a man who lied to his wife by telling her that he liked her new dress could be compared to him lying to her that he wasn't having an affair with the next door neighbor. In my eyes, there was a scale and although I didn't appreciate a small or big lie, I understood that people lied all the time. They told lies at work to their boss about how much they loved their job. They told lies about not attending a function because they were ill when in fact they really just didn't want to be there. I'd even be lying to Melanie about her birthday in order to deceive her about the surprise party. So understandably, sometimes a lie had to be told. Still, I told the truth.

"I just wanted to look something up online before we got started," I said.

Okay, so I intentionally omitted *what* I wanted to look up. I refused to allow myself to question Melanie unless she gave me grounds to do so. One thing I couldn't stand in relationships were those that question without reason; those who accuse because they think they know something when in actuality they know little, only what they are creating in their mind. Some women suggest that questions are necessary, even required, in a relationship. How can you trust your partner if you don't question their trustworthiness? It was an ass backward thought process in my opinion. Even if I had my own doubts—my own suspicions or uncertainties—I'd rather she damn near be caught guilty before frivolously questioning what I think she *might* doing. An untrustworthy person is untrustworthy, period. Even if I spent time interrogating, likely I wouldn't get the truth anyway so why bother? This was a debate I had with women in my early twenties and had vowed not be with a woman who I felt I couldn't trust. However, if I happened to find myself in that situation, I would at the very least find proof of deceit. At this point, Melanie had not shown herself as anything other than absorbed in a case and confused by the new territory of a client who wanted friendship outside of business. At least that's what I told myself.

"Let's get moving," I told Melanie.

We went into our bathroom, brushed our teeth and then changed into old, loose fitting clothes that were comfortable for painting. Melanie inserted a CD of upbeat music that we played softly until about 11 A.M. when we felt our neighbors were awake or gone to church. By that time the walls were finished and we needed to allow them to dry before painting the trim. I started a pot of coffee, the only appliance I intentionally left in the kitchen, while Melanie balled up splattered sections of newspaper and cleaned the pans of aurora orange paint.

"This looks good so far," Melanie observed.

"You know, it really does," I agreed. "Debbie did good for us."

"There's some paint left," Melanie said. "We could have a little fun with this."

I laughed. "Doing what Mel?"

"I could make some pretty designs up and down your body. Rather than paint you while nude, I can just paint you nude," Melanie suggested, reminding me of an old fantasy she once told me about in which she wanted to role play art student and subject and paint a woman nude.

"I kind of like that," I told her. "Don't put that paint too far away."

"I won't." She smiled.

By mid-afternoon we had finished two coats of trim and finally decided to shower. We entered the stall together, something we enjoyed doing whether it was a prelude to sex or just to spend quality, intimate time together. On some occasions she'd wash my hair for me, rubbing shampoo into a thick lather and massaging my scalp as she cleaned my hair. And I found great pleasure in drowning her bath sponge with her favorite liquid soap and washing her entire body for her, even *there*. The first time I wanted to wash her there she protested, fiercely objecting like we were in the courtroom. I reminded her that my fingers had already been there. My tongue had already been there. I had seen it, touched it, and tasted it at all times when it wasn't "clean" so why protest that gesture as well? She had hesitantly opened her legs slightly and allowed me to softly cleanse her delicate spot.

This afternoon we rinsed under the hot water, and assisted one another with picking paint spots off of our skin. Other than that, we washed our own bodies quickly and quietly, both of us hungry and anxious to head out for a late lunch.

Once we were both dressed in shorts and T-shirts, we were ready to walk several blocks to a nearby pub that served oversized and filling cheeseburgers. I was grateful that Melanie had not once gotten on her laptop nor checked her Blackberry all day. However, I did find it odd that just as we were about to leave, Melanie picked up her phone, appeared to contemplate whether or not to bring it, then made a decision and laid it back down on the nightstand. I could not recall a time in which Melanie had chosen to leave behind her primary source of communication.

"Let's go." She guided me out of the bedroom.

I stared back at her BlackBerry and wondered just what it was that she wanted to avoid today. I knew I didn't have to think too hard about it to know the answer.

That week Ronan and I had a welcome influx of phone calls and visits with potential new clients ready to take advantage of the turn in the upswing of the economy. Many were ready to take advantage of first-time home buying opportunities and others were seeking to refinance from an adjustable loan rate to a fixed rate. For three days Ronan and I were in the office through the evening, meeting clients, doing paperwork, and preparing for several closings.

In the office Ronan and I were the best of partners. We worked well together and our clients seemed to appreciate a sibling duo that was competent and operated smoothly. Several calls we accepted were referrals from previous clients. However, with the flow of new calls we answered that week, we also found ourselves receiving hang-up calls as well.

Businesses are not strangers to calls in which someone may have dialed the wrong number and rather than stating so, the person ends the call instead. I assumed that to be the case when I got a mute caller on that Monday afternoon. By Wednesday evening, both Ronan and I had each answered multiple hang-up calls.

The office line rang around 8:30 P.M., just as he and I were turning off the lights and preparing to leave. I was tired and ready to get home to Melanie, who also had worked late hours and who I had hardly seen since Sunday. I gave Ronan a look that said I wasn't taking the call. In response, Ronan walked back to his desk and picked up the phone.

"JR Financial," he answered, immediately slamming the phone back down. "Who the fuck dials the wrong number this many times?" he asked angrily.

"You sure it's not one of your women, Ronan? You piss one of your girls off?" I teased.

His eyes widened and I could see that the thought hadn't occurred to him. He digested the possibility. "Could be," he stated.

"Well figure out who it is and if she's not calling to get a loan, tell her to stop ringing this phone."

"I will, I will," he responded to hush me. We left the office and Ronan locked the door.

"Don't forget I'm doing a closing in the morning," he told me as we walked to our cars. "I'll be in late morning."

"I didn't forget. See you later," I responded.

Inside the car I picked up my phone and dialed Melanie's cell. She didn't answer. Next I called her office and received no answer there either. I called her cell phone back and received her voice mail again. This time I left a message to tell her that I was headed home and that I wouldn't be making dinner. I told her to grab something to eat on her way, or that she'd have to put something together herself when she got home.

I ended the call feeling lightly stressed. Although my week had been hectic and I was absorbed in my own work, Melanie had resorted back to her distracted state since Monday. We had spoken only once during each workday, which was unusual, and on Monday and Tuesday nights, we both had slept soundly on our own sides of the bed, exhausted from our day. By tonight I was missing her.

When I got home I changed into an oversized T-shirt and

got straight into the bed. I turned to a local news channel, placed two pillows under my head, and closed my eyes. I fell asleep listening to a news story about a house fire.

Around 11:30 P.M. I woke up. The television was still on and Melanie still wasn't home. I dialed her cell phone and this time she answered. I could hear a radio playing in the background.

"Where are you, Mel?" I asked, before she could say, "hello."

"Driving home," she answered. "What are you doing up?"

"I was asleep, but woke up and you still weren't here. Where have you been?" I questioned. "I was worried."

"The guys and I went out for drinks," she told me. "I only had one."

"Why didn't you call me?"

"I'm sorry."

"How long before you get home?"

"I'll be there in a few minutes."

I was silent.

"Do you need something? Are you hungry?" she asked softly.

"I'm fine."

"Okay. See you soon."

I rolled over in the bed and stared at the ceiling fan above. It spun in circles and cast a cool breeze onto my warming skin. I tried to control the racing thoughts that began to run through my mind until it felt like my head was spinning just as fast as the fan.

Quickly I hopped up, opened my laptop, logged online and went straight to Melanie's profile. I scrolled the page and saw my picture, still in its number one spot under the "Friends" section beside her sibling and a few other family members and friends. Further I scanned the page and then I saw the eyes. SunnyDay79 had left a comment on Melanie's profile two hours ago. It simply said, "Hi." I frowned and read the word over and over like she had written a paragraph. What did "hi" mean? I mean, I know what the word means, but what did it mean that she left such a plain remark on Melanie's profile? How would Melanie respond? Or had Melanie left a comment on her client's profile and this was her response? What was going on?

I shut my laptop off and laid back down when I heard Melanie enter.

"The door is fixed," she acknowledged when she came into the room.

"Yeah, I had Harry come by and work on it today," I told her. Harry was our "fix-it" man that we called upon for our condo repairs.

"Cool," she said and walked to her dresser to grab sleeping shorts and a tank. Then she went into the bathroom.

She was quiet. All I could hear was Melanie brushing her teeth and washing her face. When she came back into the bedroom she asked, "Do you want to leave the TV on?"

"Yes," I answered.

Melanie got in bed from her side and gathered the light cover over her body. She snuggled with her pillow and closed her eyes. For a moment I sat there unsure if she was really about to go to sleep without saying anything else to me. After about thirty seconds of silence I thought my insides were going to explode.

"Melanie," I said firmly.

She opened her heavy eyes. "What?"

"I've hardly talked to you all day and all I get is three sentences when you finally get home at what?" I looked at the clock. "Almost midnight."

"I'm tired, Jo."

"I'm tired too."

"So let's go to sleep."

I sat upright and stared at the TV. My body was tingling with anger and I hated the feelings that were brewing inside of me. I had sworn that I would never be a suspicious girlfriend. Never be the girlfriend up sweating at night wondering where her girlfriend was. Never be the girl who felt rejected or insecure because she wasn't sure if her girlfriend had found interest elsewhere. Yet, I could feel myself turning into just that girl.

"Where did you guys go?" I asked her.

"We went to that place on Ashland."

"What place on Ashland? There's a zillion places on Ashland."

"I don't know. I rode with Mike."

"Why did you ride with Mike?"

"Because he knew where the place was."

"You couldn't follow him?"

"He just suggested I ride with him so I did. Why are you questioning me?" she squinted.

"It doesn't make sense to me. To ride with Mike, have drinks, and then have Mike take you back to the office to your car?"

"Why doesn't that make sense?" she asked.

"It just doesn't," I responded.

"Relax and get some sleep." She reached for me and took me in her arms. I cuddled next to her and tried to collect my senses.

"Did you get my message?" I asked, unable to calm down.

She sighed. "Yes."

"So you picked up your phone, you saw I called, you listened to my message, and yet you still didn't call me?"

"Yes."

"Why not?"

"Because by the time I listened to your message I figured you were asleep."

"What time was that?" I asked.

"You're tripping, Jo. What's wrong?"

"What time, Mel?" I repeated.

"It must have been about ten-thirty," she finally answered.

"Goodnight," she added, I guess in an effort to quiet me once and for all.

I didn't respond. Instead I closed my eyes, mentally stored all the information Melanie had just shared with me, and marked it with another red flag for future follow-up.

Chapter Eight

"No, no, not yet," I whined softly when the alarm clock beeped the following morning at 6:30 A.M. I exhaled loudly, my mind pained by the thought of opening my eyes already.

"Mel," I said, trying to wake her to turn off the alarm which was on her side of the bed. No response.

"Mel!" I repeated louder. I turned over and opened my eyes to find that she wasn't resting beside me. In the spot where she should have been was nothing but scrunched sheets and tossed pillows. When I sat up I noticed that the door to the bedroom was closed. Where in the hell was she?

I got out of bed, stretched my arms far above my head, and yawned before I walked and opened the door. I peeked into the kitchen. No Melanie. I walked into the living room. No Melanie. When I passed the bathroom next to the guest bedroom, I noticed Melanie's curling iron was inside along with a few of her other personal items. She had gotten up, gotten dressed and ready in the guest bathroom, and left the house all before I got up. How did she do that after having gotten in so late the night before?

My eyes began to sting with sleepiness and tears. I headed back to the bedroom and went straight to our bathroom. Inside I found a note taped to the mirror. It read: I'm sorry Jo. Had to go in extra early today. Meet me at my office after work, okay? Te amo. Mel.

So what was she sorry for? Was she sorry for not calling me last night? Was she sorry for saying no more than a few words to me once she got home? Or was she sorry just because she had to get up early and go to work? Regardless, it didn't matter to me. I had my own share of work to complete today. However, it wouldn't stop me from leaving the office as early as I could to go see her. My heart momentarily relaxed and my nerves calmed. At least she seemed to be making an effort to rectify the uneasiness and distance growing between us.

Inside I smiled at her thoughtfulness, went into the bedroom and sprawled across the bed. On my nightstand, I grabbed my cell phone. I located Melanie's contact information and selected the option to send her a text message. I typed: I'll be there. Thank you Mel. I love you. A few moments later my phone vibrated. Her reply was a wink and a smile.

From my closet I selected two outfits for the day. One conservative, business suit for work, and a separate dress: a low-cut, short summer dress that Melanie loved. I hoped that by the time I arrived to the firm, most of the hourly employees would be gone for the day, leaving behind just a few lawyers who I didn't think would mind if they caught me entering Melanie's office in a revealing, sexy dress. Over the years I had accompanied Melanie to most of the office functions. This included Christmas parties and special functions that celebrated big cases won by some of the firm's top lawyers. Melanie had built a good rapport with them all and they all knew me as Melanie's partner.

Once at work my day remained steadily busy. I met with a few new clients, continued to work with existing clients in preparation of closings before month-end, and talked with Jillian, who had been pre-approved for a decent size loan to purchase her first home.

"I'm so excited!" she screamed in the phone.

"I'm happy for you too, Jillian," I told her.

"Does Ronan know?"

"He's not in yet, but I'll tell him when he gets here," I offered.

"We all should celebrate," she suggested.

My eyebrows furrowed at the idea. I was still a little offended by Jillian's gesture in the office upon our first meeting. At the same time, she seemed to be maintaining my brother's attention as well as now becoming an official client. I cast aside my skepticism and agreed.

"Sure, I'll have Ronan set something up."

"Thank you Jovanna. I look forward to seeing you again," she said affectionately. I almost regretted having accepted her offer.

"Okay, Jillian. See you soon," I replied and hung up the phone.

Just as I ended the call, the phone rang again. "JR Financial," I answered.

There was a muffled sound on the other end before a female voice spoke. "May I speak with Melanie?"

"There's no Melanie here," I answered. The call ended.

I placed the receiver back into the cradle and stared at the phone, wishing I had paid more attention to the information that displayed on the screen when it rang. Was it just a coincidence that someone would call my office asking for Melanie? My Melanie was not the only Melanie in the city of Chicago, however, the irony nudged at my instincts. I had a feeling it was not just chance.

I pushed the speaker button on the phone and once I heard the tone, dialed star-sixty-nine, only to be informed by an automated voice that the number that had just called was unknown. Frustrated, I hung up and then minimized the client's information I had been reviewing on my computer. Next I clicked on the Internet Explorer icon on my desktop and logged onto the networking website, something I found myself doing on a more frequent basis than I had in the past. While I had previously enjoyed the casual communication with family and friends, it was now becoming a frenzied measure in which to monitor Melanie and her client's interactions.

Once online and on Melanie's profile, I clicked on SunnyDay79's profile and my heart nearly pounced out of my chest. Although her profile was private, I could still view the status message she displayed as well as her mood at the time. Her status read: **My name is Sunday in case you wanted to know** . . . and her mood displayed: **Amused** with a bright yellow laughing smiley face next to it. When I looked into those gray eyes I could have sworn I saw glimmers of laughter and mockery at me.

What in the hell was happening? I felt like I was slowly but steadily being absorbed into a crazed online web of games. Was it simply my imagination, my own unanswered questions that had me wondering if this woman was speaking directly to me? Was it my own narcissistic thoughts that had me believing she was as preoccupied with me as I was becoming of her? Or was my mind distorting reality based upon my own insecurities that Melanie was preoccupied with her, and therefore, misinterpreting her words because of my fears?

"Hey sis," Ronan said as he entered the office. I didn't answer. "You all right over there?" he asked, concerned.

Briefly I contemplated telling Ronan what I was feeling. Telling him the nervousness I was feeling about Melanie and her client and that I was beginning to think there was more to their interaction than I knew about. However, I realized I had no concrete evidence to tell him other than the hypothetical equation I was putting together without having all of the variables.

"I'll talk to you about it another time," I responded, as I tried to rid my mind of the unfamiliar, panicking feelings that kept surfacing. The frown on my face remained intact despite my attempts to hide my feelings.

"You sure you're okay?" He sat at his desk and opened his laptop.

"Yes, I'm fine, thank you. Hey, we got a thumbs-up for Jillian," I told him.

"That's my girl," he said with a smile. I didn't know if he was referring to me or Jillian.

"She wants to celebrate with us."

"The three of us?"

"That's what she said."

"All right, all right, cool. You good with that?" he asked cautiously.

"I suppose. I mean, I'm not really about mixing and mingling business and friendship," I said, probably too aggressively. "But you seem to think it's all right so, yeah, we can do that."

"You want to hang out at the club?" he kidded.

"Melanie would like that," I said. "You know I'm bringing her, don't you?"

"Of course, the party wouldn't be complete without Mel. I'll figure something out. Let's get together this weekend. For some reason Jillian seems to really like you."

"Is that just because she's all into my brother's ass?" I joked.

"Naw, that's me gettin' up in her ass," he laughed.

"Oh, shut up Ronan! Too much information," I said with a scrunched expression.

"For real, Jo, don't hold it against her that she's a stripper. She does it because it's good money. Like most people she tries to find jobs that pay well. Trust me, she's not sexing all the men in the club."

"And how do you know that? She sexed you up pretty quick."

"Yeah, that's right. But look at me," he said cockily, half serious and half kidding.

"Whatever. Same way she grinds up on you, she grinds up on other men. How do you handle that?"

"Well, she's not my woman—yet," he added. "So it's all good.

But like I said, it's just her job. She's got to make it seem real and make the men feel good. It doesn't mean anything with those other dudes."

"Damn Ronan, you sound whipped," I told him.

"Pussy whipped, Jo? It's okay, you can say it," he laughed really hard knowing how much trouble I had with that word. In the sixth grade I was harassed half the year by a pubescent, wanna-be-sexed boy who would run up to me from behind, whisper "pussy" into my ear, and then dart off before I could say anything to him. His profane actions had warped my ability to hear, let alone say the word without an internal cringe.

"Stop," I said, though I almost laughed along.

"You are too funny, girl. How do you eat pussy but can't say the word?"

"Two different things."

"I bet Melanie would like it."

"Why do you say that?" I asked.

"Because I know women and even though some try to act like it's a nasty word, it's really a turn-on. You know how many shy girls I've been with," he said, using his hands to add quotations around the word shy. "Soon as I tell them how good their pussy is, then they really go crazy. Trust me, Melanie would love for you to tell her how good her pussy is," he urged.

"Oh my God, Ronan, I can't believe you just said that." I was almost embarrassed.

"Look, I know you and Mel have some good sex, otherwise, you wouldn't have made it this long. I can tell Mel is a freak." *How did he know that?* "Just try it out one day and you'll thank me." He winked at me.

"I can't believe you!" Maybe Ronan was right. I couldn't lie that on the inside I was intrigued by the thought. At this point I was beginning to worry about the possibility of Melanie's attention diverting to someone other than me and I'd do anything to keep her. It was time to loosen up my collar and do whatever I had to do to keep the woman I loved so much.

That afternoon a meeting with a client ran late and by the time I was ready to head to Melanie's office, it was already seven o'clock. Inside the bathroom I freshened up and changed into the second dress I brought to work with me. I added a few fresh curls to my hair, a spritz of perfume, and red lipstick which Melanie found sexy.

When I stepped out of the bathroom, I was surprised to see that Jillian had arrived. Even more shocked to find her sitting on Ronan's desk, legs apart, with Ronan standing in between her legs. Did they have no regard for my presence? Or did Jillian possess the same voyeuristic qualities that Melanie did? Well of course she did, I reasoned. How else could she be a stripper?

"Somebody's got a date tonight," Ronan teased. "Going to get some pussy?"

My mouth fell open, mortified. Did he really just say that to me in front of Jillian? Even with the conversation we had earlier in the day, his sudden comment caught me off guard and caused my cheeks to warm, but why? He was my brother and I should be used to his crass remarks by now. And further, it had been hinted to me that I needed to liven up my reserved composure and step outside of my comfort zone.

"Yes, I sure am," I said back.

Ronan raised an eyebrow and Jillian smirked. "That's my girl. We're great lovers, *hermana*, it's in our blood."

I almost gagged at the thought of him comparing me to my mother's free-spirited sexual nature, though I simply smiled. "I'm not taking any work home tonight," I told him, looking at the stacks of organized papers on my desk.

"Don't worry about it, go do your thing. I'm not taking work home tonight either," he said with a kiss to Jillian's neck.

"Okay, well, I'm leaving," I told them both. "See you this weekend, Jillian."

"I look forward to it, Jovanna," she responded, and squinted flirtatiously in my direction. I peered right back at Jillian's suggestive stare until she eventually turned her attention back to Ronan. Inside I giggled, and left the office feeling pretty good.

"Jovanna, you're looking lovely this evening," Mr. Riley, the security guard in Melanie's office building, told me after I entered through the revolving doors. Because of my frequent trips to visit Melanie for lunch and after work, Mr. Riley, the second-shift guard, and I had become acquainted. He was an older gentleman, soft in his nature and excessively polite.

"Thank you, Mr. Riley," I said as I approached the large guard station. "How are you tonight?"

He smiled delicately. "Blessed to have another day."

"That's right," I responded as I signed the visitor log in order to get to the office level. I checked the clock perched on the station to document my time. It was 7:26 P.M.

"You two doing anything special tonight?" Mr. Riley asked.

"I don't think so. We've both been busy and haven't had much time to see each other. Melanie asked me to come by tonight to visit while she works a bit."

"Have a good time Ms. Jovanna." He grinned pleasantly.

"Thanks Mr. Riley," I replied, and then headed toward the elevators.

When I reached Melanie's floor, the hall was quiet. Through the frosted glass door I could see movement just before I turned the knob. Upon entering I saw Rick, a young colleague of Melanie's, walking past with folders in his hand.

"Hey, Rick," I said perkily. "How's it going?"

"Jovanna, hey, how are you? Looking spiffy tonight," he said.

"Thanks, Rick." I touched my curls to be sure they were still in place. "Melanie in her office?"

"I haven't seen her in a while, but I think so. Good to see you," he said, and jetted toward the copy machine.

I walked past the unmanned receptionist desk and further into the firm's office. It had a professional appeal, with flat blue-gray carpeting, polished cherry-wood walls and leather furniture throughout. I peeked into the conference room next to Melanie's office, which was empty. Her office door was closed, though I heard light talking inside. I knocked gently. When Melanie opened the door, there was a genuine look of surprise on her face followed by an expression of annoyance. She quickly exited her office and closed the door, but not before I saw a set of long, crossed legs seated at the chair in front of her desk.

"What are you doing here, Jo?" she asked irritably.

"You asked me to come see you after work," I answered, confused by her snappy state.

"It's not a good time."

"And why not?" I asked, and crossed my arms over my chest.

"A client is here right now."

"Well, I'll wait," I told her obstinately.

"Jo, just head back home."

"Why, Mel? I've waited for you plenty of times when you've had clients. What's the problem?" I asked, although I knew the answer. "Who's here?"

"A client, I just told you that." The expression on her face was that of exasperation and desperation.

"Who?" I asked again.

"It doesn't matter. I'm busy right now," she said.

Just as I was about to reach for the doorknob on her door, Rick interrupted.

"Isn't she one of the most beautiful women around? Jovanna,

you need to stop by more often and brighten up this place. No offense, Melanie," he kidded.

Melanie momentarily lightened up and smiled faintly. "She's the best."

After Rick passed us and closed the door to his office, I questioned Melanie again. "Why can't I wait, Mel?"

"Please don't make a scene, Jo."

"Make a scene? Make a scene?" I said louder. "When have I ever made a scene with you? I'm not like that Mel and you know it."

Melanie didn't respond, only stared at me. I stared right back at her and for about fifteen seconds neither of us said anything.

"I'll see you at home," she stated firmly, in a tone that informed me that the conversation was over. She stepped backward, opened her office door, and closed it in my face.

I wanted to open the door, though I was too frightened at what I might find out on the other side. My insides twisted in knots as I stood in contemplation and tried to determine my next move. If Melanie's meeting with her client was indeed for business, and I opened the door in a panic and fury, surely Melanie's credibility would dampen. However, if I walked away and allowed Melanie to proceed with a so-called meeting with a woman that appeared to be a threat to my relationship, then what kind of woman was I? Then again, I still had no concrete evidence that my runaway suspicions of Melanie's peculiar interest in her client were accurate. Though my instincts were screaming yes, I had no proof that the client inside of Melanie's office was gray-eyed Sunday.

For another sixty seconds I stood outside the door. I listened to the soft chatter from inside the office, the words of which were unfortunately muffled. I was unable to decipher the conversation. My head was leaned close against the smooth wooden door, with my eyes closed in hopes that it would temporarily heighten my sense of hearing.

"She's working the late shift again, huh?" Rick asked me, startling me out of my attempted eavesdropping.

Defeated, I sighed. "Yes, looks that way. Guess I'll have to catch up to her at home."

"Well it was good seeing you," he said, and headed toward the firm's entrance.

"Hey, Rick!" I took hurried steps to catch up to him and we exited together. "Did you have a good time last night?"

"Last night?" He didn't seem to know what I was talking about.

"Yeah, Melanie said she and some of the guys tried out a new place on Ashland," I told him with my best efforts at sounding casual and not desperate. "I just assumed you went as well. What was the name of the place?"

We stood face to face outside the elevator and I felt nervous tears well in my eyes as Rick stood with a questionable expression on his face.

"Oh, my wife and I had Lamaze class yesterday evening," he told me. "I left the office early. They went out without me, huh? Wait until I get my hands on Mike, I know it was his idea," he laughed.

One of the ten pounds on my shoulders lifted. I tried to laugh with Rick. "I'm sure they didn't do it on purpose," I replied as we got into the elevator.

We rode quietly until I reached the lobby level. "See you another time." I hopped out of the elevator.

"Sure, Jovanna," Rick said, just before the doors closed and he continued down to the parking garage.

"Back so soon?" Mr. Riley asked curiously when I returned to the security station.

"Yes, unfortunately Melanie's extra busy tonight."

"She's a hard worker. Good woman she is."

I didn't respond. When I documented my departure time on the security log, 7:42 P.M., my eyes browsed the other

entries on the list. My heart sank when I saw her name. In
blue ink and with perfect penmanship, Sunday had entered
the building and logged in at 6:45 P.M. An hour later she
remained behind closed doors with my girlfriend.

"Are you all right Miss Jovanna?" Mr. Riley asked tenderly.

"I'm fine, thanks," I answered. "See you next time." I
turned around, left the building, and for the second time
in my life, sat in my car and waited to see if I could catch
my girlfriend cheating on me. I hated the unexpected and
sudden metamorphosis I was undergoing. In just a couple of
weeks I was transforming from a settled and assured partner
in a monogamous relationship to a threatened and suspecting
woman acting spastically out of my usual character.

While I sat in the car I took time to review just what had
me so apprehensive. I recalled the evening after Melanie's
first meeting with Sunday and how quiet and closed-mouth
she had been regarding their initial interaction. At the time I
hadn't considered it abnormal. After their online friendship
and Melanie's agitated demeanor whenever Sunday came up
in conversation I became concerned. Now, after Melanie's
blatant disregard for my presence in order to tend to Sunday,
I was beyond unnerved about the situation.

For twenty-five minutes I sat in my car and watched the building for Sunday's departure. Impatiently, I tapped my fingers
against the steering wheel, the console, against my thigh.
My breathing felt abnormal, as if my chest were somewhat
constrained and I needed to inhale and exhale with effort.
For only a moment I rested my eyes and scratched my head
irritably, cursing myself for resorting to such bizarre behavior.
Sure, I had hidden in the shadows of my previous girlfriend's
apartment. However, it had been worth the venture because
my suspicions had proven true. My stomach knotted again
at the thought that the skepticism I felt about Melanie could
possibly be accurate.

"I can't do this," I said aloud, to no one, and reached to turn the key that rested in my ignition. Then I saw her. She strolled out of the building confidently. Almost slyly, with a fixed half-smirk on her lips as she walked toward the curb. She stood across the street, dressed in a fitted black dress that curved snugly against her frame. Her heels, at least four inches high, accentuated her height. From a distance she appeared nearly six feet tall. Those gray eyes darted left, then right, and then left again while she determined the best moment to cross the street through cruising traffic.

My body stiffened when cars stood still at the stoplight and she weaved between them and headed in the direction in which I was parked. I lowered myself into my seat, panicked by her approach and pissed for putting myself once again in this position. I could have gone home, waited for Melanie, and addressed my concerns when she arrived. Instead, I sat in my car and attempted to blend in with the leather interior of my car while the woman who jeopardized my relationship walked directly toward me.

Sunday held her head high as she sauntered across the street. In front of my car she paused, and reached in the designer purse that rested in the bend of her arm. She retrieved her keys before she took her final step onto the curb. I could see that the grin on her face had not diminished and as brief as the moment was, it appeared obvious that the purse gesture in front of my car was intentional. Like she knew I would be waiting and gave me just what I wanted: a close-up look at her.

Her pace slowed once she was upon the sidewalk, again, as if she were purposely allowing me the moment to take in her presence. Her feet crossed one in front of the other, runway style, as she walked toward the entrance to the parking garage beside me. My eyes focused on her walk, which was graceful in an eerie manner. Sneaky like a tiger would advance toward

its prey. Her bare legs were strong, similar to Melanie's taut
running legs. Though what caught my eye was a fierce scar
on the side of her left thigh that peeked from underneath
her dress. It was a raised line, a couple of shades darker than
her skin. When Sunday reached the garage, she smoothed
her dress over the scar before she grabbed hold of the door
handle. She stood for a moment, and through the reflection
of the glass door I felt her gray eyes peer in my direction. *I see
you* they said, or so I thought they whispered to me. Sunday
held her pose a few more seconds, then opened the door and
disappeared into the garage.

Was she really taunting me the way it seemed that she was?
Or was I beginning to create in my mind an imaginary series
of events that appeared to target my emotional reasoning? Had
Melanie told her that it was me at the office door? Did Sunday
know about me? Wait, of course she had to know about me if
she was calling my office, leaving subliminal messages for me
online, and teasing me by indirectly staring at me from thirty
feet away. Still, I had no proof that the aforementioned were
true. I vowed to find out and prayed my logic and common
sense would not desert me in the meantime.

Finally, I started my car and began my drive home. In an
effort to clear my mind, I inserted a CD collage of music I had
put together of songs my grandmother played throughout my
youth into early adulthood.

"*Abuela*, I need you now," I stated into the air. How I craved
her natural intuition and ability to guide without persuasion.
She was the best at listening with an open heart and unbiased
mind, while she gently asked prodding questions that would
allow me to sort my thoughts in a manner I may not have
done so on my own.

My ride home was congested, as Chicago traffic most often
tended to be, and I contemplated calling Melanie while I sat
idling several times. She was either still at her office working,

and had not yet found the time to call me. Or she was on her way home as well, and had made a deliberate choice not to call me yet. I guess either way she still had opted not to call me to explain her aggravated demeanor. While it took concentration, I decided not to call her either. I preferred to confront Melanie in person in order to observe her expression and disposition while we talked.

When I arrived at our condo, I pulled behind the building to park in the one reserved spot we purchased with the unit. Melanie and I would alternate weeks on who would get the spot and this, fortunately, was my week. Inside the condo, I found that Melanie had not yet arrived. I took off my shoes and dropped my bag on the kitchen floor. I headed through the kitchen and dining area to the front door so I could get our mail, which was alongside a row of six in-wall boxes inside the entranceway of the building. In the hallway I used the small key to open the box and retrieve several envelopes. Briefly I skimmed the sender's address on each envelope and noticed nothing of significance. After I closed the mailbox I quickly peered outside and saw a white vehicle with black tinted windows sitting in front of the building. The headlights were on and it seemed the car was running. Who was outside? Generally I wasn't nosey, as the car could be a visitor to any tenant of the building. Or maybe a tenant had purchased a new car and this was my first time seeing it. However, the intensity of the evening's events sparked an immediate curiosity. I took a step closer to look through the glass window into the dusky night.

The car sat several minutes. With each minute that passed, my heart rate intensified. Had Sunday followed me home and now she knew where Melanie and I lived? Was she behind the black windows staring at me the way I was staring at her? Eventually, the passenger door opened and Lindsay, the seventeen year-old daughter of an upper unit tenant, exited.

She was smiling, giddy, and disheveled. Thankfully, it seemed that she hadn't noticed me. Before she closed the door she bent back into the car, revealing leopard print underwear beneath her ultra-short jean skirt, and kissed the male driver of the car I had briefly stalked. I took that opportunity to tiptoe back into our condo, and quickly closed the door behind me. I exhaled.

I went into the kitchen and headed straight for the cabinet of alcoholic beverages and mixes. A bottle of gin was the first liquor item I saw. I swiftly grabbed it, popped the top open, and took a swallow that burned my throat and sent heat through my chest.

"What's wrong with you, Jo?" I asked myself and waited in silence for an answer. Seconds later I realized that no response was coming. "Why am I talking out loud?" I asked myself another question and then shook my head angrily for doing so. I felt embarrassed in my own presence.

From the kitchen I went into the bathroom within our bedroom. I stared at myself in the mirror and began yet another conversation with myself. *What was I doing? Why was I acting like a crazy woman just because I thought my girlfriend had interest in someone else? This kind of stuff happens all the time, right? We can get past this, whatever it is. But what is 'it'?* My reflection only mimicked my confused expression and provided me no answers to my endless questions.

I turned on the shower and stepped inside. For twenty minutes I stood underneath the hot water and attempted to relax my mind in a manner that would allow me to have a rational conversation with Melanie when she got home. In my mind I prepared to ask her why she had such an attitude when I arrived at her office. I wanted to know why she didn't tell me that Sunday was her visiting client. Most importantly, why couldn't I wait for their meeting to end and spend time with her after Sunday's departure? To me the questions were simple, yet direct. All Melanie had to do was answer honestly.

When I left the shower, I towel-dried my body and slid on a short, lightweight cotton nightgown. Only when I went back to the kitchen did I realize that Melanie was home, in the living room, sitting on the couch watching television like nothing had happened. Instantly I became irritated that she hadn't bothered to peek her head inside the bathroom to let me know she was home. I calmed myself though, because it was not the first time that had happened. On many occasions in the past she had arrived home while I was in the shower, or exercising in the guest bedroom and she would allow me to finish what I was doing rather than interrupt. Before I put the gin away I took another long swig and then went to confront, or rather speak with, Melanie.

She was lazily watching a reality show about a rock star who had a bus load of fake-breasted women to choose from to be his one and only true love. I stood next to the television and only then did she finally acknowledge me.

"Hey, Jo," she said. Her eyes were tired, though they showed a hint of caution.

"Mind if I turn off the TV?" I asked.

Instead of answering, Melanie pushed the off button on the remote and sat upright as if she was preparing herself for my questioning.

"What happened tonight?" I asked. *Damn, that's not what I meant to ask.* "What I mean is why you were so upset when I got to your office? Did you forget you invited me?"

"My client showed up unexpectedly," she explained. "I didn't know she was coming."

"You mean Sunday?"

Melanie's expression shifted uncomfortably. "How did you know her name?"

"That doesn't matter, Mel. And you didn't answer my question. Why were you so upset?"

"I guess I was upset that she showed up and threw off my evening. I took it out on you when I shouldn't have."

I crossed my arms over my chest, dissatisfied by her answer. "Why didn't you tell me it was her?"

"Because I didn't think it mattered," she responded.

"I don't believe you." I had attempted to not sound confrontational. However, I realized that softly telling her that I felt she was lying to me was a confrontational move.

"What is it that you don't believe?" she asked calmly.

I had to think for a moment. What didn't I believe about her story? Sunday could have shown up without notice and that definitely could have pissed Melanie off. I knew Melanie to be an organized person who did not take kindly to disruption. She could have been trying to finish work in preparation for my arrival when Sunday came. When I arrived afterward, she vented her frustration toward me. Wait, did that even make sense? I was beginning to confuse myself.

"Okay, so why couldn't I wait for your meeting with Sunday to end? I could have stayed in the receptionist area."

"Because I needed to complete some work after she left." Again, Melanie answered in a matter-of-fact manner. She was such a lawyer.

My body suddenly relaxed a little and my head became lighter. I wasn't finished with Melanie, though the gin suddenly kicked in. My earlier concerns and agitations dissipated and my emotions became carefree.

"So tell me," Melanie said as she rose from the couch and walked to me. She wrapped me in her arms and hugged me. "How did you know her name?" she asked.

I closed my eyes and rested my head against Melanie's chest. I sniffed and inhaled her familiar scent. That was intentional and fortunately I smelled no other woman's scent on her clothing.

"I saw her profile online," I told her.

"Where?"

"As one of your friends. She had her name in her status."

"When?"

"Today. Why so many questions?" I asked.

"Just curious," she said and then kissed my forehead. "Curious just like you."

"What's that supposed to mean?" I asked defensively, and lifted my head to look into her eyes.

"Why else would you go to her profile if you weren't curious?"

"Why didn't you tell me you added her as a friend?"

"I didn't think it mattered," she answered.

"Well you were all flustered when she requested you. What made you change your mind?"

"I thought about it and decided it wasn't a big deal."

"Why not?"

"I have a ton of friends on there, most that I don't even talk to. I didn't see it as a problem to add her." Melanie's eyes softened. "Come on, Jo, what are you worried about?"

I was worried that Sunday was an intrusion into my relationship. "Something doesn't feel right. That's all I can tell you," I replied. "You seem so aggravated every time her name comes up."

"I'm not aggravated now." Her voice was gentle.

"Why didn't you tell me she was beautiful?" I asked weakly. I hated to sound jealous.

"She's not more beautiful than you," Melanie said tenderly.

I wanted to argue Melanie's statement, but what woman shuns such a compliment? I nuzzled my head closer against Melanie and she held on to me tighter. Though I strongly believed that I had not imagined Sunday's performance outside of Melanie's building and still suspected abnormal behavior on Melanie's part, I once again resorted to securing proof before I challenged Melanie further. As Melanie would tell me, we are all innocent until proven guilty.

Chapter Nine

"You're late," I scolded Melanie that Saturday when she arrived home after an early afternoon run. Ronan and Jillian were due to arrive at three and Melanie hadn't started the grill and begun to barbecue the steaks we had purchased the day before and marinated all night long. Melanie wasn't the cook of our house, though she had the skills. She had offered to do the meat after I told her about our weekend guests. It was also after our troubled encounter at her office.

"I'm sorry." She walked to give me a sweaty kiss. I allowed her to lean her warm, damp body against my skin and I kissed her back. Despite the recent upsetting interactions we had, Melanie continued to own my heart. There was nothing I wouldn't do to preserve our relationship.

Melanie washed her hands at the kitchen sink. "What are you working on?" she asked.

"Finishing up the coleslaw. Jillian made some beans and we can do the corn on the cob when they get here in about an hour."

Melanie rested against the counter and sighed. "I had a good run today."

"That's good. Crowded?"

"Sure was. Seems like everybody wanted to get out in this weather." The temperature was a perfect seventy-five degrees with a blue sky and mild breeze.

"It's a gorgeous day for a cookout so get started, Mel," I told her. "I need to get this kitchen cleaned up too."

"*Si, senorita,*" she said and smacked me on the ass. Melanie went to the small patio outside the kitchen door, which was the back door entrance, and started the gas grill.

"I'm going to get this going and then take a fast shower," she said loudly so I could hear her from outside.

"Good idea," I yelled back.

"Take one with me?" she asked, and this time peeked her head through the doorway.

"Love to," I smiled and hurriedly placed saran wrap over the bowl of coleslaw. I placed used utensils and containers into the dishwasher and then wiped the counters clean. From the cabinet I retrieved our mojito fixings along with four glasses. Quickly and expertly I prepared two mojitos for Melanie and me. Just as I finished, Melanie re-entered the kitchen and I handed a glass to her.

"You're the best," she told me as she frequently did.

"Don't you forget that," I warned. We laughed and took cool swallows of the fresh drink. Thirsty, we finished them in just a couple of minutes.

"Let's go." She took my hand and led me to the bedroom then into the bathroom. Melanie started the shower and I began to undress.

"No, let me do that," she said. Melanie faced my body toward the mirror and stood behind me. From behind she lifted my fitted T-shirt over my head and dropped it to the floor. Next she unfastened my bra and slowly slid the straps over my shoulders until the cups slid down my belly and revealed my brown nipples. They hardened as I watched Mel eye them through the mirror. She unbuttoned and then unzipped my jean shorts and lowered them over my hips and down my thighs and calves. Finally, she removed my panties until I was naked. My body was on fire. Melanie leaned her hips into mine and my clit began to throb. My heart began to race and my throat became tight. *Should I?* Although our interactions had resumed their loving and cordial nature, we hadn't made love in days. And like I said, I'd do anything to keep my woman.

"Melanie," I whispered. Melanie ran her hands up my belly and took hold of my breasts.

"Hmm?" She asked with circular strokes over my nipples.

"I want to eat your pussy," I told her.

Melanie halted the grind against my backside and her fingers got still. Her eyebrows raised and she smirked at me through the mirror. "What was that?" she asked.

I turned around to face her and looked up into her surprised eyes. "I said I want to eat your pussy," I repeated.

For another moment Melanie stared at me, perhaps waiting to see if I was going to laugh. However, my eyes remained connected to hers and with each second the anticipation increased. "Right now," I instructed.

Without a word Melanie removed her tank, sports bra and running shorts. Though she was taller than me with a mild tomboyish appeal, sexually she allowed me to do to her whatever she did to me, and that meant spreading her legs whenever I craved her sweetness.

Melanie came best in a seated position. She attributed this to years of adolescent and teenage grinding against chairs as she experienced her first orgasms. And for this reason, Melanie loved to sit on my face as much as I loved the feel of her strong legs around my head. I laid on the plush bath rug and Melanie cradled my face with her middle. She looked down and watched me part my mouth to greet her lips. I sucked them and tasted her saltiness. We remained in that position for a while; Melanie lightly circled her hips as my tongue pleased her. The moment began to intensify and I could tell that Melanie was nearing climax. Suddenly she stopped and lifted her body a couple of inches off of my face. She gazed hungrily into my eyes.

"Is it good for you, Jo?" she asked.

"Your pussy is so good," I told her. "So damn good."

She moaned with excitement, lowered her body once again, and came a few strokes later.

"What got into you?" she asked several minutes later, after the calm and after I resisted her wish to return the pleasure. We were in the shower and rushing to get ready.

"Just want to show you how much I love you," I answered.

"By talking nasty to me?" she laughed.

"It's no nastier than you wanting everybody to see us getting busy."

"So true. See, I knew with enough time I could bring out the freak in you," she stated proudly. I only smiled at her. I couldn't tell her that as unorthodox as it was, Ronan was the one who had urged me to liven it up with the previously unspeakable word.

"We have to hurry and get those steaks on the grill," I said.

"Right."

We finished our shower and dressed speedily, Melanie in indigo-colored fitted jeans with a red T-shirt and me in black capri pants with a yellow tank top. Over the next fifteen minutes Melanie had placed the four flavor-filled steaks on the grill along with the corn on the cob while I prepared the newly decorated kitchen for company. I turned off the central air, opened the sliding patio doors, and moved the table alongside so that we could enjoy the summer air that breezed through the screen. On the table I placed colorful dishes, cloth napkins, and turned the radio to Chicago's V103 station for old school and current R&B.

One similarity Melanie and I shared was the presentation that accompanied hosting. Although we did not have company every weekend or even every month, when we invited guests over, we were sure that the condo was clean, neat, fresh smelling, and comfortable. We treated our guests like customers to a restaurant; we wanted them relaxed during their stay and anxious to come back for seconds and thirds.

The bell rang in perfect timing with my fixing Ronan and Jillian's first mojitos.

"I'll get it." Melanie stood and left the kitchen. I wished I had a camera ready to capture her expression when she returned with the duo. It screamed, *Dayum!* in a good kind of way. I feared my expression was more of a flabbergasted nature and I fought hard to maintain my composure. It looked like Jillian had been twirling the pole, hopped off the stage, and came straight to our house. She wore red platform heels, jean shorts that left an intense camel toe impression, and a red lace top with no bra. Shameful as her outfit was, she wore her hair pulled into a bun with little makeup on her face, revealing milky clear skin.

"Hi, Jovanna," she said sweetly and rushed to kiss my cheek. I found the gesture inappropriate as she was still my client. How could I protest Melanie's interaction with Sunday when here I was, allowing my own customer to connect on a more personal level? It seemed I was using double standards to my benefit, however, I rationalized that at least in my case there were no awkward encounters aside from voyeuristic indiscretions with my brother. Surely there were no interactions that would cause stress between Melanie and I.

"Hey, Jillian, good to see you. You met Melanie?"

Jillian smiled in Melanie's direction. "Yes, I did."

"What's good, Jo?" Ronan asked me after he placed Jillian's beans on the counter. He was a stylish contrast to Jillian, dressed metro-cool in relaxed, loose fitted jeans and a black T-shirt with a newsboy cap.

"Hey, give me that hat," I teased him.

"Is it your birthday?" he asked and smiled.

"I'll have it before the end of the night, don't worry," Melanie kidded with him. "Let me check the steaks."

"I have fresh mojitos for you two," I said, and handed Ronan and Jillian a full glass each.

"My sis here makes the best mojitos around," Ronan bragged before taking a swallow. Jillian followed suit and nodded her head.

"Tasty Jovanna," she said.

"Hey, the kitchen is cool," Ronan commented on the new décor.

"You like? Melanie wanted to brighten it up."

"Looks good. Why don't you show Jillian around?"

Ronan knew the condo just as well as Melanie and I did, but I didn't protest. "Sure."

Jillian followed close behind me, her heels clicking across the kitchen floor and through the hallway. I showed her my and Melanie's bedroom, both bathrooms and guest bedroom. She admired the dining area and the coziness of the living room.

"You have a beautiful home," she said after the tour.

"Thank you. Come back to the kitchen and have a seat."

"Steaks shouldn't be too much longer," Melanie told us when we returned.

"Need help with anything?" Jillian asked.

Ronan answered for us. "They appreciate your offer, Jill, but don't worry about it. These two get a kick out of serving people."

"Your beans look great," I told Jillian when I took off the aluminum foil and smelled the mixture of beans with bacon, onion and green peppers.

"Thank you. Hope you like."

I placed the beans in the oven to keep them warm then set the side dishes on the table. I refilled our drinks and waited for the steaks.

"So, have you been house hunting?" Melanie asked Jillian.

"Just a little bit. I've had my eye on a place for a while now.

I'm thinking I may go ahead and put an offer on it. Ronan and my realtor both suggest that I check out a few other places to be sure that's the one I should get."

"Not a bad idea to see what other options are out there. Then again, if your heart is calling that one, go for it."

"I think so too. But I was trying to appease Ronan just a little," she said with a rub to Ronan's leg with a red heel.

"I bet he appreciates it." Melanie winked at Ronan.

"Jovanna says you like the strip club." Jillian looked at Melanie.

Melanie, who was midway through a swallow, coughed into her glass. I shook my head in denial and Ronan turned a guilty shade of pink. Melanie pointed a finger at herself to say *who, me?*

"No, Jill, I told you that," he corrected her.

"You did?" Melanie grinned, and then turned her head sideways to me. "How did your brother know that?"

I eyed Ronan evilly and he mocked me with a humorous wicked glare.

"Well, you know, we talk about all kinds of stuff all day long," I explained to Mel.

"I think you have a cute relationship. The way you share things," Jillian said coyly.

Melanie bit her bottom lip, certainly in an effort not to laugh. Ronan shook his head, and I took a sip of my drink. Did no one else find Jillian's comments inappropriate? Soon as the thought crossed my mind I realized that I was, indeed, finding myself uneasy in a client's presence. Is this how Melanie felt? Did Sunday make her uncomfortable and that's why she chose not to speak about her? And that's why she became aggravated by Sunday's presence?

"We are not yet friends online," Jillian stated to me.

"I'll get the steaks," Melanie said, and went to the patio.

"What do you mean?" I asked.

"I sent you a friendship request. You have not yet accepted. You are not ignoring me, are you?" She smiled.

"No, I didn't know you sent it, I apologize."

Ronan spotted my discomfort. "Jovanna here is still getting used to the idea that business can sometimes cross personal lines."

"Yes, I remember you said that," Jillian said to me. "Don't worry. I won't bite you through the screen."

"Sure, I'll remember that."

Melanie re-entered the kitchen with smoking steaks on a silver tray.

"Oh yes, Melanie too. We can all be friends," Jillian said excitedly.

We both ignored her and for a moment, our perfect hostess crowns fell off and were crushed under the weight of the forbidden social networking topic. I hadn't logged onto the site since the day I saw Sunday in person. Although my curiosity had not diminished, I refused to stress myself and look for something that may or may not be there. At least that's what I had agreed to within myself the past few days.

"Let's eat," I told them and double checked the table to make sure that everyone had what they needed, including steak knives. "You all are going to love the steak sauce. Melanie made it and after all these years she hasn't told me what's all in it. This is the only time I can get my woman to grocery shop," I laughed. Melanie smiled too.

We all sat around the table and began to prepare our plates. Melanie and I allowed Ronan and Jillian to choose their steaks first. We passed around the side dishes and when I was ready to eat, I waited for one of them to take the first bite. Instead, Jillian surprised me.

"Let us pray." She held her hand out to Ronan on her left and Melanie on her right. Melanie eyed me while I eyed Ronan. He bowed his head. Melanie and I did the same, though we nearly laughed when we caught one another peeking with one eye. It wasn't that we found prayer humorous, we were simply surprised by Jillian's act of gratitude.

"God, we thank you for the company of friends and loved ones and for the serving of this food before us. Bless those who prepared this meal and those fortunate to receive. Almighty God, we honor and thank you."

"That was nice, Jill," Ronan said. She smiled in response. Melanie and I exchanged a 'not bad' expression.

Both Ronan and Jillian began an easy slice into their warm steaks. Jillian poured sauce onto the cut portions and then took a bite. She closed her eyes and hummed a delicious moan. It sounded like a light orgasm.

"This is so wonderful," she purred. Melanie thanked her and finally, she and I began to eat our own food.

"Your beans are really good," I told Jillian.

"*Gracias*," she said, and continued to devour her steak.

"So what's going on at the firm?" Ronan asked Melanie.

"Same old stuff. Trying to do the best for my clients."

"Any interesting new cases?"

Melanie glanced at me in question, displaying a concern and subtle accusation that I had mentioned something to Ronan. My eyes told her that I hadn't said anything. "Nah, not really. Don't want to bore you with work right now," she answered and took a sip of her drink.

"That's cool. It's the weekend, right? Too bad my baby here has to work tonight."

"Really?" Melanie asked.

"Yes. Saturday is the best night for the club. That's why I mentioned it before. You two should come with Ronan tonight. I'll make it worth your time."

"How so?" Melanie asked. I kicked her under the table and she grinned at me.

"I will make sure to reserve a table up front and keep your drinks filled all night long, on the house of course."

"What do you say, Jo?" Melanie urged.

Three sets of eyes were focused on me and I felt the pressure to say yes. Internally I contemplated my response. I would have felt a bit more enthusiasm, maybe, if we had at least closed on Jillian's loan and she was no longer an official client. Again, how could I defend my feelings about Sunday and Melanie fraternizing online if I was out watching my own client dance naked on stage? That only provided Melanie the perfect justification she'd need to befriend Sunday if that were her choice.

And let me clarify that it wasn't that Melanie couldn't have female friends. Although we primarily shared our group of friends together, Melanie had made casual acquaintances with a few women over the years and it hadn't affected our relationship. In fact, Melanie always insisted that I meet the women and our relationship was acknowledged early on. Still, my gut feeling told me that Sunday was not a casual acquaintance or someone with whom I wanted me or Melanie to be social with. Inside I sighed and cast aside the rampant wave of thoughts as they were not going to assist me with the matter of the moment. I looked at Ronan whose expression was curious. Jillian's was anxious and Melanie's was a distinct dare.

"Come on," she instigated. "Think about the progress you already made earlier today." She winked at me, my body flushed, and I accepted the invitation.

"Sure, let's go," I agreed.

"Check you out, girl," Ronan said. "What happened today, huh?" he inquired further.

I winked at Melanie to silence her.

"Ahh, I know what happened," Jillian cooed. "Remember what you asked her in the office the other day?" She grinned at Ronan. He didn't seem to remember his suggestion that I was going to get some pussy when I left the office dolled up and on my way to see Melanie.

"*Nothing*," I spoke in a low, aggressive tone. How embarrassing it would be for Melanie to know I hadn't spiced things up on my own. And based upon her response, I already knew that she was going to ask for more.

Jillian smacked her lips to me in the air and Ronan still appeared clueless. Melanie, perhaps still floating from our earlier romp, didn't inquire further.

"Let me fill up your glasses," I offered.

"Last one for me," Jillian said. "While our customers are usually buzzed, I prefer to stay sober while working. It's all the more fun for me to see the pleased expressions on their faces while I dance and make them happy."

"So you enjoy what you do?" Melanie asked, although the answer was apparent.

"Oh, yes. Some girls do it just for the money. And some of them have to drink their way through the night in order to perform. For me it is a talent, a skill. I have learned to dance well from the many years of lessons I had growing up. I took many classes on how to move with and around the pole. It's not easy you know. I also like to have satisfied customers and make people feel good. In the end, most jobs are the same; to make money by bringing customers in and keeping their business. My goal is to open my own club someday."

"See, my girl's got a strong business mindset. I like money, she likes money. We can be the next Russell and Kimora. Minus the divorce," he laughed.

"Damn Ronan, how long have I known you? This is the first time I've ever heard you even hint around to settling down," Melanie prodded.

"Now that you mention it," I chimed in with Melanie.

"You never know," he smiled.

I laughed on the inside, perhaps feeling light from the mojitos. Surprised I was, to find that Ronan was taking such a liking to Jillian. The more I thought about it, I realized that she had remained in his number one spot longer than any other girl had. Unfortunately, my mind wandered to Sunday at the thought of the online site and I had to refocus my thoughts once again.

We spent the next couple of hours eating, drinking—except for Jillian who switched to bottled water—and playing Melanie's favorite card game of Spades. Early in our relationship I found Melanie to have a competitive nature, I presumed because of her day-to-day role as a lawyer. She was no different with a card game in that she wanted to win. Initially I was fairly inexperienced at how to strategize the game and determine the right number of books, however, despite my early novice practices, Melanie never allowed us to lose a game. In fact, we've never lost a game and Melanie vowed to maintain our streak. This evening we proved consistent and we beat Ronan and Jillian in several rounds. At six o'clock Jillian needed to get to work and Ronan told us that he'd see us at the club later.

"She's all right," Melanie commented as I began to clean the kitchen with her assistance.

"They were on good behavior tonight," I told her. "They didn't act like they were about to have sex in front of you the way they've done me."

Melanie smirked. "This is going to be fun tonight."

I rinsed out the glasses and placed them in the dishwasher. "I suppose. A little too close for comfort if you ask me, but I guess it'll be all right."

"Why? You're still talking about working with her?"

"Yes."

Melanie sighed. "Sometimes those lines can be crossed. It's all right this time, don't you think? Ronan actually seems to like her."

It took a moment for me to respond as I replayed her first words in my head. I simply wasn't in the mood to discuss business and client line crossing when inevitably the conversation would turn to Melanie and Sunday. Well, maybe not with her prompting but likely with mine.

"Yeah, he does," I replied.

We cleaned the kitchen and quieted the evening with a relaxing pause by lying on the couch next to one another and watching *Brown Sugar*, a movie we had seen so many times before but loved like brand new each time. At ten o'clock we dressed and left for Sweet Tea, the club where Jillian worked. Melanie had told me that the owner's name was Leno Tea. When I asked why she would know such information she told me that prior to his opening a strip club, he owned several liquor stores on the south side of Chicago that were often in trouble for license issues. This she knew through word of mouth at the office. I exhaled, grateful to learn that she wasn't hawking strip clubs in such a manner that she knew the owner's names.

Tightly Melanie held my hand and led me into the club. The entranceway was dim and dull with a small window in which to pay our fee to the older gentleman behind the glass. Once Melanie opened the door and we entered the first level of the club, the atmosphere turned artistic. The room was cleverly decorated with large black and white photos of nude women adorning the walls. Raunchy they weren't. Rather, they were tasteful, and reminded me of photos I'd see in a Victoria's Secret catalog, without the clothes.

The space wasn't large. It fit about twenty-five tables in front of a performance stage that contained three poles, one on each end with one on the end of the runway in the middle. The clientele consisted of a couple of tables filled with young men, maybe celebrating a bachelor party by the manner in which most of the guys singled out one particular friend when the dancer on stage bent over in front of their table. Many of the other tables were occupied with older gentlemen in groups or alone. There were a large number of women of all ages throughout the club, though men certainly outweighed the women.

We stood for a moment and peered across the tables until we saw Ronan sitting in the front row. He sat alone at the table labeled for six. We made our way through the crowd and joined him. He appeared happy to see us and also seemed to be holding a steady, but calm buzz.

"What's up mamas?"

"Nice spot," Melanie said appreciatively, admiring the twelve inch distance we were from the stage.

When the dancer noticed Melanie and I took our seats, she seductively made her way toward us. She was a white female with a deep, natural tan or one that was sprayed on to perfection. While her body wasn't necessarily firm, she sauntered toward us in long, sexy strides swaying her curvy hips and poking her large breasts upward, all to the beat of the bass groove.

To Ronan's left was a stack of one dollar and five dollar bills. Quickly he divvied the pile between the three of us. Without reserve, Melanie picked up a single and stood to place it in the garter that rested on the woman's thigh. She smiled at Melanie, then at me, and once again moved across the stage.

A waitress arrived at the table and Melanie ordered a mojito. In an effort to relax quickly, I asked for a shot of tequila along with a long island iced tea. Both Ronan and Melanie smirked at me and I smiled in return. We each leaned back in our chairs and enjoyed the rest of the performance by the dancer. She ended with a wide-legged twirl around the pole and landed in a split. She stood, gathered the bills strewn about the stage, and exited blowing a kiss to the crowd. The deejay to the right of the stage thanked Apricot for her performance and introduced Berry as the next entertainer. Quizzically I looked at Ronan.

"All the dancers are some form of a tea," he explained. Melanie burst out laughing and I shook my head. It was a cheesy idea in my eyes, however, if it worked, it worked.

The stage lights darkened for a few moments. When they lit again, Berry stood center stage dressed in a form fitting hot pink dress. Her makeup was extreme, but flawless, and her hair was short up top, with an obvious long and flowing hair piece in the back. She tapped her five inch silver platform heels three times against the floor and then "Addictive" by Truth Hurts began to play. Berry took strides down the runway to the beat of the music. When she reached the pole, she began to grind it, wrapping her legs around it with her dress hiking up inches with every movement. Customers cheered at the sight of her thong. She took that opportunity to swiftly lift her dress over her head, whirled it in the air, and tossed it backward so it landed far at the edge of the stage. Berry soon removed her bra and bills immediately flowed onto the stage. The rest of her dance was impressive in my opinion, though when the performance ended, Melanie said to Ronan, "She was all right." Ronan agreed. I guess I had more to learn.

There was a short break and our drinks finally arrived. The shot burned my throat although the follow-up swallow of my drink cooled it slightly.

"You all right, Jo?" Melanie asked me.

I closed my eyes for a moment, placed my chin in the palm of my hand, and re-opened my eyes to smile at Melanie. "I'm good," I told her. She leaned forward and puckered her lips. I leaned forward as well and kissed her.

"You all ready?" the deejay asked over the massive speakers. "She's one of Sweet Tea's most treasured delights! The always flavorful, always tangy, always satisfying, Cinnamon!"

Ronan clapped louder than any customer in the place and howled at the stage. "That's my girl right here," he announced excitedly. Melanie and I exchanged an amusing look and turned our attention to the stage also.

Jillian came onto the stage from the right dressed in a vintage cabaret costume that reminded me of the sexy items worn in the film *Moulin Rouge*. The shiny black outfit slimmed her waistline, accentuated her bust, and snuggled against her hips. She wore knee high stockings, a lace garter around each arm and one on her thigh. To complete her accessories she sported a bow tie, sequined top hat and tapped a cane at her side. Then the music started: "Lady Marmalade" by the Labelles. That's when I began to understand why Jillian referred to her dance as a craft and ability. I realized that her performance was not only a strip act, but an actual choreographed dance routine. Jillian moved in sync with the song, her hips sashaying side to side with the lyrics and beat. She used her cane in manners that simulated pleasurable intercourse, though it was performed in a tasteful style that wasn't obscene, but erotic. Once Jillian removed the top hat, corset and bottoms, she was left standing in a sparkling g-string that glittered between her legs. The second half of the song she danced up and down and around the pole, flowing fluently with the music and flaunting her strength, rhythm and trained skills. By the end of the song, the stage was donned with bills, with Ronan having thrown at least seventy-five dollars himself. Men whistled. Even the women wore expressions that said, *damn!*

Jillian's body was shiny with faint body glitter and sweat as she scooped up her money. Her makeup was intense with long, full fake eyelashes, heavy coats of liquid eyeliner, with bright red cheeks and lips. She smiled widely at the three of us before she left the stage.

"She'll be back y'all so be sure to stick around to see the sexy Cinnamon again," the deejay told us. The customers clapped louder.

"Now that right there . . ." Melanie began, though the sentence remained unfinished.

"That's what I'm telling you. She leaves you speechless," Ronan said proudly.

"She's good, Ro," I added. Both he and Melanie looked at me like a naïve child.

"Good? Girl, please," Melanie said.

"Well she's great, actually," I corrected. "I mean, she's truly talented."

"Yeah, that's my baby."

"You're really feeling her, aren't you?" Melanie inquired just before she finished her mojito.

Ronan suddenly became bashful and didn't answer. I guess some people really do fall in love with a stripper.

The next dancers were entertaining, though none compared to Jillian. As I sipped on my second drink I found myself antsy and anxious to see what her next performance brought.

"You think you can do that for me?" Melanie whispered in my ear, and pointed to a dancer on a small section of the second level who was performing a lap dance.

"Whenever you want," I answered.

"I like that." Melanie rubbed her hand up my thigh.

Jillian was the final performance of the night and she didn't fail to satisfy. This time she performed to a slowed salsa beat in a red two-piece outfit with black lace trim. Even I stood to toss bills on the stage in honor of her delightful talents.

After the club closed and most of the fellow patrons had left, we were allowed to remain inside and wait for Jillian. Several employees had become familiar with Ronan and even the owner, Mr. Tea himself, acknowledged our presence.

When Jillian joined us from backstage, I almost didn't recognize her. She wore a comfortable, loose fitting and lightweight jogging suit in a shade of light gray. Her face was freshly washed and her hair hung loosely in blond curls. She kissed Ronan on the lips.

"So glad you came. Ronan and I almost bet that you wouldn't." She directed that to me.

"You were wonderful," I told her. My words were slightly heavy.

"Thank you, Jovanna. And what did you think, Melanie? Yes, I am fishing for compliments," she teased.

"It was all right, you know. You got a little something, something going on," Melanie teased.

"Where to? You hungry?" Ronan asked.

"I think we'll head home," I answered on our behalf. All three of them eyed me like I was up to something when I wasn't. I was simply ready to resume my position of lying in Melanie's arms and falling asleep.

"Well let's go home too," Jillian said. "Back to my place. I'll make you some breakfast.".

Ronan kissed her in response and they walked in front of us, their arms around one another in a manner that was most often seen among teenage couples. I had to admit that it was endearing, and I chuckled to myself when I made yet another mental note to play T-Pain's "I'm in Luv (Wit a Stripper)" at work on Monday. Clearly he was falling.

"What's funny?" Melanie asked.

"Nothing, sweetie," I answered and we walked to the exit. I held her hand and then kissed it. "I love you, Mel."

Melanie smiled in response and held open the door for me with her free hand. She was such a gentlewoman most of the time and that was one of the reasons I loved her so much. I vowed to keep her mine.

Chapter Ten

Over the next four days Melanie became a hermit, confining herself to the second bedroom when she wasn't at the office. I hadn't realized that the court date for Sunday's case was fast approaching and Melanie needed to spend time preparing their position while still tending to her other cases. Melanie shared that she was confident that the not guilty plea would stand in court and that Sunday would be free of any charges.

Our conversation about the case was brief, as Melanie was engrossed in her work as she always was prior to court. Surprisingly, there was no tension as Melanie explained her desire to win the case for Sunday. I wanted to inquire about the amount of interaction she and Sunday may have had leading up to the Thursday morning court appearance, though I refrained from asking since I had never questioned about clients in the past. Melanie was busy and distracted, yet her disposition toward me was sweet-tempered. If she remained pleasant, I wanted to give her the same in return.

Even so, I still found myself logging online every day, several times a day actually, to check for updates on Sunday's profile and for any sign of interaction between the two of them. I was embarrassed by my behavior, even if I was the only one who knew about it, but I still felt the internal nagging need to monitor Sunday for a bit longer. The day after our visit to the strip club, she had updated her status to read: **Even Sunday rests on Sunday.** Her mood was changed to **quiet**. Every day thereafter I looked for a change in mood or headline, however, there was none. She remained quiet.

Years prior, a few months after Melanie set up her account and we had gotten comfortable with our dual online networking, sometimes we would log on and review profiles and status updates of those on our lists of friends. It had become a form of entertainment in which we'd observe women who flirted with one another, then dated, updated their headlines with professions of a lifelong love, only to break up thereafter and delete each other from their list of friends completely.

We witnessed one particular relationship gone sour that resulted in one of the women hawking the other's profile day and night, with constant check-ins to see if her ex had found interest in someone else. We became privy to deeper details as the woman who was being tailed, Jessie, frequently attended Murmur events and had been introduced to us by Prestin. Melanie and I would gawk in amazement at the computer screen when Jessie's ex—she was also on our list of friends—would update her status messages with direct apologetic comments for Jessie. And within a day if Jessie did not respond, her apology flipped to angered, harassing comments aimed back at Jessie. The drama was captivating, though distressing to watch at the same time.

One time the ex's headline pleaded by way of a sentimental quote: "You may not love me today, tomorrow, or ever, but I will love you until it kills me, and even then, you'll be in my heart. I love you Jessie." Jessie ignored the publicized proclamation of love and in response, the woman next screamed at Jessie with embarrassing and intimidating threats: "Watch out bitch or I'll post those nasty ass naked pictures of you. Bet all your friends would love to see that shit."

On several occasions Jessie had told us of her ex's haunting behavior that we couldn't see. The ex would e-mail her with questions about the new friends on her profile, or text her with inquiry as to why women left certain comments on her page. On a couple of occasions Melanie and I had to be the ones to inform Jessie that her ex had arrived at the Murmur party and we then had to assist her with an inconspicuous exit from the club. Melanie and I only had Jessie's word to go by and not the ex's. However, we resorted to awkwardly helping her when she reached out for support.

I had begun to remind myself of Jessie's ex with my persistent and consistent reviews of Sunday's profile. When I checked my dictionary for stalker and learned that it meant to pursue, approach or prey, I felt a twinge of relief as I refused to define myself in that manner. I told myself that I was merely monitoring the activity of a woman I wanted to maintain a certain distance from Melanie.

Thursday morning Melanie woke earlier than usual. When the monotone beep of the alarm sounded, I awoke to an empty bed and had an immediate flashback to the day Melanie had darted out early and left a sweet note to meet her later, only to disregard the request when I saw her. I rolled my eyes at the memory and scratched my itchy scalp through tangled curls. The white T-shirt I wore to bed was damp. We had turned off the air and slept with the bedroom window open. Humid air swirled inside and steamed the bedroom.

I peeked outside the bedroom door not anticipating Melanie to be home. But there she was, dressed in the plaid girl boxers and tank she had worn to bed, humped over her laptop staring uncomfortably at the screen. My impulse was to run into the room to catch what she was viewing before she had a chance to minimize the screen or shut down. Then her expression changed. Her eyebrows relaxed and she began to smile. Then laugh. When she sat upright and began to type, I walked into the room.

"What's up, Mel?" I asked. My voice was a bit raspy from sleep.

She looked up, startled. "Morning, Jo."

"What are you up to?" I asked.

"You've got to come read this joke that Ferris sent to me. This shit had me confused at first, but it's funny as hell." She reached her arm out to grab my waist and bring me close to her.

After I viewed the humorous joke about a lawyer, Rabbi, and Hindu, I laughed, though felt a pinch of guilt for having immediately suspected Melanie of an early morning online rendezvous with Sunday.

"That's funny."

Melanie logged out of her e-mail account and shut down the laptop before she stood up and kissed me lightly on the cheek.

"Ready for your big day?" I asked. I couldn't help it.

She closed her eyes for a moment. "Yeah, it's just another day in court," she said nonchalantly.

I followed her into the bedroom, feeling a sudden sense of anxiety in visualizing Melanie sitting next to Sunday in the courtroom in defense of the accusations against Sunday. What kind of picture would she paint of Sunday? As an innocent ex-girlfriend who hadn't caused anyone any stress by violation of a restraining order?

"You nervous at all?" I asked.

We were now in the bathroom and Melanie had begun to wrap her hair. "No, not at all. This really isn't that big of a case."

"Has anything weird come up at all?"

"What do you mean?"

"You know, in your meeting with Sunday and research." I was curious. The energy I felt from Sunday was dark and from what I learned from Ali, I needed to respect what my intuition was telling me.

"Actually, yes. How did you figure that?"

"Just a guess. What did you find?"

"Remember that day you came to the office?"

How could I forget? "Yes, I remember," I told her. I was fully engaged in what she was about to tell me.

"That day word had leaked back to me that Sunday had threatened to kill her ex. Even though I didn't know Sunday was going to show up that day, I asked her about it."

My heart pounded faster. "What did she say?"

"She told me that it was the other way around. That her ex tried to kill her. That her ex had flipped it all on her to make her look like the guilty and crazy one."

Could that be?

"She has this scar on her leg," Melanie continued. "She said her ex stabbed her."

I remembered the scar. But I didn't say anything to Melanie considering I hadn't told her about Sunday's production in front of my car.

"She showed you the scar?" I asked.

"Well it's on her leg, Jo," Melanie said, unaware that I knew the entire wound could not be seen unless Sunday had lifted up her dress.

"So her ex tried to kill her by stabbing her in the leg? That doesn't make sense." I reached for my toothbrush and toothpaste and began to brush my teeth while waiting for Melanie's response.

"She said her ex aimed for her chest but when she blocked her, the knife pierced her leg."

"That's a lot of she said," I mumbled through mint flavored gel.

"It's my job to listen to the he said and she said." She then turned on the shower and stepped inside.

In my mind I attempted to envision Sunday as the victim; not the attacker but instead the target. Even though I didn't know her, I had difficulty believing that story, even with the scar. An innate speculation screamed that Sunday was not only suspect, but guilty of a yet unidentified wrongdoing and I already looked forward to the end of the day when Melanie could share with me the events in the courtroom.

After her shower Melanie dressed in a black business suit with yellow collared blouse that brought warmth to her skin. She unwrapped her hair, which was growing longer as it always did in the summer, and feathered it into layers away from her face. Next she applied one coat of mascara and clear, shiny lip gloss. Just before she was ready to leave I gave her a thermos filled with black coffee that I had just made. She took a sip and smacked her lips.

"All right, I'm out of here," she told me before she grabbed her briefcase.

"Okay, Mel." By this time I had just ended my own shower and had picked out gray slacks and a white blouse to wear to work.

Melanie bent to kiss my lips. "Mmm, you smell good."

"Thanks. New body wash. You didn't see it in the shower?"

"No, but it smells great on your skin. Call you later, okay?"

"Please," I responded anxiously.

Melanie left and I went into the bathroom to apply my makeup. That's when I noticed that Melanie had left behind her BlackBerry. It sat in its case on the vanity behind the sink and the red light flashed indicating she had a message. I picked it up and held it in my hands.

Aside from my dislike for liars, I had greater disdain for those who invaded privacy. Okay, so maybe in a roundabout way, sitting outside my ex-girlfriend's house and Melanie's office was an indirect intrusion into their space. And it was a deliberate act in order to uncover something in which they may have been keeping a secret. Yet, I rationalized that it didn't trespass what was their private property. Whereas I hadn't experienced a personal violation of my privacy, Landon had once shared with me the embarrassing details of a woman she dated for a short period of time that had rummaged through Landon's possessions after Landon left her at her apartment while she went to grab doughnuts for them.

In twenty minutes time the woman had swiftly viewed Landon's photo albums, read e-mails from Landon's computer which was unlocked, and had gone through her mail, reading bank statements and bills from creditors. Oddly, the woman had no shame for her actions. When Landon returned with their breakfast, the woman commented to Landon that she didn't know that drivers could make such decent salaries. In response Landon casually agreed that it was definitely possible. After the woman quoted Landon's exact payroll deposit amount, Landon realized the woman had gone through her things. Their interactions ended that day, though Landon trusted no one in her apartment for quite some time after the incident.

I slid Melanie's BlackBerry out of the case and pressed the rolling ball in the middle so that the screen would light up. It revealed that Melanie had one text message and a new e-mail. I could read each of them and then mark them both as unopened, but why would I do that? Why would I now choose to read Melanie's correspondence with the assumption that Sunday was contacting her? Would Sunday have Melanie's cell phone number and personal e-mail address? If I read Melanie's text and e-mail and found interaction with Sunday, then I would likely have the proof that the nagging in my belly was validated.

"Forgive me," I said aloud and scrolled to the message icon. Before I could press the ball to open the message, Melanie re-entered the condo through the kitchen and I heard her heels run across the kitchen floor. Quickly I put her BlackBerry back in its place, picked up my black eyeliner and with shaky hands, began to apply it. My eyes began to water from immediate disapproval at what I had almost done as well as nearly being caught doing it.

"Forgot my phone," Melanie said when she reached me. She grabbed it and bolted from the room. "Bye!"

I didn't reply, only applied my makeup in the quiet stillness of the condo. I silently prayed that by the end of the day, Sunday would permanently depart from our lives.

"You look so pretty tonight," Jaye exclaimed loudly over the house music playing at Murmur.

"Thanks, Jaye. Got a new hat today." I ran a finger across the brim.

I was wearing a sexy black halter-style capri jumpsuit that snugged my waist and puffed delicately at my knees. On my feet I wore open-toe black pumps and on my head a funky black fedora hat over my straightened hair. Earlier that day at the makeup counter I experimented with false eyelashes for the first time and used those along with black liner and shadow for a dramatic evening look. Melanie was crazy about my appearance that night and hadn't let go of my hand since we arrived.

"You two have a good time," she told Melanie and I. "Prestin and I will catch up to you in a bit." Jaye walked away and continued to mingle about and assist Prestin as women began to pack the club.

Melanie and I had secured a table conveniently located next to the bar and waited for the rest of the ladies to arrive.

"I'm so glad to get out," Melanie said.

"I know love. You've worked so hard this month. It's time for you to relax."

Melanie bobbed her head to the music and sipped on her drink. Soon after, Ivy and Donna arrived with Ivy giving smooches to every woman she knew. Donna stood nearby until she tired of waiting for Ivy and finally came and took a seat at the table.

"How you doing, Donna?" Melanie asked.

"Good, good," she replied. Generally Donna appeared unimpressed with whatever was happening around her if it didn't have something to do with Beverly. She'd put forth efforts at participating in engaging conversations at times. However, most often she was friendly, but remained in an aloof state. For a moment she livened as her eyes darted through the club, no doubt checking for Beverly's presence. Disappointed, she sank into her chair.

"How's writing going? Working on any new pieces?" I asked her.

"Not right now," she answered, almost fully present again. Second to Beverly, the topic of writing usually brought a sparkle to Donna's eyes. "Actually, I'm considering writing a book. Tossing around some ideas in my head."

"That's wonderful, Donna!"

"Thank you, thank you." She grinned slightly.

"Hey, beautiful women," Ivy crooned when she approached the table. Melanie and I were greeted with the usual provocative kiss. Donna's mood dimmed once more and I wondered if her book might end up being about the struggle of losing a true love and winding up in an unsatisfying relationship. I knew that artists tended to use real life experiences in their works.

"Holy fuckin' shit," Melanie suddenly mumbled with her eyes bucked forward.

"What?" I asked softly and followed her gaze. "Oh my God!"

Headed toward the table were Ali and Noni, with Noni walking in front of Ali. Noni wore a nervous expression. Behind them, near the entrance of the club I could see Prestin and Jaye staring with shocked looks on their faces. Donna, who had been gazing blankly at the dance floor did a double take when they took their seats. And for once, Ivy was silent.

"Hey, girls," Noni said in a low voice.

No one responded.

"What's up, ladies?" Ali asked smoothly. She leaned back in her seat, opened her legs and relaxed an arm near her crotch. She eyed each of us confidently and awaited our reactions. Speechless, I stared at Ali. Gone were the gentle soft curls that reflected her sweet, natural style. Now she wore a nearly bald, tapered hair cut. Her usual colorful jewelry was replaced with large diamond studs in each ear and a pinky ring on her left hand. She wore a baggy, pin-striped suit in navy with a white T-shirt underneath. Personally, I had absolutely no issue with the way a lesbian woman dressed. To each her own, but I knew that Ali's presentation was not a true reflection of her being and in the long-winded discussion I had with so many women, the consensus remained that a woman should remain true to herself and allow that truth to reflect both her inner and outer self.

"How you been doing?" Melanie asked and finally broke the ice.

"Been good," Ali answered. Even her tone had changed from the tender voice we all knew to a more aggressive, firm inflection.

It seemed no one really knew what else to say. After several minutes of heavy silence, Ali asked if anyone wanted something to drink. Everyone answered yes.

"I'll go with you," Melanie offered and the two of them stepped a few feet away to order drinks.

Noni's eyes widened and sent an obvious cry for help in my direction.

"What happened?" I mouthed. Both Ivy and Donna leaned forward to catch our exchange.

Noni peered behind her to check Ali's distance. She spoke low, though loud enough so we could hear. "One day she just came into the salon and asked me to cut her hair off. When she told me how, I asked her why she wanted to do that. Ali only said because she's kind of natural anyway, so I didn't see it as all that big of a deal. Next thing I know she shows up at my place dressed in sagging shorts and a beater."

"Get out of here!"

"Girl, yes. Again, I asked her what she did that for and she said she wanted to try out a new look."

"What have you told her?" I asked.

"Nothing really. I mean, it's her body, her style, her life," Noni sounded resigned, although the grimace she wore revealed her true feelings.

"Do you like it?" I asked, even though I knew the answer.

Once again Noni eyed Ali. "Honestly, I don't dislike it," she admitted. "I just don't understand the sudden change. She was beautiful before and she still is. She's just...just going through something I think."

I wasn't sure if I should tell Noni about the conversation I had with Ali and the reason she had altered her appearance so drastically. That the purpose was to secure Noni's place in her life once and for all by becoming more masculine. Instead of saying anything I decided to wait and get Melanie's opinion.

"Here's your drink, baby girl," Ali told Noni when she and Melanie returned.

Melanie flashed me a comical expression and I lowered my head to conceal the smirk that crossed my face.

"How are my favorite women doing?" Prestin appeared at the table and questioned. She made eye contact with everyone at the table, lingered on Ali for a moment and then peered at me. Next to Noni, she knew I was the closest person to Ali. Apparently she didn't know what to say either.

"Let's check out the shoes, Prestin," I said excitedly with an attempt to turn everyone's attention away from the overwhelming awkwardness we all felt.

Prestin smiled and kicked her right leg backward to display

a lustful black and gold stiletto shoe. "You like? These would go great with your outfit," she told me.

"Hand 'em over," I teased. She laughed like I should know better.

"Showtime is at eleven, okay? Christina is in the back warming up." Tracy, one of the members of Murmur's management team, interrupted and told Prestin she was needed to say hello to a special guest. Prestin excused herself. So did Melanie and I so we could dance and compare stories. We stood close, our bodies touching at the hips with my arm draped around Melanie's neck. Side to side we swayed, in unison with the beat, and spoke into each other's ears.

"What got into Ali?" she asked.

"I guess I didn't tell you. A few weeks ago she was telling me that she wanted to change her hair for Noni. Jokingly I told her that she might want to dress like a man."

"What in the hell made you say that?"

"I said that men were the reason Noni wouldn't commit to her. I know it was stupid, and now look at her." We both glanced toward the table at Ali. Her exterior disposition seemed cool, yet, I could only guess that the inner Ali hadn't caught up to the outer Ali.

"I know women that have changed, but I've never seen anything like this," Melanie said.

"Talk to her again, Jo. Make sure she's all right with this. What did Noni say?"

The song we had been bobbing to ended, and a faster paced bass sound blew through the speakers. We parted slightly to allow the other space to move, yet we remained close.

"She doesn't seem happy, but she said it's up to Ali to look how she wants to."

"I guess," Melanie acknowledged. "Though don't you go pulling that on me."

"You wouldn't love me if I wanted to go bald?" I asked.

She ran her fingers over the ends of my hair. "Whatever makes you happy. But you know how much I love sweating out your hair, right?"

We laughed and finished our dance to the song. When we returned to the table, Ali had just stood up to leave for the restroom. I took advantage of the opportunity to go with her. We walked around the dance floor and past the second bar into the bathroom. A few women stood in front of the mirror touching up makeup and spraying various perfumes on their bodies. I waited for Ali alongside the sink and checked my nails to ensure the polish was smooth and had not flaked.

A young woman, a newbie I had never seen at previous Murmur parties, began to stare at me while she applied a purple shade of lipstick. I smiled at her then resumed my nail inspection. She tapped me on the arm. I looked up again.

Is that your girlfriend? She mouthed the words to me and tilted her head backward toward the stall that Ali was in. I shook my head side to side to indicate no.

She relaxed her posture and turned her body to face me. "Do you have one?"

"I do."

"She sure is one lucky woman," the young woman responded. She picked up her purse, eyed me up and down, and then left with the other women that had also finished applying fresh makeup. I shook my head in amusement.

Ali exited her stall and began to wash her hands. "Thought you had to go?" she asked.

"Really I didn't. I wanted to talk to you."

Ali reached for a paper towel. "What's up?"

I sighed. "What happened, Ali? What's up with the new style?" I touched her suit jacket. "I've never seen you like this before."

"We talked about this already. I told you I'd do anything to make Noni mine. If she's not sure if she wants a man or woman, I can be both."

I wished it didn't sound so easy and logical, but it did.

"Is it working?"

"She hasn't said anything," Ali said softly, a moment of her tender side resurfacing.

"Well, have you asked her? I mean, you've gone through all of this and you don't know how she feels about it yet?"

"It hasn't been that long. I've been waiting to see how she responds."

"And how is that?"

Ali thought for a moment. "Well, she hasn't said we could be together if that's what you're asking."

That wasn't exactly what I was asking but since she brought it up. "You probably want to tell her what this is all about, Ali. So she can have a better understanding of why you made this change. Then you can at least know if you want to continue on like this or not," I urged gently.

Several women entered the restroom and Ali and I left. The deejay stopped the music as we were en route to the table. I recognized the familiar voice of Satin, one of Chicago's finest female deejays. She was an outgoing woman with a sexy, short spiked haircut. She and Prestin had "come up" together; friends from the early days when Prestin's parties involved a small circle of women and later grew to attract hundreds. Satin had always been the woman playing the tracks that everyone grooved along with. To the heartbreak of many women, several years ago Satin married a man and put an end to the ongoing question of whether her bisexuality would land her with a man or woman in the end. Still, to everyone's pleasure she was faithful to Prestin and to her female following, therefore, remained a constant presence at all of Prestin's functions.

At Satin's announcement, the crowd quieted and Christina was introduced as the evening's special guest performer. From the edge of the dance floor Christina emerged and walked to its center. She looked gorgeous and confident and her expression screamed appreciation as everyone applauded her introduction. Satin put on a track that began with a soft piano melody and Christina began to perform "Gently," the song she sang for us after the Pride Parade.

During the performance, several coupled women danced slowly while others smiled at one another in tribute to the sweet words Christina sang. Melanie held my hand once again and when I saw Ali reach for Noni's hand, and Noni accepted, my heart warmed.

At the end of the song, everyone at our table stood to cheer and whistle at Christina for an amazing song. Prestin greeted her on the dance floor and with Prestin's own microphone declared that Christina's performance was the first of many at Murmur. In response, patrons clapped louder. Christina smiled graciously, bowed, and ran to hug Landon who was waiting next to the bar.

"She's going to be a star," Donna said suddenly, and we all looked her way in surprise that she initiated a conversation.

"I think you're right," I agreed as we observed Christina accepting various congratulations from women. By the time Christina and Landon arrived at the table, Ali had removed her blazer and was resting comfortably in her chair, the only sober one in the group.

Christina welcomed hugs from everyone. When she reached Ali she stepped backward first. "Ali? Damn girl, you look sexy as hell," she squealed.

Ali looked like she wanted to do a cartwheel and a backflip. It must have been the first compliment she received. "Thank you," she said proudly.

For the remainder of the night we partied in our usual Murmur fashion. We each danced to the songs we favored most, people watched all the women, and cut Landon, Donna and Melanie, the designated drivers, off drinks well before club closing. We lagged behind a short while after Murmur closed its doors for the evening. Before Prestin retired to the back office, I caught her and apologized for interrupting a conversation she was having with Satin.

"You're looking good tonight," Satin complimented me after we hugged.

"Thanks, you too," I told her and then turned to Prestin. She spoke before I could. "What's up with Ali?" she whispered.

I trusted Prestin. "She did it for Noni," I told her. Her expression was confused. "She thought that since Noni still digs guys too that she should masculine up a bit," I explained.

"A bit?" Prestin questioned.

"I know . . . We'll get to the bottom of it. But for now, are we all set?" I quickly asked because Melanie was approaching.

"We sure are. Talk to me this week and I'll give you all the details. She's going to love it," she smiled.

"Thanks," I whispered. "I'll give you a call. Bye Satin!"

I beamed with joy, grateful to Prestin, grateful for Melanie, and eager to honor Melanie on a special night with family and friends. She deserved it.

Chapter Eleven

"All right, sweetie. I'll see you tomorrow. You all have fun tonight. Tell the kids I said I miss them."

"We will and I'll tell them."

"Love you, Mel."

"Back at you," she replied.

I disconnected the call and laid the phone at my side. On the couch I nestled comfortably against a pillow and turned on my laptop. Melanie was gone for the night and I had a Friday evening alone. Early in the week Ferris had called Melanie and asked if she could watch his kids while he and his wife, Barbara, went to dinner. Melanie offered to babysit the kids all night, well aware that her brother and his homemaker wife rarely spent time away from the children. It took a day of convincing for them to submit to Melanie's suggestion and then only under the arrangement that Melanie watch the kids in their home. Even under the safe care of Melanie, Ferris and the Mrs. booked a hotel room less than two miles away to ensure easy access home if there was an emergency.

I typed the familiar name of the networking site into the search bar and logged on. Ever since Melanie won the case involving Sunday a couple of weeks ago, my preoccupation with Sunday's profile had lessened. In fact, I had only logged on one other time since and that was to accept Jillian's friendship request that she had phoned me twice about and had sent a message through Ronan.

Melanie had informed me that although they won the case

and Sunday had not been found guilty of violation, at the request of the ex, the restraining order had been extended an additional six months and Sunday was warned to oblige and have no contact with the ex.

Casually I browsed through the photos of those who wanted to be friends. I accepted most and declined a few that had left indecent comments along with their request. It never ceased to amaze me the vulgarity and brazenness of so many people online. It seemed that so long as they hid behind their computer screens, they believed they could say and do whatever they pleased and be whomever they wished as well.

Less than two minutes after I approved new friends and while reviewing my cousin Leandra's latest updates, I received a pop-up notification that one of them had left a comment on my profile. I clicked on the icon to view it and saw that it was from a woman who called herself Khamai0606. Her profile was not of herself, but a photo of an animated kaleidoscope design in a medley of vibrant colors. The comment she left simply said, "Thank you." Although she was obviously logged on at the same time, the online alert didn't show next to the picture and I realized that she, too, kept her online status hidden.

Because I had approved her friendship without viewing her information, I decided to browse her profile to learn more about her. Overall, I knew very little or nothing about the majority of my online friends. With some there was an initial introduction such as the one Khamai had just left. For others there was limited, harmless interaction via e-mails or comments left on one another's profiles. And then there were the women, and some men, that pushed virtual limits in their desire to connect and with the tap of a key, were deleted from my list.

I was surprised to find that I was only Khamai's second friend next to the automatic acquaintanceship of the creator

of the site. It seemed her profile was recently created as there
was little information to look at other than a few personal
items that detailed her age: Twenty-nine. Height: Five foot
six inches. Location: Chicago, IL. Ethnicity: Black. Sexual
Orientation: Lesbian. If she was "family" she was all right
with me so I returned her comment and said, "You're
welcome. Have fun on here." Afterward, I resumed browsing
Leandra's most recent blog on why there were no good men
in Milwaukee where she lived. Just after I responded to the
blog and suggested that maybe she had been a little harsh
in her depictions, I received another notification, this time
informing me that I had new e-mails. When I viewed the
messages in my inbox, I was surprised to find that the e-mail
was from Khamai. The subject line read: **Hi.** Even though it
seemed innocent enough, I already prayed that I wouldn't
have to delete this woman. I left the e-mail unread.

For the next hour I skimmed a few more profiles, left
Melanie a message that I knew she wouldn't see for days, and
then played online Spades, losing two of four games. I stepped
away from online activities for a moment. In the kitchen I fixed
myself a couple of tacos, which were leftovers from the night
before. When I returned to the couch and finished eating the
spicy, warmed food, I prepared to shut down my laptop and
retreat to the bedroom for a movie. Before I could sign off,
another e-mail popped up. **How sweet**, the subject line stated.
Again, it was from Khamai. This time I didn't ignore it and
opened the message immediately.

You make a beautiful couple, she told me. I went back
and read the first e-mail which stated: I am happy to meet
you. I opted not to respond to either message, only sighed
in gratitude that she had taken the time to peruse my photos
and acknowledge my relationship. My experience showed
that most women respected that boundary, though there was
that 1.5 out of ten ratio that did not. Because there was little

description about her in order to gain an understanding of her personality, I wasn't yet sure in which category Khamai would be placed. I left Khamai and my laptop alone for the night and retired to the bedroom.

I'M GOING FOR A RUN. THEN I'LL BE HOME. That was the text message Melanie left for me at 9 A.M. the following morning. Melanie had that annoying habit some possess of typing in all caps as if the recipient of her messages were being scolded by the loud words screaming through the phone. On many occasions I had asked that she stop yelling at me in writing, yet it seemed to be a habit she couldn't break.

I assumed she sent the message under the belief that I would have taken her absence as an opportunity to sleep later than usual, hence the reason she didn't want to wake me by way of a phone call. However, atypical of my usual Saturday morning behavior, I had already gotten up to review files for a new client that I had failed to check on Friday. When I remembered that I had asked him to forward additional documentation to me through e-mail, I found myself back on my laptop.

After I located the information from the work message system, I decided to quickly check my personal account. I was fairly certain there wouldn't be anything new in my box from overnight. I saw an e-mail notification that a friend from Texas had left a comment wishing me a happy weekend. Quickly I logged onto the site to approve the posting of her message to my profile.

Before I could sign off I saw a pop-up alert, which was a duplicate to the simultaneous e-mail notifications, that I had just received a new e-mail. Surprise, surprise, it was from Khamai. I logged off the site and went back to work. By 11:30 A.M. I was on my second cup of coffee and curious as to why Melanie hadn't made it home yet. I called her cell phone even though I knew she didn't carry it on her runs. It went to voice mail after five rings as I expected. By 1:30 P.M. I had gotten nervous that something had happened so I called again; no answer. I decided to send her a text message and ask that she call me when she returned to her phone. **Call me love,** I wrote. Thirty seconds later she responded: **Shortly.**

What the hell? Obviously she had just ignored my call if she was able to immediately reply to my text. Instantly aggravated I sent another message: Where are you? This time she didn't answer. I closed my eyes and groaned while I caught glimpses of déjà vu visions of red flags waving before me. I had assumed that with the closing of the case, my feelings toward Sunday had been futile; that in actuality, she wasn't pursuing my woman, that my woman had no interest in her, and that their interactions would cease. However, I remembered something that my grandmother had always told me: to listen to my instincts as they would always guide the way, even when I didn't know to where.

Intuitively, I went online and navigated my way to Sunday's still private profile. She had changed her picture to a close-up of her eyes. They were accentuated in a charcoal, smoky eye design which only enhanced the fierceness in her eyes. My body shuddered in impulsive discomfort. My uneasiness intensified when I read her status: Case closed. But it's not over.

Who was she talking to? To what was she referring? Was "it" not over in reference to her ex-girlfriend? Or could "it" be regarding Melanie? I didn't know.

I sat in contemplation for the next thirty minutes. I debated whether or not I would ask Melanie if she knew what Sunday meant. But then Melanie would know that I, for an inexplicable reason, had checked Sunday's status again. I considered requesting Sunday as a friend. It would not be odd in light of the fact that she was already on Melanie's friend list. And that way I could monitor any interaction she had with Melanie. I also deliberated leaving daily messages on Melanie's profile with descriptions of my love for her while I confirmed the strength of our relationship. It was catty, childish, and not my character; I refused to be that female who "had to make it known" who her woman was in order to keep others at bay. Sadly, I realized that I just may be turning into her. Finally, I decided that I would grant Melanie an opportunity to explain her whereabouts; if her alibi was acceptable, I'd let her slide. If her account deemed suspect, the examination would begin. I'd trust myself in the moment.

"Hey." Melanie coolly walked in the condo and sat next to me on the couch. She wore black, capri running pants with a sky blue fitted top.

I waited for her to elaborate but in typical Melanie fashion, she waited for me to question.

"Where have you been?" I asked.

"Running," she answered, then casually began to take off her shoes. "Then I ran a couple of errands."

"You didn't say you were going on errands when you sent your message this morning," I continued.

"I decided to make some stops after I went for my run."

"Melanie, why is it so hard for you to answer a question?"

"What question?"

"Where did you go?" I asked slowly, sarcastically.

"I-went-running," she mocked like we were in the midst of a light-hearted conversation. I squinted my eyes at her.

"Relax, Jo. After my run I went to pick up some toys for the kids that they told me they wanted. Then I went back to Ferris' house and dropped them off."

"So why didn't you answer when I called?" It was abnormal for me to inquire about the items she purchased for her niece and nephew, but I was too absorbed with uncovering Melanie's tracks the past several hours.

"Only because Barbara had me hemmed up in a conversation about some new linen she wants to buy. Believe me, I wanted to answer, but you know how sensitive she is. When you sent the message, I typed back real fast."

"Yet, you didn't call," I added.

She was quiet.

"Melanie?"

"I wanted to surprise you with that corn dish you like. I didn't call because I didn't want you to know."

Melanie was referring to a Mexican corn dish in which I would indulge only a couple of times a year. I also knew of a place on the way home from Ferris' that made it best. The biggest problem remained: she had no corn.

"Well where is it?"

"I ran into a client outside the place."

"And?"

"And then I forgot to get it."

I exhaled loudly. "Who did you run into?" I asked, though I would have bet my entire hat collection that I already knew the answer.

"Sunday," she replied.

This time I was quiet. Just for a minute. I think Melanie thought she was off the hook. She repositioned herself, laid sideways on the couch, and placed her sweaty feet on my lap.

For several weeks I had granted Melanie the benefit of a doubt. I had not questioned her about Sunday, at least not to the degree in which I could have. I had agreed that I would wait and give it some time prior to placing her on the stand and interrogating her with what might be insufficient evidence. I wanted to trust her enough to know that, one, if Sunday had ulterior motives she would tell me; and two, that she would have no desire to entertain Sunday's hidden agenda if one did exist. All I knew at this point was that my confidence in Melanie was quickly deteriorating.

"So she happened to be at the same place you were?"

"Obviously."

"Look Melanie, I've been more than patient with this. The least you can do is not give me attitude about it."

"Patient about what?"

"About you and Sunday. You being all uptight and evasive when we talk about her."

"That's not true. How many times have we even talked about her?"

"Several times!" I said loudly.

"When?"

"Don't try to flip this on me, Mel."

"Flip what? I don't even know what you're talking about."

"Twirl this around like I'm making stuff up in my head."

She stared at me. An insulting gaze that suggested I acknowledge that I was indeed allowing my imagination to create fictitious scenarios.

"So how long did you talk?"

"I don't know," she lied. Of course she knew.

"What did you talk about?"

"We talked about how she's been doing since the case,'" she said vaguely.

"And how is that?"

"Why do you care?"

"I care because this doesn't seem right."

"What doesn't seem right?" she questioned.

"You and her!"

"There is no 'me and her,'" she said calmly. It wasn't often that Melanie and I argued, but when we did, I became heated while she remained unaffected. It pissed me off.

"Forget it," I said, and removed her feet. I stood up. "I'm done."

"Done what?"

"Talking about this." I began to walk toward the bedroom.

"Good," she muttered.

Slowly I turned around to look at her.

"What was that?" I asked.

She returned the eye contact. "I said good," she said arrogantly.

"Okay, Melanie," I laughed in a patronizing manner. "Don't let me find out you're lying to me."

"Or what, Jo?" she shot back.

"Or you'll regret it," I told her.

Now she laughed. "So you're threatening me? Wow, all right." She stood up and walked toward me until we stood face to face. "You want to be like Sunday's ex and send threats my way?"

My face flushed with anger. "Excuse me?"

"You heard me," she responded.

My body began to shake and I took a moment to calm down.

"Don't you see what this is doing to you? What it's doing to us? Every time you're around that woman you treat me like shit; like I'm the one with the problem."

She didn't say anything, only walked into the bedroom and closed the door. For a while I stood motionless, shocked by my and Melanie's encounter. We had disputes in the past, though never to the escalated point of intimidation and provocation. What was it about Sunday that causes such a stir within both of us? Was I truly causing an unnecessary crisis between us? Or was the sounding alarm in my belly a distinct warning of the intentional fire Sunday wished to create?

Even with the caffeine racing through my system and the frustration weighing on my heart, my body had tired and I sought refuge in the second bedroom. I laid down for a nap and the final thought I remember before falling asleep was that I needed to cut to the chase; to figure out what was happening and to move forward from there, wherever there was.

***

Melanie and I didn't speak the rest of the day on Saturday. We each secluded ourselves to our own spaces and when we happened to cross paths once in the kitchen, we pretended as if the other were invisible. My heart was unsettled and my spirit in a state of unrest. Yet, I remained steadfast in stubbornness and ignored her. By evening, the tension could be felt between both rooms and behind closed doors. Neither of us attempted to initiate communication. Not until morning at least.

I heard a light tap against the wooden door and assumed Melanie would enter. When the knock became louder I lifted the down comforter I had been resting under and rose to open the door. I cracked it slightly, just enough that she could peek inside, and I got back in bed with my back to the door.

The door creaked and opened slowly. Next I could feel her standing beside the bed. Even though my eyes were closed, my heart thudded and my mind was spinning. What did she want?

"Jo."

"What?" I asked, without moving. She sat on the edge of the bed.

"There's something I need to tell you," she said softly.

So here it is . . . the big confession. I turned over so I could look her in the face.

"Sunday did make a pass at me," she began. "Yesterday when I saw her she asked if I wanted to get together sometime. I told her no."

Her eyes shifted from mine and she stared at a picture on the wall. I waited for her to continue, yet she remained fixated on the black and white photo.

"That's it?"

"What do you mean 'that's it?'" Her gaze met mine once again.

"So she asked you out and you said no. Now that's the end of it?"

"It should be."

"Why should? Why isn't the answer just yes?"

She exhaled. "Because I can't control her. I'm hoping she accepted my answer."

I thought for a moment and then asked, "Is there a reason you think she wouldn't?"

She didn't answer.

"Let me rephrase my question, Mel. Have you ever given her a reason to think you want to go out with her?"

"The day we went to court, she and I had lunch afterward," she confessed.

"And what happened?" I asked louder, my voice more intent on securing an answer.

"She was really happy we won and wanted to celebrate. I didn't have much on my calendar the rest of the day so she had a glass of wine and I had a mojito. After awhile she started telling me more about her ex-girlfriend and how much she had loved her, but the ex treated her so bad. Would tell her stuff like she was fat and unattractive and that no one would want her . . ." Melanie's voice trailed off.

"So you came to the emotional rescue, right?" I asked sneeringly.

"I didn't want her feeling worse. She started asking me if I thought she was pretty and if I was single would I date her."

"And let me guess, you said yes? Unbelievable, Melanie, why didn't you tell me this before?" I asked, surprised by the ease in which I asked. While a part of me was still angry, another part was grateful that at last, Melanie was telling me the truth. Now I could rest in confidence that my instincts were accurate. But what about the thought I had the day before? That I needed to figure out what was happening. Was this all there was to it? Chapter closed, end of story?

"I didn't tell you because I knew how you would respond. You already don't agree with mixing friendship with clients.

In my mind I told myself that it was no different than you meeting your clients out for lunch or an appetizer while you talk business."

For several minutes I pondered her words and then mentally retraced the events of the day they went to court. Melanie had been sweet in the morning and calm in the evening. I had attributed that to winning the case and added relief that it was over. Both which I'm certain are accurate, however, now that I tied in with the knowledge that she had intentionally hidden her lunch date from me, I became skeptical at the ease in which she omitted that information.

"You should have told me," I said.

Melanie shrugged her shoulders as if to say "that's neither here nor there."

"Well," I continued, "I think you should delete her from your friend's list."

Her expression became confused. "Why?"

Did she really have to ask? "Because, Melanie. She's already tried to cross lines with you, even knowing we're together."

"That happens all the time online," she defended.

"This wasn't online," I reminded her. "Have you ever talked about me with her?" I was suddenly curious.

"Not really."

"What do you mean 'not really?'"

"I mean, over lunch she commented that we were a nice looking couple. She asked how long we had been together..."

"What else?" I asked, knowing she was again, intentionally dismissing part of their conversation.

"She wanted to know if I was happy."

My teeth clenched. "And your answer was?"

"Come on, Jo. You don't have to ask me that," she stated like I had asked her an outrageous question. I sat up, propped a pillow against the headboard and leaned against it.

"You know what, you're right, I shouldn't have to ask you that. I never thought we'd even being having this kind of conversation. But right now, I don't know what to think anymore. All I know is you have some woman coming on to you, you kept it a secret, and now you don't want to let it go."

"Let it go? Let what go? Just because I don't want to delete her online? Jo, it's the internet, it's not that serious. And don't forget, I did win a case for her. Regardless of how you feel about it, she could bring in new clients if this is handled the right way."

"It *is* that serious to me. But okay, you just make sure you handle yourself the right way."

"What's that supposed to mean?"

"It means no more run-ins with Sunday. It means no more secret lunches. It means she's nothing more than a previous client."

"I can't control being in the same place at the same time," Melanie told me.

"Whatever." I said, as I lowered the pillow and laid back down.

Could she not appease me for one second in this situation? Melanie lifted the comforter and scooted her body underneath. She snuggled her body against my backside and her warmth immediately brought calm to my distress. I wanted to stay mad. I wanted to remain indignant for just awhile longer, but, the love I felt for Melanie wouldn't allow me to maintain that type of hostile chemistry.

"I don't want to spend another night without you," she said.

I was quiet, certain that an *I'm sorry* would follow. It didn't.

"Don't do anything else that causes us to spend another night apart," I cautioned.

She didn't acknowledge my warning with a response, only tightened her grip around my waist and held me close. Silently, and willingly, I accepted her unspoken apology.

Chapter Twelve

"Okay, so what happened when you told Noni?"

Ali had just arrived at my office and brought lunch for us. She disregarded my order for a cheeseburger and fries and instead purchased a second lentil burger identical to hers and placed it in front of me like we both were vegans. I retrieved a small bag of chips from my desk drawer and opened them. I'd have to eat later.

"She was really surprised," Ali told me. Ali was wearing relaxed fit jeans, a wife beater, flip flops and a baseball cap. Not an outfit I'd necessarily consider studly, though not one I had seen her wear in the past.

"What did she say?"

"Well, she told me that she loved me just as I was before. Then she said that it wasn't necessary; that I shouldn't have done it if that was the reason and she wished I had talked about it before."

"So what does this mean?"

"I'm not sure."

"Why aren't you sure?"

"It backfired. She said she could kind of understand if I was just going through something. But now she realizes just how much I love her if I went through all of this to be with her. She went on to say that I deserve someone else who can appreciate all the love I have to offer." Ali took a bite into her burger and searched my face for a response.

"No offense, Ali, but come on now. You've been stuck on

Noni for how many years and she didn't know how dedicated you are to her? What, now she feels guilty for taking all your love and not giving it back the same?"

"I guess. She makes it seem like it was a crazy idea to change my appearance for her. Like it's doing too much and she can't handle it."

"Are you saying she broke up with you, or whatever it is with you two?"

Ali put her burger down and lowered her head. "All these years I've been so faithful to her. All this time I've tried to show how much I love her hoping that she would one day give in to us." She lifted her eyes to me. "Now I finally realize she'll never love me the same way that I love her. If this is all it took to push her away, she wasn't ever really here," she concluded.

I felt sad for Ali. I knew the depth of the love she had for Noni and the longing for the day that Noni would be hers. "I'm sorry, Ali."

She nodded her head in appreciation.

"What now?"

"What now is right," she said. Her eyes expressed bewilderment. "I need time . . . time to heal and understand. If this is really over, I want to know what the lesson is and somehow, someway, trust that there is something else— someone else— out there for me."

She sounded like Ali again. "I'm here whenever you need me," I assured her.

She smiled. "You know, I used to dream that me and Noni would be together and buy a condo by you and Melanie and the four of us would double date and have dinner and we'd all have so much fun together."

I poked my bottom lip out. "That would have been nice."

Ali sighed. "You're fortunate, Jovanna. You and Melanie have something so special."

I looked away and stared through the window beside my desk at passerby on the busy sidewalk. Pieces of my heart agreed with Ali; Melanie and I truly shared a connection to be treasured. If I were to divulge my and Melanie's recent conflicts, I wondered if Ali would still feel the same. I was beginning to feel like those image perfect couples that looked the part, and hid their controversies behind closed doors.

When I didn't respond to Ali's comment, she inquired. "Is everything all right?"

Ali possessed a certain spirituality that at times came off as spacey and bizarre. I actually found it comforting with her ability to make the best out of any situation, just as she resolved to with the end of her and Noni's affair.

"It's okay," I answered. "We hit a few rocky spots lately, but everything will be fine."

"You know you can talk to me too, right?"

"Of course, Ali. Thank you." I realized that in the time Melanie and I had been together, I hadn't needed to consult with a friend about any woes that Melanie and I faced. Should I be grateful that we were challenged with our first ordeal five years into our relationship?

"You're not going to eat your burger?" she asked.

My head cocked sideways. "Sorry, you can't convert me. I'm a meat lover for life."

She squirmed and made an intentional squeamish expression. "All those poor animal spirits," she said. Statements like those are when her spirituality seemed a bit extreme. Still, I desired her input on my current circumstance. I asked indirectly.

"Why don't you belong to any social networking sites, Ali? It seems like everyone is doing it these days."

"Oh, I have one," she said quickly.

"You do?"

"Yep. But I use it strictly for online group spiritual networking. I don't have *real* friends on there."

"Why is that?" I asked, curious as to why she didn't want to interact with us online.

"First, I see and talk to you guys all the time so I don't really see it as necessary. Second, that can get messy and I'm not into that. I've heard stories."

"What kind of stories?" I wondered if they were similar to some of the insane accounts I had heard about and witnessed.

"People lying about who they are and pretending to be something they're not. People getting in relationships then finding out that person doesn't live up to the image they created. Then you have all these so-called friends that get connected and start interacting and all it takes is one messy person to interrupt the whole dynamic. One person starts sending e-mails talking about somebody else and telling someone's business. I've heard it all. And then there are people who get all addicted and attached to being online until the point when they can't live without it." Ali shook her head.

"How do you know all this?"

"In talking to other people and hearing their experiences. Most of the people I do volunteer work with are all online and they tell me stuff. I have to ask them why they put up with it. Some of them feed off the drama and some of them stay clear. It's good you and Melanie haven't been through that crazy stuff," she added.

"Right."

"I belong to five groups and if any one person brings any form of negativity to the group, the administrator deletes him or her right away. No drama allowed."

"That's good, Ali. What do you all do?"

Her face lit up. "We spread enlightenment. We uplift and encourage one another every day. Say someone has a job interview and shares that with the group, we all spread positive love and energy to that person. Maybe share an inspirational quote or passage. We honor one another's being."

I was quiet for just a second. "Did you talk about you and Noni?"

"Yeah. Honestly, no one agreed with my decision to change. Everyone told me that I needed to honor myself and shouldn't have to adjust to be something I'm not in order to gain her love. But that's why I appreciate the group. We all respect each other and what we do. There's no judgment and no trash talking. It's all love."

"That sounds really cool. I see why you like it so much."

"I really do. I'm not online that much but when I am, it's such a welcoming place. So, no offense to you all, but I choose to keep you separate from that. Most of the people in our group do."

"I understand that. I won't take it personal." I grinned.

Ali removed her hat and revealed springy curls that had begun to sprout from her scalp again. "Think I'm going to grow it back," she said.

"Yeah?"

"I miss them." She rubbed her hand over the new growth.

"What about the clothes?" I asked, cautiously.

Ali looked down at her baggy jeans. "I'm not sure yet. I get a lot of attention from pretty girls when I am dressed like this." She laughed. "Once I'm over Noni, this might work in my favor."

"You'll see what your group says?"

She thought for a moment. "Maybe. See what the Universe says first."

I smiled on the inside. She was still Ali.

"Oh, Ali, wait a second. Before you go, I wanted to ask you something. Do you know what it means to dream about snakes?"

"Well, I'm not completely certain, but, I believe it can mean both good and bad. It depends on what's happening in your life. It's an individual thing."

"Okay, thanks. Maybe I'll look it up."

"You might want to do that. Think about what's going on in your life and see if there's any connection to the snake. What is the snake doing in the dreams?"

I didn't want to answer. "It's trying to hurt me."

"Maybe it symbolizes a trial in your life. Something you will need to overcome. I'm not sure, Jovanna, I think you should meditate on it."

I smiled at her. "Thanks, I will."

After Ali left, I was still in the office alone. Ronan was out meeting with clients and I was inside handling paperwork. The talk about online networking caused me to question why I was online. In the beginning I signed up to stay in contact with family, which I did. Along the way I gained hundreds of friends, most of whom I did not know on a personal level, yet was privy to the details of their daily lives like we were best friends. It was interesting to say the very least. But like Ali said, I already had a steady flow of contact with my true friends. The ones I loved on a day-to-day basis. Was it necessary that I know that one of my 697 friends had a doctor appointment? Or that another had just eaten at a great new restaurant? Sure, that's what networking was all about: to share information, did it benefit me?

And I already had Melanie. The woman I loved and planned to spend the rest of my life with. We had a beautiful circle of friends that touched our lives differently and in manners we welcomed. Did I need to meet and sometimes interact with others? I understood the joy Ali found with her online friends. There was meaning behind their encounters. Were the communications I participated in beneficial to me and others, and just as importantly, were they conducive to my relationship?

Nonetheless, I logged onto the site and viewed the most recent updates of my friends. I skimmed through my top friends and found that Melanie had no recent updates; Ronan was making money and Leandra had given up hope of finding Mr. Right. I deleted my previous headline and simply changed my mood to contemplative. Inside I wondered, did anyone care that I was contemplative?

Within seconds I had my answer. Khamai sent me an instant message that read: **Happy to see you. What r u thinking?** I cursed at myself for having forgotten to turn the IM capability off so that no one could send me a message. I debated if I should respond. She knew I was online and it would be rude to ignore her. But I didn't know her so who cares? I gave in.

About life, I typed.

What about it? she wanted to know.

What's good for me and what isn't? Why was I telling her?

U r not happy?

I'm VERY happy, I told her.

Is something wrong?

My hands rested over my keyboard without typing. *Who was this person asking all these questions?*

Who are you? I asked.

The space for her response remained blank for about sixty seconds.

A friend, she finally replied.

Do I know you? Have we met before?

Another delay, we have not met.

Before I replied, I clicked on the colorful photo to open and view her profile. No additional information had been added and I was still only her second friend.

Why am I your only friend? I inquired.

Because you are the only one I want to be friends with, she answered with a yellow smiling face.

My impulse was to close the instant messaging box, delete her e-mails and remove her from my list of friends. Curiosity overpowered and in less than three minutes I had realized how quickly a person could be absorbed into ambiguous babble. That is, only if he or she allowed it and in that moment, I granted permission. Something told me to.

There are many you can be friends with, I responded.

You intrigue me most . . .

I am not here to intrigue you. I have a girlfriend, I typed quickly.

LOL. I know. I don't want to be your girlfriend. Just your friend. I didn't respond.

U did not respond to my last e-mail, she typed.

What e-mail?

I sent last week.

I moved my cursor to the inbox icon and clicked. Then I remembered that Khamai had sent messages the night Melanie was babysitting and I had chosen not to respond.

Thank you, I wrote in response to her previous compliment that Melanie and I made a beautiful couple.

U r welcome. U have a nice profile, she typed back.

Thanks again. My mood suddenly switched to aggravation. **Look Khamai, I appreciate your compliments. But you may want to find other friends. I'm not here for that.**

There was no reply for a moment and then she wrote: **Then y r u here?**

Exactly. Bye Khamai.

I closed the box and immediately updated my security settings to disallow instant communication.

"Come here Melanie," I yelled from the kitchen later that evening while I prepared dinner for two that consisted of smothered pork chops, rice, and broccoli with cheese.

"Yes?" She had been in the bedroom watching a WNBA game and wanted to get back to the television. I could tell by the haste in her voice.

"Do you think we should keep our online profiles?" I asked.

"What?" She sounded impatient.

"Why do we have them?"

"Well I have one because you had one when I met you. So you tell me why we have them."

"To stay in touch with people."

"Well there's your answer," she stated and began to walk away.

"Is it bad for our relationship?"

"What do you mean? Why would it be bad for our relationship?" She frowned. "Is this about Sunday?"

It was about Sunday. It was about Khamai. It was about the conversation I had with Ali.

"Kind of," I answered.

"Don't worry about Sunday."

"What do you mean 'don't worry about Sunday?'"

"It's taken care of."

"What's taken care of?"

"Just leave it alone, Jo." She walked back into the bedroom.

After I finished cooking, I placed healthy-sized portions on a plate for Mel and took it to her in the bedroom. She accepted, mumbled a soft thank you, and began to eat without taking her eyes off the woman who was preparing to shoot a free throw.

"Yeah!" she shouted when I turned my back and headed to the living room. I guess she made the point.

I found comfort in my usual position on the couch and out of Melanie's view—she wasn't paying attention anyway— to log onto the internet. From Melanie's list of friends I found Sunday and clicked on her photo. Shocked, her profile opened to reveal its contents. The privacy setting had been removed.

When the song on her page began to play, Jennifer Hudson's version of "And I'm Telling You I'm Not Going" I fumbled to press the mute button before Melanie could hear it. After the song silenced I peeked around the corner and saw that Melanie was still engrossed in the game.

Scanning Sunday's profile I learned that she was five feet eight inches, originally from California, had no siblings, was outgoing, and that her favorite food was salmon. She wrote about her love for poetry, travel, late night walks by Lake Michigan, and passion for children. According to her description she believed in God, prayer, love and faith and at the end of her bio had added that she fully believed in having all that she desired, no matter what it was, it was attainable.

I browsed through the comments some of her friends had left. Some older postings read **Congratulations,** I assumed in reference to the win in court. Others said they had dropped by just to say hello. A few remarked on her appearance, and called her **exquisite** and **striking.**

Sunday had five of her nine hundred friends in the tops section. I didn't bother to click on any of them, only took notice of their names and photos to check if they were mutual friends of mine at another time. When I scrolled back to the top of her page and finally noticed her status, it read: **Welcome, friend. I knew you'd come . . . ;-)**

Humored I wasn't. Confused I wasn't either. I was certain she was speaking to me. How coincidental was it that she opened her page for public viewing just after she asked Melanie out? What did she want me to see? And why? One thing I knew for sure was that I was going to find out.

"Get those e-vites out 'cause we're good to go," Prestin instructed.

We were sitting at her kitchen table discussing the finalized details of Melanie's surprise party. Prestin's clout had influenced the restaurant to the extent that Melanie's party was being granted free of charge. The owners wished to secure Prestin's business for future functions and if they satisfied her with Melanie's party, she had assured the likelihood that she would utilize their venue again. She had asked me if I minded testing them by way of Melanie's party. I told her no. I trusted her judgment and knew that she wouldn't set up a poor event.

"Okay, I'll send it out soon as I get home."

I'd be lying if I said some of the initial enthusiasm I felt about Melanie's party hadn't diminished because it had. The wish to make her birthday special remained, though our recent upsets had lessened my earlier fervor.

We heard their front door open and then close. Jaye walked into the kitchen dressed in loose fitting dark gray slacks with a sleeveless pink blouse. Her weave was pulled back into a ponytail and she wore silver framed eyeglasses that made her eyes appear double their size. She gave Prestin a long, closed-mouthed kiss.

"Hi, Jovanna," she then said.

"Hey, Jaye, how are you?"

"I'm well. Long day and glad to be home." She exhaled.

"Where are your contacts, sweetie?" Prestin asked Jaye and then winked at me.

"Don't start," Jaye laughed and then removed her glasses. "One of them was irritating my eye earlier and when I took it out, I dropped it and couldn't find it." She looked at me. "Prestin always talks about me in my glasses," she explained.

"Did you see them coke bottles?" Prestin teased.

"Don't get me to telling on you, Prestin," Jaye razzed. "She can't see a lick when those contacts come out."

I laughed at both of them and the light banter exchange.

"I'm going to shower," Jaye said. She walked toward their bedroom and then turned around. "What's for dinner tonight?"

Prestin looked over each shoulder. "Who's cooking?"

Prestin and Jaye were known for going out to eat at least five times per week. Even with their large modern kitchen and appliances, neither of them expressed the desire to grill, fry, or bake anything inside of it. Besides, just like the ease with which Prestin receives stiletto after stiletto, she receives a greater number of dinner invitations and requests for her patronage at restaurants all over Chicago. She and Jaye received V.I.P. treatment everywhere they went.

"Where are we going?" Jaye asked, excited.

"You'll see."

"Dress?"

Prestin looked up at the ceiling and thought for a moment. "How about a dress . . . comfortable, but sexy."

"I can do that," Jaye smiled and left the kitchen.

"I don't know how you two stay so in shape with all that food you eat," I commented.

"She has me going to exercise classes a couple of times a week now. Even before then I'd be locked up in the room with her doing Tae-Bo in the morning. And look who's talking with all that good home cooked food you eat. Melanie runs it off, what do you do?"

"That's usually my biggest meal of the day. I eat, but don't overeat throughout the day. I guess that helps."

"Seems to be working."

I looked down. Prestin was still as charming as ever. Any woman with the slightest weakness of heart could easily find herself enamored by Prestin's innocent appeal.

"Prestin, you've been doing online social networking for a long time, right?"

"Yeah, I have."

"Have you ever had any problems with it?" She looked concerned. "What kind of problems?"

I selected my words carefully, even though I knew Prestin would be able to see through any ambiguity I displayed.

"People trying to interfere with your relationship," I said calmly.

"Oh yes, all the time."

Of course I should have known that, with the way women threw themselves at her when they thought Jaye wasn't looking.

"How do you handle it?"

"Well, this is business for me. My name is important for all that I do so in that case, I have to use caution in how I respond to people. If someone sends me a compliment, I'll thank them and invite them to the next Murmur party. Some people leave it at that. If that doesn't work and they continue on, I usually have to ignore future attempts to interact. Sometimes I run into the women at the parties. If they catch me they'll ask why I didn't respond. If Jaye is nearby I'll point to her and let her know that's the reason why. Or simply tell them I was busy, which isn't a lie."

"Some women are bold, aren't they?"

"You should see some of the stuff they say to me!" Prestin shook her head. "It's unbelievable."

"So you've never been tempted to connect with anyone?"

"Sure, before Jaye. And offline. I can't have my business out there on the internet. So if someone of interest made a pass at me online, it was likely that I'd see her at a Murmur event. We'd connect and chat there."

"Oh, I see how you work, Prestin," I joked.

"Don't act like you forgot." Once again she shook her head, likely at the many quiet rendezvous she participated in years ago. Prestin was never loud about the women she entertained, although we all were aware that the number of broken hearts was high after Jaye arrived.

"You met Jaye online. What was different about her?"

She thought for a moment. "I guess the way she came at me. I had heard it all . . . and initially I put her in the category with all the others. I liked that she was mature and smart and didn't act like all she wanted was one night with me. Or that she wanted to get next to me to see who else she could get next to. Not someone just looking for the spotlight. And it didn't hurt that she is beautiful."

"How does Jaye handle all the women hitting on you?"

"She's great. Well, I mean, I'm sure she could live without it. It's funny to her that these women think they're being slick when they approach me behind her back. Trust me she has eyes in the back of her head. She sees it all." Prestin laughed. "I think what keeps her secure is that she knows I wouldn't do anything to cause doubt in her mind. She's my woman and everybody knows that whether they respect it or not. The majority of women do, but there's always those few, you know?"

Yes, I did know.

"So why are you asking these questions, Jovanna? Is there someone acting out of line?"

"I think so," I answered.

"To you or to Melanie?"

It seemed that both me and Melanie were her target. "Both I think?"

Prestin's smooth skin crinkled into a frown. "Someone is trying to get with both of you?"

"No, not like that. It's complicated," I said, unsure how to describe it without having the facts I needed. "I was just curious if you had been through anything and how you handled it."

"Well, it comes up often enough, but nothing over the top crazy, no. And if someone did try to go there with me, I wouldn't have it."

"So you would handle it?" I was seeking some sort of confirmation that my drive to investigate further was not without basis.

"I don't know what you mean by handle it, but I would make sure that I put an end to whatever was going on. It's one thing to have someone trying to mess with you by talking and saying stuff about you, who cares about that. But it's another if someone is truly trying to cause an interruption to your life. I'm not with that. I'm professional because I have to be, but no one is going to mess with me and Jaye and get away with it."

That was how I had begun to feel and maybe Melanie's nonchalant assurance that we didn't have to worry about Sunday should have appeased me. But Sunday's implicit comments toward me online prevented my mind from rest.

"Thanks, Prestin." I rose to leave. Prestin slid paperwork regarding the restaurant into a folder and handed it to me.

"Anytime. I don't know what's going on and I don't think you're going to tell me, right?" She smiled.

"Right." I laughed.

"Just don't get caught up in nonsense, okay?"

"I won't."

Prestin gave me a quick hug. "When are we coming over for one of your Puerto Rican meals anyway?" she asked, reverting back to our earlier conversation.

"Maybe Mel and I can have everyone over around Labor Day or something."

"Now you know we'll be in Atlanta that weekend. That's one of the few times I get to go out and enjoy all the hard work someone else invested into putting the parties on."

"Right. Okay, I'll cook another time. Speaking of Atlanta, Melanie and I should come this year." I had no idea what I would uncover with Sunday and what would unravel. Despite my discomfort, my goal was to renew the strength I had felt until recently with Melanie and stabilize our relationship.

"Works for me. Let me know and I'll get us all hooked up."

"No, Prestin," I resisted. "You've done enough hooking up with this party."

"It's good. You know I do what I can for my friends."

"We appreciate it. Thanks again for everything. See you in a few weeks."

"Okay. Now let me see that invitation before the end of the night," she reminded me.

"Got it." We walked to the front door and she let me out. "Tell Jaye I said bye, okay?"

"I sure will."

Chapter Thirteen

Weeknights were my choice of time to grocery shop. It didn't matter if it was Monday through Thursday, so long as it wasn't a busy Saturday or Sunday when many folks opted to cruise up and down aisles, checking lists and piling carts up with food, drink, and toiletries. All day long while at work I had jotted down items to add to my already extensive list.

When Melanie and I first moved in together, she enjoyed shopping with me. Once she realized that I'm a coupon-clipping, sale hawking consumer, our shopping partnership dwindled to shorter trips in which we may be purchasing items for a particular meal she requested. Now I most often shopped after work with my iPod in my pocket and music playing in my ears while I eased my way about the store.

I had just completed this week's shopping and was standing in the last aisle reviewing my list to double-check that I had picked up every item. That's when I realized the unimaginable had almost happened again: Melanie's treasured snack wasn't in the cart. I turned the heavy cart around and went to the refrigerated section to grab four small cartons of her favorite brand chocolate pudding.

On my way to the front of the store I was softly humming to a song while walking down an aisle of shelved crackers and cookies on one side and bottled water and flavored drinks on the other. I noticed a tall woman walking in front of me. She wore skin tight black leggings, high heeled shoes, and a loose-fitted top that hung off of her right shoulder. In her hand was a box of pudding, Melanie's favorite pudding.

She walked fast and I quickened my pace. The wheels on my cart began to squeal as I caught up to her. Just as I was about to pass her on the left, she snapped her right finger and stopped.

"Oh right, the wafer cookies," she said aloud, though speaking to herself. "Sorry, excuse me." She looked at me with dark brown eyes before she turned back down the aisle.

"Sure," I replied. I stood still for a moment to gather my breath and allow my heart to resume a steady pulse. With or without Sunday's help it seemed my mind was performing involuntary hallucinations. Had I taken one additional minute to fully focus, I would have observed that the shopper's jet black hair was a short style that in no way resembled Sunday's brown, shoulder length layers. Relieved I was to find an empty line, load up our groceries, pay for them, and get out of the store.

At home I put all the canned and boxed items in the cabinets, frozen vegetables in the freezer, and fruit in the bowl on the counter. I changed into my usual shorts and tank "at home" outfit and then phoned Melanie.

"Hey, *mi amor*," I said when she answered her office phone. I made a conscious effort to sound as normal as possible after my imaginary near run-in with Sunday. It was the same perky energy I had been exerting since my decision to expose Sunday for the crafty, schemer I felt her to be. I hadn't determined when, or if, I'd let Melanie know about the cunning perception I had of Sunday.

"Hey, what's up?" she asked. Her voice was calm.

"I'm not cooking tonight. Not up to it. Can you pick something up on the way home?"

"Sure, what do you want?"

"Corned beef sandwich on rye, please." My mouth rejoiced at the thought.

"No problem. I'm wrapping up and will be leaving soon."

"All right, see you when you get here," I told her.

"Okay, bye." She hung up and I laid my cell phone to my side.

Instead of turning on the television to watch a sitcom or movie, I used the remote and pressed buttons to locate one of the satellite radio channels offered with the cable provider. I flipped through an R&B and then old school station until I settled on a station of 1980s rap. I turned the volume low then picked up my laptop.

Online I read a response Leandra had made after I commented on the severity of her blog about no-good men. At the end of her sermon she stated that if the mindset of men didn't change, she may find herself jumping the fence and joining my team. I groaned aloud and decided to wait before I responded.

On my own profile I accepted the request for friendship of two new women. I didn't recognize having seen them before and wondered if our lifetimes would offer us any interaction other than this brief transaction here.

My mailbox had three new messages. When I viewed them, one was from Jillian asking me to check out the new photo of her and Ronan on both their profiles. Now that I had to see for myself. If Ronan had posted a picture of him and Jillian, he had undoubtedly escalated their relationship to another level.

The second message was from a woman out of North Carolina who had a trip to the Windy City on her calendar and wanted to know of places to go and parties she could attend. Politely I responded and sent her a couple of website travel links about Chicago and directed her to Prestin's page in case she'd be in town during a Murmur weekend.

Khamai had sent the final message. When I opened it she had written: **I did not mean to offend u the other day. I am sorry if I did. Here 2 be your friend.**

I didn't reply to her message. Interaction with Khamai

was a distraction to the current matter at hand. I took my usual route to Sunday's profile by way of Melanie's, which I scanned only for a comment from Sunday; there wasn't one. Sunday had once again altered her photo. In this picture she was posed leaning against a rock. With the blue waters in the distance and path of people behind her, I could see the photograph had been taken at Lake Michigan.

She wore a white cotton dress with no bra. Small brown nipples showed thru the thin material and her hair blew across her face. Yet her eyes shined mischievously into the sunlight and directly into the camera. I leaned closer. When I did, my eyes focused not on Sunday, but centered on a runner positioned about twenty feet behind her. It seemed the runner may have just passed Sunday seconds before the picture was taken. She wore black capri length running pants and a blue top. There was no mistaking the runner was Melanie. This picture must have been taken the same day Sunday had coincidentally been at the same diner where Melanie went to buy my bi-annual corn dish.

I debated whether or not to bring the photo to Melanie's attention. If Melanie saw the photo she'd have to admit that Sunday had followed her and intentionally situated herself to have the photo taken at the precise moment Melanie ran by. Then I wondered if Melanie had already seen it. For all I knew, she and Melanie could have just engaged in conversation. That would have been another lie by omission on Melanie's part. In my mind, Sunday had just proven herself not as the hopeless victim she portrayed herself to be with Melanie, but as a sneaky vixen with a fixated preoccupation on Melanie.

What should I do? Melanie had indicated that there was no reason to worry about Sunday. Either she was wrong about Sunday's determination, or a willing collaborator in the entire game. What was the game?

My cell phone rang and cut into my thoughts. It was Ronan.

"Hey, Ro," I answered.

"Hi, Jovanna, actually it's Jillian."

"Oh, hey Jillian. How's it going?"

"Wonderful. Got good news!"

"What's that?"

"I found a house!"

"Great." I tried to share her enthusiasm. "The one we talked about?"

"No, I found another home that's *perfecto*."

"I'm happy for you," I told her. "So your realtor will be getting the offer to me?"

"Yes, I'll be speaking with him tomorrow and then set up time with you."

"With me? Why is that?"

"He told me that you can go over with me what the next steps will be."

Ronan knew exactly what would follow the offer as far as an appraisal and inspection and the many details that are all integral to the home buying process. I gave in. It seemed he wanted us to be friends.

"I'll call you tomorrow morning when I'm back in the office. In the meantime, can you e-mail me the address of the place? I just want to check it out."

"Yep, I'll do that."

"All right, talk to you tomorrow. Congratulations."

"Thanks. Hey, Melanie home?"

"No, she hasn't made it yet."

"Tell her I'm going to take it personal if she does not accept my friend request soon. Did she not like my performance?" She laughed and so did I. She was too much.

"I'll tell her, Jillian."

"Oh yes, I'm looking forward to the surprise party too!"

So Ronan had invited her with him. "Glad you're coming."

"Yes. Do you need entertainment for it?" she asked.

Stripping? I hoped that wasn't her suggestion. "No thanks."

"Anytime you do, let me know. I do private events too."

"Really? Does Ronan know that?"

"Of course he does, he trusts me. And I take security with me for those so it is safe too."

"Good to know."

"Okay, see you soon," she said.

"See ya," I replied and hung up.

When I brought my attention back to Sunday's profile, I noticed that her headline stated: Countdown: 10, 9, 8 . . . to number 1. She had increased the number of her top friends from five to ten and who was in tenth spot? Melanie. She was really pushing it with this move and insinuation that Melanie would soon be her number one friend.

My next step was undetermined. I contemplated adding Sunday as a friend but what purpose would that serve? Then she would have full access to my profile and details of my life that I'd rather she didn't. On the contrary, at least then she could view the history of sweet comments Melanie had posted to my profile and maybe then she'd fully realize the depth of the love Melanie and I shared, however, my psychology courses taught me that a twisted mind like Sunday's had difficulty with the ability to grasp reality.

I could send Sunday an e-mail. An e-mail that informed her that I knew of her advances on Melanie and that I could see through the innocent charade she was putting on for Melanie. Before I made any contact with Sunday, I first needed confirmation that Melanie absolutely had no reciprocal interest in Sunday. How could I do that without stirring up adversity between us? I'd have to figure that out.

Melanie entered through the kitchen and I could smell the hot meat and spicy mustard as she walked to greet me with a grease-spotted white bag in hand.

"Smells so good," I said. Hurriedly I logged off the website and turned my attention to her and the food.

"Hey," she said, and lowered her body to kiss my cheek. She sat down, opened the bag, and handed a sandwich to me followed by a handful of napkins.

"How are you sweets?" I asked.

"Hungry," she answered, then took a large bite. "This was a good idea," she said through a mouthful of corned beef.

"Yeah, thanks for picking it up."

She swallowed. "Anytime. You deserve breaks from cooking."

"So we can start going out to eat like Prestin and Jaye?" I joked.

"I didn't say that now," she laughed. Her eyes caught site of my laptop and lingered on the screen. I turned my head and saw that even though I had signed out of the website, I had failed to close the box. In the past this had never been an issue, concern or second thought. Times had changed.

"Um, Jillian wanted me to tell you to accept her friendship request online," I told her.

"I will. I haven't been online too much."

"Okay. Well when you have a minute, just do it so she won't have to ask me again."

"No problem." She stared straight ahead and took another bite. We ate quietly while listening to Lil Wayne and Bobby Valentino rap and sing about a sexy female cop.

"Melanie," I said.

She raised an eyebrow and looked at me. "Hmm?"

"Your birthday is coming up . . ." I smirked.

She frowned fiercely. "Do you know what? I can't believe this shit," she said. "I found out today that the firm is sending us up to Wisconsin for a meeting the morning after my birthday. We have to leave Friday, *on* my birthday to be at the social event that evening."

I laughed on the inside. *Got her.* "Are you serious, Mel? That's not fair." I pouted and focused on pretending to be disappointed.

"I can't remember the last time I couldn't do something fun on my birthday." She was such a birthday brat.

"Well when will you be back?"

"Saturday afternoon."

"We can celebrate then." I sighed to cover up a rising laugh.

"Yeah, I guess."

"It's okay love. I'm sure the guys will make sure everyone knows it's your birthday and show you a good time."

"In Wisconsin?" she asked sarcastically.

"Yes, sweetie, even in Wisconsin."

"Let me throw this away." She took the aluminum wraps, paper bag and dirty napkins to the kitchen. Finally I allowed a smile to cross my face. Rick had obviously done a great job. The plan had been for Rick to come to Melanie and inform her of a conference the firm wanted its lawyers to attend. Melanie's response was a predictable argument that it was her birthday weekend and that she and I always made plans. Rick bluffed that he, too, was upset considering his wife's due date fell that weekend and he couldn't believe the partners were forcing him to travel during that time.

"And you know Rick's wife is due that weekend and he has to go too?" she yelled from the kitchen.

"Wow!" That's all I could think to say.

On the day of her birthday, after work and prior to the train ride to Wisconsin, Rick and the other lawyers were going to suggest treating Melanie to a quick drink for her birthday. They would bring her to the restaurant hosting the party where the rest of her friends and family would surprise her. It seemed to be the perfect setup. I was grateful to Prestin who helped me concoct the plan.

"I've had a stressful day, Jo," Melanie said when she re-entered the room.

"Me too."

She sat next to me and ran her hand over my thigh. "Are you really tired?" she asked.

"I'm tired, but not too tired." I knew what she was hinting toward.

"Help me unwind?"

The new complexities of our relationship confused me at times. One day we'd exchange loving pleasantries and share a cozy evening at home nestled in each other's arms. And the next day might be filled with anxiety and tension between us caused by no particular action, but instead by an obvious obstruction—Sunday—that maneuvered its way in and out of our day-to-day activities. Even with the up and down rockiness, the one constant was that I'd do anything for Melanie.

"What would you like?" I asked.

"Slide on some flip flops. Come with me," she instructed.

While I retrieved a pair from the closet, Melanie quickly undressed and put on boxer shorts and a T-shirt. We left the condo and got into Melanie's black Yukon. She drove to Belmont Street and headed east until we met Lake Shore Drive. Melanie parked in a lot overlooking the water, turned off the engine, and locked the doors. The sunroof was cracked open. She turned to face me.

"Please," she said.

"Please, what Mel?"

"Here. Me and you . . ." she told me.

I looked around at the additional cars in the lot and wondered when their owners might return. "In the car?"

"Yes," she pressed. Her voice expressed urgency, heightened eagerness. "Get in the back."

I crawled over the console and sat behind the front passenger seat. Melanie pressed the automatic button to move the seat forward before she climbed into the back with me.

"Take off your shorts," she instructed.

I removed them as did Melanie hers. She wasted no time. She grabbed my waist and slid my body forward, straddling my body under hers with our middles touching. Her body was hot. She kissed me and I tasted the spiciness from the corned beef sandwich. Our hips rocked up and down until we began to sweat. She stopped.

"Do it," she told me. I knew exactly what she wanted. Not that sex was predictable. Obviously it wasn't, but I was aware of the positions that pleased her most.

I sucked my third and forth fingers and rested them on my thigh. She rose, and then lowered her body onto them. They disappeared and I moaned with pleasure at the warmth and wetness I felt. I rested my palm open and allowed Melanie to grind while I circled my two fingers inside of her. She moaned too, and got louder and louder until I began to feel nervous that someone would hear her. I kept my eyes open, partially turned on by the frantic nature in which Melanie rode my fingers, but also to lookout for people about the parking lot. After awhile her expression twisted and she came hard. Her breathing sounded painful, though I realized it was the result of muffled attempts to hush her orgasm.

She slid her body back and forth over my fingers for another minute and then opened her eyes. "Thank you so much."

Melanie lifted herself off of my fingers and I brought them to my side. She knelt before me in the large space between the front and back seats and opened my legs. She sucked my lips and flicked her tongue over my clit to tease me. Then she lifted my hood and began to please me. Her tongue felt like silk and my juices flowed instantly. My body was so heated and ready that it didn't take long to climax.

"Melanie . . ." I murmured softly. I relished in the sweet sensations caressing my lower body while Melanie continued to hold me in her mouth. Finally, my body became still and I opened my eyes.

"Melanie!" I screamed.

She jumped up. "What?" She was concerned by the panic in my voice.

"That person right there," I pointed wildly at the tinted window to my right.

Melanie squinted. "I can't hardly see out there, Jo."

"Someone was watching. I saw somebody standing on the side of that car over there," I told her. I spun around to look out the back window, but saw no figure through the darkness.

"Well, Jo," Melanie said, and kissed my lips. "That's kind of the point." She winked and sat next to me.

I reached for my shorts, pulled them over my waist and unlocked the door. I hopped out into the cool air and ran toward the red sedan parked two spots to the right. There was no one there. Left to right I searched, but only saw one couple strolling slowly on the path near the water.

Dressed again with keys in hand, Melanie ran over to me. "What's wrong?"

"Someone was here," I repeated.

"It's a public place. That's very possible," she rationalized.

I placed my hands on my hips and walked back and forth angrily. Melanie grabbed hold of my arm. "Look. You had to know one day someone was going to see us. That's the excitement. That's what makes it so hot, but we don't have to do this again if you don't want to," she comforted. She embraced my body with a hug.

I rested my head into her bosom. "That's not it," I said.

"Then what are you freaking out about?" she asked, and lifted my face to hers.

"Nothing. Let's just go home."

We walked back to the truck and got inside. On the ride home Melanie apologized.

"I'm sorry, Jo. I didn't know actually being seen would be that weird for you."

I stared out of the window and replayed the shadow I had seen outside the window. Granted, it was dark, and within seconds the figure disappeared, but there was no mistaking what I saw. Her eyes were too distinct, too fierce. Like a cunning snake in the grass, she hid while studying her prey. I knew it was Sunday.

"It's okay, Mel. You're right, that's the point of it all. You know I'll do anything for you. This doesn't have to be the last time." I forced a smile and she looked so relieved.

What I did know was that was the last time Sunday would ever get that close to me again.

Chapter Fourteen

Hi. It looks like u no longer want 2 talk 2 me. I wish that were not the case. only wanted 2 get 2 know u. U seem nice. Would it help 2 know I have more friends now?

That was an e-mail I received from Khamai late night after my and Melanie's lakeside adventure. I was at work, browsing information about the house which Jillian wanted to make an offer, when I took a break to log online. What did this woman want? I clicked on her profile and saw that she had obtained five more friends, bringing her total to seven. A couple of them even left comments after the earlier one I had posted the night Khamai and I met.

Khamai, it's not that I don't think you're a nice person or anything, but I think you're looking for a form of friendship and interaction that I'm not. Before you wanted to know why I'm here and the answer is to stay connected with people. There is very little I know about you . . . you have no information about yourself on your profile and I don't even know who you are. I don't talk to many people here and especially not those who don't reveal much about themselves . . . you will meet more people here.

I pressed the send button and hoped she would understand my position. I picked up the phone and dialed Jillian's number.

"Jillian," she answered cheerily.

"Hey, Jillian, it's Jovanna."

"Hi!"

"How are you?"

"I'm wonderful. I was practicing a new routine before I lie down for a nap."

"Oh, okay. Well, you can come in Friday morning to chat if that works for you."

"Friday, yes, I sure can."

"Good. About eleven?"

"Will be there," she said enthusiastically. "I have a question for you."

I prayed it wasn't about Melanie. "Sure, what is it?"

"This routine I'm working on. It's kind of a tribute to Jennifer Beals and *Flashdance*. Remember the scene when water poured on her body? Well, that is too much for my club which is why I can't wait to have my own because there I can do it. Anyway, since I can't do that, how should I get water on my body?"

I moved the receiver from my ear and frowned at it. "Jillian, really?" I asked when I placed it back to my ear.

"Yes, really, what do you think?"

"You're the performer, don't you know?"

"I was thinking maybe having water bottles with me and pouring water down my body at different points in the performance."

"Okay, good. That sounds nice," I rushed.

"You think so? That's a good visual to you?" I heard her smile on the other end.

"Does my brother know you talk to me like this?" I asked her. Sometimes I was uncertain about Jillian's indiscreet coquetries. Her ambiguous statements were confusing, given my understanding that she was both straight and in love with Ronan.

"Like what, Jovanna? I just want your opinion so that I can put on a good show," she answered innocently.

"Looks like you already know how to put on a good show," I told her.

"*Gracias*. Okay, I will see you Friday."

I hung up the phone before she could say anything else. Unsurprisingly, when I returned to my laptop, Khamai had responded to my e-mail.

U have not asked me anything 2 get 2 know me . . . can I IM u?

Reluctantly I removed the restriction to block instant messages. I reasoned that I'd chat with Khamai and either terminate her persistent attempts to befriend me or at least create a mutual understanding. I sent her a message first.

Why are you so insistent in talking to me? I typed.

I told u, u interest me.

There are millions of women on here. Why?

Y not?

What do you do? Why are you always online?

I work from home. On the computer. Y I am online. She explained.

Do you go out?

All the time.

Where? I asked.

All over. She wrote.

Why don't you have pictures of yourself on your profile?

Because I want u 2 get 2 know me first.

I don't understand.

The cursor blinked for a while. U may not talk 2 me if u knew what I look like.

Was she an obscene, gargantuan creature on the opposite end of the computer?

Do you not like the way you look?

I luv the way I look.

Then what's the problem?

I will reveal myself to u soon, k?

Sure I typed, curious, but not really caring if she did or didn't.

How have u been?
Great.
R u still contemplating?
Somewhat.
What will help u decide?
Answers.
2 what?
To questions I have.
About your girlfriend?
No I lied.
No?
No. Why do you ask anyway?
Relationships cause the most contemplation.
Are you in one?
Not right now. Soon.
I relaxed slightly. **So you have interest in someone?**
Very much.
I hope it works out.
Thank u. That means a lot coming from u.
Should you get back to work? I asked.
Yes. U 2?
Yes.
Thank u 4 talking 2 me. ;)
Sure. Bye Khamai.

I closed the box, unsure if she sent a response, and began to draw up the paperwork to put an offer on the home Jillian wanted to buy. Around noon I called Melanie while I thought she'd be out for lunch.

"Hi, love," I said after she answered.

"Hey you," she replied.

"What are you up to?"

"Went for a walk to get some air. Now I'm sitting outside near Millenium Park."

"You really needed to get away, huh?"

"Yeah, it's one of those days. Real busy, that's all. And I'm still mad about my birthday too," she said.

"You're such a baby. It'll be all right, Mel, don't worry about it."

"And what are you doing?"

"Just finished getting some things together for the house Jillian wants to buy. She's coming in on Friday."

"So she found one?"

"Yeah, she did. It's nice, too!"

"That's good. Ro is really feeling her?"

"He really is." I almost slipped and added that Ronan had invited her to the party.

"I was thinking about grilling chicken tonight," I told Melanie.

"Okay, and how about . . ."

Hey, Ms. Lawyer, I heard a female voice say in the background. I heard the phone shuffling about and it sounded like Melanie almost dropped it. *Pudding sure looks good,* the woman added.

"Hey, back to you!" Melanie said excitedly.

"Melanie?" I said loudly.

She didn't answer and all I could hear was muffled talk and faint music in the background.

"Melanie!" I yelled.

The call disconnected. Immediately I pressed redial to call her cell again. It went to voice mail. I dialed three more times and each call left me with her message greeting in response. Fifteen minutes later the office line rang and I saw Melanie's number on the caller ID. I picked up on the second ring but said nothing.

"Jo?"

"What, Melanie?"

"I'm sorry," she said.

"What happened to 'don't worry about Sunday' and 'it's taken care of?' What happened to all that, Mel?" I yelled into the phone.

She was silent and then laughed. "What are you talking about?"

"Sunday! Wasn't that her?"

"Where?"

I scrunched my eyebrows between my fingers. "Stop playing with me, I'm not in the mood."

"Jo? Oh my God. Are you all right? That was Beverly I just ran into."

"Beverly? Donna's Beverly?"

"Yes. Why in the hell did you think it was Sunday?"

I groaned in partial embarrassment and partial disbelief of her explanation. "Why didn't you answer my callback?"

"I accidentally turned the phone off when I hugged her. I turned it back on but then we got to talking and I didn't even hear it ring. You know I keep the volume low."

We were quiet and I could hear her heels against the concrete while she walked back to the office.

"How's she doing?" I eventually asked.

"You won't believe this," Melanie said. "She's single again."

"For real?"

"Yes. After she asked about you the very next question was about Donna, wanting to know if she and Ivy were still together."

"Damn, that's so crazy," I said. The irritation I felt minutes before completely resolved at the potential thought of a Donna and Beverly reunion.

"Well, I had to tell her that they're still together. I mean, we all want to see Donna and Beverly as a couple but that's between them."

"Is she going to tell Donna?"

"It didn't seem like it. She said they hadn't been in contact for almost a year and meanwhile, she's been going through this break-up. She looked disappointed when I told her they were still together."

"Should we tell Donna?" I asked.

"I don't know," she answered. "It doesn't seem right."

"If we tell her it's not like we're trying to break her and Ivy up. Don't you think it's normal conversation?"

She flipped and personalized the situation. "Let's say next time we're out Ali tells me that she ran into my ex. The one I was living with before you, okay? And my ex told Ali that she's single again and asked about me. Do you think that's appropriate?"

When she put it that way the answer was a flat-out no, but I wasn't certain if I was being hypersensitive due to my current concerns about Melanie. Plus, Melanie wasn't a fiend for her ex and lost in a loveless relationship with someone who didn't respect their union.

"I see your point."

The sound of passing cars vanished. "I'm back at work now," Melanie said. "We'll talk about this later."

"All right."

"And," she continued. "We'll talk about Sunday too."

"No, we won't," I told her in response.

She didn't say anything.

"See you at home," I said.

"Okay," she replied and left it alone.

After we hung up I sat at my desk for several minutes with my eyes closed. I had to get a handle on my emotions. With the misunderstanding over lunch I began to fear that my attention to reality was on a steady decline and if I didn't watch myself, Sunday and I would be sidekicks in the psych ward. I was still certain that Sunday was playing games with me, though the lack of proof and then error of the day didn't support my beliefs.

I hadn't logged off the site yet and just to indulge myself, I visited Sunday's profile. When her profile displayed I gasped and stared incredulously at the screen. The photo was the same; her eyes stared tauntingly into the camera through wind-blown strands of her hair. What temporarily stopped my heart was her update twenty-five minutes ago. She had written: It's my turn to buy her pudding. And then there was Melanie's smiling business photo, right in Sunday's prime number one spot.

Immediately I picked up the phone and dialed Melanie's cell phone. No answer. I called her private office line and received no answer. Next I dialed the general number to speak with the receptionist. After I frantically asked to speak to Melanie, she checked Melanie's calendar and told me that she was in a meeting all afternoon.

"Is this an emergency? I can certainly interrupt if so," she said with worry in her voice.

"No, no thank you. I appreciate it." I hung up.

How did Sunday know of Melanie's adoration for chocolate pudding? Had Melanie told her? Had Melanie eaten pudding in her presence? Had she followed Melanie today and observed her over lunch? The answer to all of those questions truly didn't matter. The fact was the picture and her status were the evidence I needed to show Melanie that Sunday was fucking around with us.

Come straight home I typed via text message to her. Then I gathered my briefcase, threw some unfinished paperwork inside, locked up the office and left.

"Ro, I had to leave the office. I'll see you tomorrow," I told his voice mail when I called him from my car.

By the time I reached home, my nerves were less frazzled. I kicked off my sandal heels and propped up pillows on the bed to lean against for cushion. For the next hour I worked from the bedroom. I made a few phone calls and finalized two closings for the following week. With work behind me, I began to prepare dinner. Instead of grilling chicken as I had told Melanie prior to Beverly's arrival, I decided to bake the chicken breasts. In the quiet of the kitchen I cut a head of lettuce, and sliced tomatoes, cucumber and avocado for a fresh salad. Finally, I turned on the oven, wrapped two potatoes in aluminum foil, and set them inside.

At four o'clock dinner was complete. I changed into an old Lauryn Hill T-shirt I had purchased over ten years ago at one of her concerts and had managed to wear only a few times over the course of its life. In Lauryn's honor I slid her most popular CD into the player and blasted *Everything is Everything*. Next, in tribute to the moment I played "Forgive Them Father" from the same CD.

"I'm almost home," Melanie told me when she called a few minutes later. "My meeting ended early."

"Good," I said stiffly. "I'll see you when you get here."

"That music is loud, Jo," she commented. "You know Mrs. Kerrigan will come knocking any second."

The walls throughout the condo were thick and not much sound escaped through the vents either, but Mrs. Kerrigan was one of those older neighbors who found reason to create unease whenever an opportunity presented itself. Twice in the past we had answered our bell to find Mrs. Kerrigan on the other side of the door to address the volume of our music. The first instance was understandable. It occurred when we hosted a housewarming only a month after we moved in and invited all our friends and family. The second was when Melanie and I danced around the house and pretended to be our favorite musicians by putting on concerts for one another.

"I'll turn it down when you get home," I said.

I retrieved two plates and two salad bowls from the cabinet and set the kitchen table for two. I folded cloth napkins at each setting and laid a cutting knife, salad fork and regular fork on top of each one. From the refrigerator I got a bottle of Italian dressing for Melanie and Thousand Island for myself and placed both on the table. Finally I prepared Melanie a mojito, which was ready the minute she got home. When she walked into the kitchen she turned off the music and I handed her the glass.

"Thanks." Her voice conveyed concern. "What's wrong? You told me to come straight home."

"Let's eat and talk," I responded.

She removed her jacket and took it with her briefcase into the bedroom.

"You did some work from home," she observed. "You're not feeling well? Pregnant?" she joked.

I smiled and prepared her plate and then mine.

"How was your meeting?" I asked once we began to eat.

"It was cool," she said. "One of the partners is retiring within the next six months."

"Oh, so you're up, right?"

"Wouldn't that be something?" She giggled at the thought. "Someday."

"You like the chicken?" I asked.

"Of course I do," she told me. "Hey, I thought more about Donna and Beverly and I don't think it's all that bad to mention it casually. What do you think?"

After my viewing of Sunday's profile, Donna and Beverly hadn't crossed my mind again all afternoon, although I was all for bringing the two of them together. "I agree. If there's something to tell someone that might create good in the end, even if someone may be hurt in the meantime, you should tell, right?"

"I don't know what you just said, Jo."

"Donna is in love with Beverly?"

"Of course."

"Beverly is in love with Donna?"

"Most likely."

"Is Ivy any good for Donna?"

"Not really."

"So if we tell Donna about Beverly and the two of them connect, Ivy might be hurt, but if she was no good for Donna anyway, it all works out because two people are happy in the end."

She looked bewildered. "You'd make a lousy lawyer with that kind of explanation."

I knew I wasn't making sense and trying to compare the Beverly, Donna, Ivy threesome to our trio was absurd. I had to show Melanie what I was referring to before she locked me up in the straightjacket herself.

"Come with me." I stood and walked into the bedroom. Melanie followed and stood behind me while I sat on the edge of the bed and entered my e-mail address and password to sign on. I went to Melanie's profile and viewed her list of friends.

"What's going on?" She sounded nervous.

"You'll see."

I scrolled to the letter "S" and opened the page to reveal all of her friends whose online name began with the letter. When I got to SunnyDay79 my face scowled in disbelief.

"What the . . .?"

Gone was the photo of Sunday at the lake with Melanie running in the background. She had replaced it with the original smiling photo I had seen the first time I saw her. I clicked on the picture. Her profile was set to private again.

"This can't be happening, this cannot be happening," I groaned.

"What are you doing?" Melanie asked.

"She changed it," I said. "She changed it so I couldn't show you."

"Show me what? What are you talking about and why are you so obsessed with this girl?"

I tossed my laptop to the side and stood to face Melanie.

"Me? Obsessed? I can't believe this! I'm not the one who's obsessed, it's her! Earlier today her status said it was her turn to start buying the pudding. And now it says what?" I bent to read the screen. "Right. Perfect. Now it says to have a happy day."

"Why are you so strung out over her? It was just lunch, Jo. You don't have to keep checking up on me, I'm not doing anything."

"She's playing with me, Melanie, don't you see that? She even had a picture of herself with you in the background. And," I said, with a point of my finger at her chest, "you were in her number one spot."

Melanie grabbed hold of both my hands and held them. "Jo, her profile isn't even open. And you're trying to tell me that Sunday had a picture on her profile with me in it? *And* you're also telling me that today she said she was buying pudding?"

"Yes, that's what I'm telling you."

"Now tell me why you were on her profile anyway."

"Because I thought she followed you while you were on your walk."

"You went to her profile before I told you it was Beverly?" The lawyer in her had surfaced.

"No, I went after but that's not the point."

"So even after you knew she didn't follow me, you still took it upon yourself to go online and look her up."

"I did, but you don't know the whole story."

"What's the whole story?" she asked with cynicism in her tone.

"She leaves messages directed at me on her headline and then that picture with you. Oh, and that day you had your meeting with her, I was sitting outside and when she came out she stood right in front of my car."

Melanie shook her head back and forth. "You waited outside my office?"

"Yes, and when she left she crossed the street and walked right in front of me. She's messing with me, Melanie. I'm not making this up."

"Sit down," Melanie instructed.

Slowly I sat back down on the bed and Melanie knelt on her knees in front of me.

"Listen to yourself. Do you know how you sound? You're trying to tell me that a woman you've never met is sending you subliminal messages online."

"She is."

"How do you know?"

"I just do." I hated that I didn't have proof and I despised the way I looked from Melanie's standpoint. This was the precise reason I hadn't brought any of my thoughts about Sunday to her attention because without the evidence, I'd emerge as the crazy one.

"What's this all about? You're really stuck on the lunch she and I had? Or that she was at the same restaurant I was?"

"That's it! What was she wearing when you bumped into her?"

"I don't remember." She was getting aggravated, I could hear it in her voice.

"A white dress, right? How would I know that if I hadn't seen the picture?" I felt redeemed. She had to believe me now.

Melanie rolled her eyes upward to recollect memories from that day. "No, she wasn't. She had on jeans and a halter top."

"Are you sure?"

"Of course I'm sure. I remember now because it was just like one you have."

I was desperate. "See?"

"Come on now, there's a million of those shirts walking around." Her expression changed to pity and I wanted to scream. "Look, I admit, it was wrong of me to have lunch with her and not tell you right away. But seriously, I can't imagine that's got you so shook up that you're making stuff up in your mind."

"I'm not making this up," I said weakly.

Melanie's eyes slanted. "I never would have pegged you as the jealous type."

"I'm not jealous!" Frustration began to form and I lowered my head.

She didn't respond. Her troubled disposition said it all. I was speechless also. Anything I said would only further discredit me as well as Melanie's perception of my ability to judge and recognize what was fact from fiction. I understood Melanie's skepticism; if roles were reversed, likely I would doubt her as well. If I hadn't seen the photo and status updates myself, I'd probably let it go like Melanie had ordered. However, Sunday's conniving actions of the day provided evidence that the game was in full motion. With the departure of Sunday's ex and withdrawal of Melanie, we were down to two players, yet the cards had been dealt. Who would trump who in the end?

Chapter Fifteen

Jillian and I had been in the office about fifteen minutes before she stopped me midway into my explanation of what would occur if the seller accepted her offer.

"Jovanna, there is really something else I want to talk with you about."

I crossed my fingers and laid my hands on my desk. "You do?"

She sat in front of me, on the opposite side of my desk, and stared anxiously into my eyes. "It's about Ronan."

Of course. Jillian wasn't the first woman who sought me for guidance on how to deal with my brother. "What is it?" I asked.

"I really like him. Your brother excites me and fascinates me in a way that men usually don't. Many of them are so typical. They come into the club acting all macho or they come in desperate. Ronan was neither." She searched for an explanation. "He was just so cool and confident. It turned me on and still does."

Ronan's laid-back demeanor mixed with discerning self-assurance was a captivating combination for many women. Some were intrigued by the quiet humbleness he sometimes displayed; that despite his success, he looked down on no one. And on the other hand, when he cruised around suited up in his sporty Mercedes, he exuded an impressive strength that women were drawn toward.

"Okay," I said, expecting that she would continue.

"There is no problem, except that I know I am falling in love. I believe he is falling in love with me too, but . . . your brother has been single a long time. How do I know it is real? How do I know he will not leave me? I was engaged once and he could not handle my job and left."

"You were engaged?"

"Yes, about three years ago," she told me. "He felt that my work was not a right fit for a wife."

"Then why did he propose?"

"I am not sure. I guess he thought I would eventually agree. Anyway, I don't want to talk about him. My question to you is, do you think Ronan is capable of falling in love?"

"That's a heavy question. Don't you think you should be asking Ronan?"

"I have and he tells me that he believes he is falling in love with me too. You know him best though. You've been with him your whole life and I'm sure you have seen him with women."

I nodded my head. Falling into the trap of speaking on Ronan's numerous ex-loves was not on my agenda.

"I'll tell you this," I said, deciding to grant her a portion of my viewpoint. "Ronan likes you too. I can say he speaks favorably about you all the time. Yeah, he's been single a long time. But do I think he's capable of falling in love? Yes. Maybe the time has come when he's ready to settle down, I really don't know for sure. I'm not in a position to offer much more than that."

"Thank you, I appreciate that."

"I hope it helps."

"It does because, as a woman, I don't believe you would steer me to believe something that would be false. If Ronan were playing me and really not worth my time, I think your choice of words would have been different."

She was right. In the past when women wanted my counsel,

I didn't put Ronan's head on the cutting board, but I also didn't lead the women to believe that he might actually commit to them. From what I had observed, I had no doubt that Ronan had deep feelings for Jillian. To a large degree, though, that was for him to express and her to accept without needing my input and confirmation.

"Are you wearing something special to Melanie's party?" she asked me. It seemed she had cast aside our initial discussion about her home purchase.

"I am, although I haven't been shopping yet. I want to find an outfit that I know she'll love."

I spoke the words, yet felt no passion behind them. Since my Wednesday night conversation with Melanie, she eyed me with belittling sympathy as if I needed an abundance of coddling to soothe my deteriorating mind and overactive imagination.

"What are you doing?" she had asked the night before when I was online checking my bank account information. The real question was, "You're not trying to hack Sunday's profile, are you?"

"Did you get that?" she asked me while we watched a comedian tell a joke about Adam and Eve. Like the lunch misunderstanding had injured my competence in understanding a joke.

And the worst was when she attempted to tell me that Ferris and Barbara had invited us for a backyard picnic with the kids on Sunday. Before she could complete the word—she had begun the "S" sound—she altered her selection of words to "this weekend, after they get home from church." I winced and rolled over to go to sleep. She rubbed her hand on my back like a mother would a child as if to say, *Poor baby, it's okay.*

"I would like to wear something special too. Can we shop together?" She appeared thrilled by the idea and I was enchanted also. If we went together, I could make sure she didn't show up at the party wearing an outfit suited for work versus an evening social affair.

"We can do that, sure."

She smiled.

"I'm about to use the restroom, I'll be right back."

"Okay. Hey, can I use your computer for a minute? I would like to check something."

I minimized several work applications that were opened and then clicked on the Internet Explorer icon. "There you go," I said, and went into the bathroom.

When I returned, Jillian was as enthusiastic as ever. "Melanie has accepted me finally!"

"Oh, that's great," I responded, surprised that Melanie had been on the site in the last few days. She must have done so after I told her to accept Jillian on Tuesday night.

"Let's see what she's got going on here," Jillian said as she began to read Melanie's profile.

I fumbled about the office while I waited for Jillian to complete her review.

"Aw, this is so sweet," she commented after reading the piece in Melanie's bio in which she speaks about the two of us.

"Look at them!" she exclaimed as she watched the photo slideshow and pointed to Melanie's niece and nephew. "So adorable."

She was quiet for a moment until she said, "What is she doing on here?"

I looked up. "Who?" I was at Ronan's desk looking for the phone number of someone he had asked me to call.

"Her! Sunday!"

My heart beat fast and I rushed to my desk. Jillian was staring at the earlier comment in which Sunday had simply written: **Hi.**

"Do I know her? *Si*, I know her. This bitch is *loca*! Crazy! Why is Melanie friends with her?"

"What? How do you know that?" My voice sounded urgent and high-pitched.

"She worked at the club years ago. Was one of the best dancers we ever had. She was unstable, very crazy. She used performing to boost up her self-esteem."

I grabbed the chair from the front of my desk and brought it next to Jillian. "Tell me everything."

She did. "I've been at Sweet Tea about six years. She came about two years later. I don't know where she was from, but because of her beauty, Leno hired her on the spot. She was a nice enough person—at first—but she had these mood swings that would make all the girls nervous. One day she'd be calm and excited to perform, and the next she'd come in crying talking about how much she hated her life because no one loved her. And on really bad days she would flip it and get mean, downright nasty. If you so much as walked behind her she would snap and act like you were about to attack her or something. So she would get defensive first, tell you not to mess with her and that you better watch your back. It's not a perfect world backstage, but she made it hell. Some of us would complain to Leno but he kept her because she was so pleasing to the crowd."

Jillian paused to catch her breath. "She had this way of latching on to the patrons that was not normal. It was like she needed the attention from them as much as they wanted the attention from her. There were a few regulars that would come to see her and if one of them missed a night, she'd think they didn't like her anymore. After performing she'd rush backstage and start crying, saying that so-and-so wasn't there and what did she do wrong. Was she not pretty enough? Did she need to lose weight? Were they somehow mad at something she had done? We tried to explain to her that our customers have lives too and that sometimes they would not be there. She didn't get it. She always blamed herself. Or she'd get mad at us for even trying to help and tell us to stay out of her business. She had this manipulative way of playing on our feelings depending on her mood. She'd make you feel sorry for her with her tears and stories about her hard life, and then she'd make you feel like shit for extending a hand. There was just no way to win with this girl."

"Yeah, that sounds emotionally unstable and confused for sure. How was she crazy?"

"All of that is crazy but I'm getting to the worst part. This had gone on for over a year, dealing with her loony personality. But then she found something—someone—that calmed her down for a while. Even though we all thought she was into guys by the way she would butter them up, she fell for Rochelle, who was one of our woman customers. I was there the night they met. Rochelle had come in with a group of her lesbian friends one night to celebrate a birthday. We all made really good money that night. Sunday did a great job and Rochelle, on behalf of the group, had given her a couple hundred dollar bills. It was the worst mistake Rochelle ever made. From that moment forward, Sunday thought of nothing other than Rochelle.

"She would perform almost every night hoping that Rochelle would come in again. She bugged all us girls about who we knew to see if anyone knew Rochelle. And actually, one of the dancers who is a lesbian knew who Rochelle was. She didn't tell Sunday though because we all knew Sunday was crazy. Well, somehow it got back to Rochelle that Sunday had interest in her so Rochelle was in the club about three weeks later. After performing, Sunday got offstage and went straight to Rochelle. I mean, we have to admit that Sunday's beautiful. Anyone would be flattered if she expressed interest and that was the case with Rochelle. She adored Sunday. They started dating soon after and then they moved in together."

"What happened?" I asked, sitting on the edge of the padded seat.

"Well, she became obsessed with Rochelle's every move. Rochelle is a painter and would get work in people's homes and businesses and it made Sunday very nervous that Rochelle would be out interacting with people. Sunday claimed to have no family and no friends so she clung to Rochelle like glue. Sunday would sometimes pop up at jobs where Rochelle was just to make sure she was there and no other women were around. Or she would do things like play sick and have Rochelle leave work to care for her. It got to the point where some of Rochelle's loyal customers were not willing to send her name for referrals anymore."

"Wow."

"That's not it, Jovanna. It got so bad that Sunday would have Rochelle come to work with her at night just to know where she was. That turned out not to be good because then Sunday got mad every time a girl performed and Rochelle would watch. She didn't want Rochelle to see any of the other girls so when Sunday wasn't performing, Rochelle had to either go in the bathroom, or turn her back to the stage."

"Get the hell out of here!"

"Yes, I know. Crazy, right? That didn't last long. One time I guess Rochelle had enough and she watched one of the other dancers, her name was Lilah. Sunday saw it from behind the curtain and came rushing on the stage and dragged Lilah off. It was a very bad moment for the club. Finally Leno fired her that night.

"Now, we knew all that had been going on with the two of them from the other dancer who knew Rochelle. Well we heard that one day Rochelle had packed up all of Sunday's things and told her she had to move out. Sunday, as usual, tried to play on Rochelle's sympathy and begged her to stay. At first Sunday was sad, but then she got angry when she realized Rochelle wasn't giving in. So she goes to get a knife and pretends like she's going to kill herself."

"Jillian, are you serious?"

"This is what I was told and because I worked with Sunday for so long and know how she is, I believe it. Rochelle tried to take the knife from her and they were tussling around with it. Finally Rochelle got it but at the same time, Sunday wrapped her hand over Rochelle's and forced the knife into her own leg. Gouged this huge hole into her leg. Rochelle called 911 and when the paramedics came, they saw that there was a domestic issue and the police came too. Well, Sunday completely flipped on Rochelle and said that she was trying to leave the relationship and move out and that Rochelle got mad about it. She said that they were arguing and Rochelle got a knife and while they were fighting over the knife, she got stabbed in the leg. She was nice enough not to say Rochelle did it on purpose—she later told Rochelle that she loved her too much to get her into trouble, but nevertheless, she made it seem like Rochelle was the crazy one."

"Sunday moved out and things were quiet for a while, but then Sunday tried to creep back into Rochelle's life with phone calls and popping up at the old apartment. That went on for months before Rochelle finally got a restraining order."

I was in shock. Not only had Jillian confirmed my belief that Sunday was a disillusioned woman, she also scared me with the degree to which Sunday would extend herself to get what she wanted. How far would she go with Melanie?

"So I ask you again, why is Sunday a friend to Melanie? That should not be," Jillian asserted.

"I don't even know what to say," I told her. Even with all the information Jillian had just shared with me, I wasn't sure how to process it and what to do with it. If I went to Melanie with it and exposed Sunday as the crazed individual she was, how would Melanie handle it? Would she finally believe all that I had told her? Would she feel unsafe with the knowledge that Sunday had been following her? How would she feel knowing that Sunday had followed us both online and offline?

"What's going on, Jovanna? I do not think this is someone Melanie should associate with, even if it's just online."

"She was Melanie's client."

Her eyes widened. "For what?"

"Melanie defended her for violation of the restraining order. They won."

"Are you serious?"

"Yes, and now that I know the whole story it had to be Rochelle they were against."

"There is more to this, I can tell by the look on your face," she observed.

I stood up, crossed my arms over my chest, and began to pace while I told Jillian what had been happening.

"Something didn't feel right about this case. It was like, right after Melanie met Sunday, her entire mood changed. And every time Sunday's name came up, Melanie would get short with me or clam up. I didn't know what to make of it because she's just kind of like that with work. She gets real absorbed in it and it consumes a lot of her time. It was different with Sunday though. And then when Sunday requested her online friendship, Melanie was all distraught about it. I understood that it was new for her, to have a client on a social networking site, even though I disagreed with it, she eventually accepted Sunday. With what was going on with you and Ronan and being our client, it didn't help the situation at all. I couldn't defend you and Ronan, and then act like she couldn't be friends with Sunday so I had to accept it."

Jillian sat quietly and listened to my every word.

"Then everything just got suspicious to me. I saw Melanie a few times on Sunday's profile. Or at least I assumed that's where she was. One day she asked me to come to the office and then got mad at me when I did because Sunday was there. I sat in my car and waited for Sunday to leave and when she did, I swore she was playing with me. She stopped right in front of the car. I think she wanted me to know who she was."

"After they won the case my feelings about Sunday were up and down. At first everything seemed all right and Melanie and I were fine. Then Melanie ran into Sunday at a restaurant and admitted that Sunday had made a pass at her. By this time I was going to Sunday's profile all the time, checking to see what her headlines were because it seemed like she was talking to me, sending me messages, but it was making me feel crazy because I had no proof that she was. Then Sunday posted a picture of herself with Melanie in the background and talked about how much she liked chocolate pudding and all of this was messing with my head. On top of that, I think she watched us make love one night."

Jillian inhaled loudly. "She knows where you live?"

"I don't know, probably, but we weren't at home."

Her expression turned quizzical and then relaxed. "Oh, I see." She smirked. "This is not funny but I get what you're saying."

"So anyway, I thought she followed Melanie over lunch the other day and when I finally told Melanie everything that has been happening, she twisted it on me and she's looking at me like I've lost my mind."

"Sunday is good, Jovanna. I bet she had Melanie feeling all sorry for her, didn't she?"

"Yes. She told Melanie that her ex—Rochelle—tried to attack her and that's how she got stabbed."

Jillian adamantly shook her head side to side. "We've got to do something about this."

"I'm not sure what to do. She wants Melanie and I'm not sure how far she'll go to get her."

"I don't like to ask you this, but you are certain that Melanie has not fallen for Sunday's temptations, right?"

"Melanie has told me several times that there's nothing going on."

I sat back down next to Jillian and we each were consumed with our own thoughts for several minutes.

"Does anyone else know about this?"

"No. You're the only person I've told. I didn't want everybody looking at me like I was crazy."

"Not even Ronan?"

"No. I think he knows something is bothering me, but I never told him."

"Let's keep it that way."

"Okay."

She spoke slowly. "I have an idea, Jovanna. But it is risky. I think we both know how far Sunday will go to get what she wants, but how far will *you* go to keep what you have?"

"I'll do whatever it takes to keep Melanie," I answered confidently. "She's everything to me."

Her face brightened. "I like to hear that. Now tell me this. Do you have access to Melanie's online information?"

"What do you mean?"

"Do you have her sign on information?"

"No, I don't," I answered.

"Hmm, okay. We must find a way to get her password."

And then I remembered. "Wait a second."

I opened my desk drawer and retrieved my wallet from my purse. It was overstuffed and filled with credit cards, store savings cards, coupons, and receipts. I fingered through the crumpled papers until I found the old post-it note I was looking for. Jillian and I both smiled when I handed it to her.

"Good. Now this is what we need to do."

Nervously I crossed the street in a residential Hyde Park neighborhood where I was to meet Sunday. I doubled checked the address on the piece of paper in my hand and walked toward a beautiful three-level brownstone. The door was unlocked as expected, and I entered the first floor unit.

The flat was spacious, with hardwood floors, vaulted ceilings, and large windows throughout. The smell of fresh paint permeated through the air. I took a seat on a small twin sofa located in the living room, one of the few items throughout the recently purchased property. I checked my watch. It was 2:45 P.M. She was due to arrive in fifteen minutes.

I closed my eyes and said a silent prayer with hopes that our plan would succeed. Two days after Jillian and I met in the office, I had logged onto the networking site under Melanie's e-mail address and password. It was then that I found that Melanie had been honest with me about her interaction with Sunday. I went against my every conviction in reading Melanie's e-mail, however, Jillian and I agreed that if I found exchanges between the two of them, that I would have to read the content to ensure our plot would make sense.

After their court victory, Sunday had sent Melanie an e-mail thanking Melanie for representing her case and for taking her to lunch when they won. She then complimented Melanie on her success, her appearance, and said that I was a fortunate woman to have her. She also told Melanie to let her know if she ever became single because she'd be waiting.

Melanie replied several days later with a cordial, but brief message. She told Sunday that she didn't log onto the site often, but happened to do so and saw her e-mail. Melanie agreed that she was happy they had won the case. She told Sunday that she appreciated her compliments and while the offer was kind, she need not wait for her to become single; she expanded that she loved me and treasured the relationship she was in with me. Because I know Melanie's personality and her wish to keep things light, the e-mail ended with a sentence that the only thing that might sever our relationship was if I went crazy on her and that wasn't going to happen.

From Melanie's response I gathered that Sunday walked away with two things. One, she could taunt me online without Melanie's knowledge because she was then aware that Melanie didn't log on often. And second, I realized that Sunday must have taken Melanie's comment to heart. It was just like an unsound mind to pick what was false as the truth and ignore reality entirely. She disregarded Melanie's statements of love for me and instead focused on what it would take to sabotage our relationship. She began to utilize her manipulative talents to torment me online; she showed me what she wanted me to see with an attempt to make me look irrational and unstable in the end.

It was a gamble to send a message to Sunday. We weren't sure if she'd respond to the e-mail or worse, call Melanie's office after receipt. Jillian and I carefully chose the words that would embody the e-mail. We decided that Melanie would tell Sunday that she wanted to meet with her and that there was something special she wanted to share. In the e-mail I typed that it was too risky to meet in a public place and gave her the address to a friend's newly purchased condo where we could meet. I asked her to please not reply because Jovanna had been acting weird and I wasn't sure if she was reading my e-mails. In fact, I was going to delete this e-mail from my sent box just in case and asked that she delete hers too. I ended the message by telling her I looked forward to seeing her.

I stayed online. When I checked the status of the e-mail several minutes later, I saw that Sunday had read the message. I deleted the e-mail from Melanie's sent folder and logged off. Shortly after, Sunday updated her status to read: She's mine. This time I laughed.

There was a creak in the foyer and I stood up.

"Oh, hey," I said to Jillian when she walked into the room.

"Hi, Jovanna. How are you?"

"A little shaky honestly."

"It's okay. We've got to put an end to this so you and Melanie can move on. I've seen how damaging Sunday can be."

I sat back down and Jillian took a position near the front window. The air blowing through the vents was the only sound we heard.

"I see her," Jillian said softly. She turned to face me. "Let's do this, Jovanna."

Moments later we heard the front door open. "Hello?" Sunday said. Her voice surprised me. It was light and child-like with a youthful tone.

"In here," I said as calmly as possible.

I heard her take a few steps through the foyer. She stopped when she turned the corner and saw me.

Sunday wore dark, slim fitted jeans over her long legs with a red low-cut short sleeve blouse. Her hair hung delicately to her shoulders and when she removed the black sunglasses covering her face, her eyes sent a violent scowl in my direction. The intensity had me taken aback.

"What are you doing here?" She glared at me. "Where is Melanie?"

"Melanie isn't here," I told her. "You're here to see me."

"What is this? What are you talking about?" she demanded. "Melanie invited me."

"No, Sunday, she didn't. I did. And we need to talk."

She took a step toward me. "Why would I want to talk to you?"

"I know what you're doing and it's got to stop," I said. Even though she soared over me by nearly six inches in her heels, I took a step toward her as well to show that I was not intimidated.

She laughed. "Jovanna, right? What makes you think that you can tell me what to do?" She slowly took three more steps until she stood right in front of me. "Don't you know that what I want, I get?"

"Not this time."

"And what are you going to do? From the looks of this, you

called me here to what, threaten me? This doesn't look good for you, Jovanna."

"It doesn't look good for you either," I told her.

"Tell me why that is," she said with sarcasm.

"Because you're violating your restraining order."

She squinted her eyes. "What are you talking about?"

Jillian and Rochelle appeared behind her.

"You shouldn't be here," Rochelle interjected.

Sunday spun around and for a moment, appeared unnerved.

"And from the looks of this to *me*, you followed me to work, and you know as well as I know that you're not supposed to be anywhere near me."

"You can't prove it," Sunday said, though I caught a hint of uncertainty in her voice.

"Yes, we can," Jillian said. "Rochelle was contracted to paint this condo by the new owners a couple of weeks ago. The contract is right here." Jillian held up a piece of white paper. "See, this is what it looks like for *us*. Rochelle thought she had seen you following her to work. She wasn't going to let you get away with lying in court and winning against her again, so this time she took pictures of you outside. She also took pictures of you walking through the door."

I took several steps away from Sunday and Jillian swiftly took oto of Sunday standing in the middle of the living room alone. Jillian caught Sunday with a surprised expression, mouth wide open, clearly caught off guard.

"And now we have another photo of you inside. What do you think the judge will say about that?"

Sunday gave each of us an evil gray eye. "I can't believe you'd do this to me," she said to Rochelle. "All I ever wanted to do was love you. Why would you hurt me like this?"

Rochelle held up her hand. "I don't want to hear it. Love isn't needy, clingy, possessive and obsessive. Get some help, Sunday. Really. You can't spend your whole life making people feel sorry for you and then stalking them."

Sunday was speechless. She peered at Rochelle but didn't respond. Then she fixed her eyes on the camera in Jillian's hand; her head hung in sad defeat. Finally she lifted her eyes and met mine with an icy stare.

"You're not as foolish as I thought you were," she said to me. "But be careful who you talk to online. We're all chameleons; we can be whoever we want to be."

I didn't comprehend the meaning of her warning and at the moment it didn't matter to me. "Leave Melanie alone," I told her. "Delete her from your profile, don't e-mail her, and stop following us. And keep your mouth shut about all of this."

She gave one more shot at seizing control. "Or what?"

"Or we'll make sure those photos are shown in court and you land in jail," Rochelle spoke.

Sunday gave us each another once over and then placed her sunglasses on the top of her head.

"I could get you all back for this," she warned.

"Just let it go, Sunday," Jillian advised. "Leave Melanie *and* Rochelle alone and move on. It's over."

Sunday wore a look of acceptance. I was near convinced that she completely understood. She nodded at me, readjusted her leather purse over her shoulder, and walked toward the front door. She placed her hand on the doorknob then turned around.

"I'll always love you, Rochelle." She walked out before anyone could respond.

Jillian immediately ran over to me. "Are you all right?"

"I'm okay." I looked over to Rochelle. "Thank you so much."

She walked toward me. "I'm glad I could help."

Rochelle was a mature woman in her late thirties. She was fairly nondescript in appearance, but had a likable disposition with a sweet nature.

"When Jillian told me about everything that happened with

you and Sunday, we wanted to be sure that she left you and Melanie alone from this point forward. I'm so sorry about the case; we didn't know."

"It happens. Scary though, isn't it? To know that guilty people get away with crazy stuff all the time. It's easy to overlook until it hits home."

I thought about the potential lengths Sunday may have taken in order to obtain Melanie and I shuddered. "You're right. Thanks again. Let's hope we don't hear from her anymore."

"I hope not too. It's been hard for me to move forward with a crazy ex lingering in the background," Rochelle said.

"Yeah, I can imagine."

"Are you ready to talk to Melanie?" Jillian asked.

"I don't know," I admitted. "I'm not sure how she'll take it."

Although Jillian and I had discussed whether or not to tell Melanie about our plan, in the end we decided to proceed without letting her in on the arrangement. The more I had considered it, I was pretty sure Melanie would have believed all that Jillian had told me about Sunday's past, but what we didn't know was if Melanie could resolve the problem. Sure she could have told Sunday to leave her alone and remove her from her friend's list. However, Jillian and I felt a certain obligation to help Rochelle also and felt it best to leave Melanie out of the process. Melanie, having just defended Sunday against Rochelle, could have no part in that.

"Let me know how this goes," Jillian said.

I gave Jillian and Rochelle each a hug before I left. Inside the car I called Melanie and with a bit of hesitation, I asked if I could stop by her office. We had moved rapidly with our plan. It was Wednesday afternoon, just five days after I learned about Sunday's troubling history.

"Actually, I think I'm going to leave early today. Meet me for a drink?" she asked.

That would be perfect. "Absolutely."

"Where?"

I told Melanie the name of the place I wanted to meet. "Nice. I'll see you soon," she replied.

When I arrived, I was grateful to find that the table where Melanie and I sat on our first date was empty. The hostess allowed me to sit there and placed down two menus.

"Your server will be right with you," she told me. I thanked her and scanned over the appetizer list.

During the ten minutes that I waited for Melanie, I mentally replayed various moments of our relationship in my mind. In this spot I learned that her favorite drink was a mojito. I recalled the first time she kissed me, many months later, while we stood outside my car. She had wrapped her arms around me from the back, leaned her head into my neck and placed her lips on my skin. A smile crossed my face when I remembered the time I dragged Melanie into a pet shop and begged for a small, furry ball of a Pomeranian puppy. Melanie near cursed me out in the store. It wasn't funny at the time, but in hindsight I found humor in Melanie's aggressive stance about not wanting a dog. I never brought the topic up again.

"What can I get for you?" Natalie, a young waitress, asked.

"I'll have a mojito," I heard Melanie say from behind me just before she approached the table. She ran her hand across my back before she took a seat. "Hi," she smiled at me.

"Hi, back to you," I said. "I'll have a lemon drop martini," I told Natalie.

"I'll get those for you right away," she said.

Melanie spied my comfortable clothing: boot-cut jeans that curved my waist, an oversized sheer white top with tank underneath, and an army green colored newsboy cap "Did you work today?"

"I didn't."

"You didn't tell me you were taking the day off. What'd you do?"

I looked for Natalie but she wasn't yet en route with the drinks. "That's what I wanted to talk to you about."

She looked curious. I lowered my head and searched for the right words. There was no way to say it other than what it was. "I saw Sunday today," I told her.

"You what?" Her voice heightened in pitch and her expression menaced in disapproval.

"Hear me out, Melanie," I said before she could start telling me I was being ridiculous. "There's good reason for it."

"There better be." She adjusted her body on the stool, leaned forward, and for the next forty-five minutes I shared with Melanie every detail of my conversation with Jillian the past Friday. I told her that after she accepted Jillian's friendship, that Jillian noticed Sunday as a friend on Melanie's profile. I gave her near verbatim documentation of the talk that ensued after; that Sunday used to work with Jillian and how Sunday really got the scar on her leg. Finally I told her the specifics of the plan we devised and the reasons we opted not to share them with her.

We both had finished our drinks and Melanie ordered a second mojito.

"Jo, do you know how dangerous that was?"

"Yes, I do. What would you have suggested?" I asked.

"I don't know, but if she's really as crazy as you just explained, who knows what could have happened."

"I'm just glad it all turned out fine. Do you believe me now, Mel? Do you realize she was playing mind games with me?"

Melanie took one of my hands and caressed the palm. "I believe you, Jo. I wanted to believe you then . . . there was just no proof. I'm sorry."

"Let's just be grateful it's over," I told her.

"You know, there's one thing she got right."

"Who? Sunday?" I asked, doubtful that there was any facet to Sunday that was right.

"Yep. She told me that I was fortunate to have you," Melanie said. "And I am."

"Thank you, Mel."

She leaned over the small table and kissed my lips. "I love you," she whispered—my three favorite words.

"What was that? I didn't hear you," I teased.

"You heard me." She laughed. "I have to use the restroom, okay?"

"Sure. Hey, can I use your phone real quick? I want to check something."

Melanie removed her BlackBerry from the pocket of her blazer and handed it to me. As soon as she walked away I clicked the internet browser button and logged onto the social networking site. Straight to Melanie's profile I went and scrolled through the friends section. SunnyDay79 was gone. A smug grin turned the corners of my mouth upward. Quickly I checked my own profile and noticed that one of my comments had been removed from Khamai. I wasn't bothered. Friends were added and deleted all the time, though I admit to being curious. Still, I shrugged it off and closed the browser. The most important matter had been resolved: Melanie and I had our lives back and the efforts it took to salvage our relationship were worth every ounce of risk. I'd do it again.

Chapter Sixteen

The week after, on a humid Friday morning, I awoke at six A.M. to cook a breakfast of scrambled eggs with cheese, sausage and homemade waffles, with freshly cut cantaloupe on the side. I stirred and turned the eggs softly in the skillet. I poured mix onto the waffle iron grill quietly and fried the sausage on medium-low to dim the sizzles and pops of grease.

On a plate I added helpings of the warm food and placed it on a tray with a cup of steamy coffee. When I opened the door to the bedroom with the hope of surprising Melanie with her birthday breakfast, she was lying on her side with an arm resting under her head looking right at me. Although the white sheet covered her mouth, I could see that she was smiling by the small crinkle in the corners of her glowing eyes.

"Happy birthday to you, happy birthday to you, happy birthday sweet Melanie, happy birthday to you," I sang horribly while I walked the tray of food to her. I kissed her forehead. "Sit up, love."

Melanie sat up and bunched two pillows behind her back. Carefully I placed the tray over her body and then turned on the morning news. I went back into the kitchen, made myself a plate, and picked up the butter-flavored syrup which I had forgotten.

"This is good," Melanie told me when I re-entered the bedroom.

"Thank you. Enjoy."

We ate and watched the morning co-host team tell viewers about Friday the thirteenth superstitious tales.

"Damn, Fred is going to be a fool tonight on the train," Melanie said before taking a bite of her waffle.

"Why do you say that?"

"He's so scared. And then to take the train on Friday the thirteenth . . . he's going to be sweating bullets," she laughed.

I laughed too, but on the inside. Melanie was still clueless with regard to the surprise birthday party that evening. Last night I had packed her overnight bag and made up a small story about plans we had for Saturday after she returned from Wisconsin. I had told her that we'd be connecting with Prestin and Jaye for an early dinner at a swank place downtown and that she'd have to wait and see how the rest of the evening unfurled. I figured I had twisted the events of Friday enough already and didn't feel the need to go overboard with an extravagant lie about Saturday.

"I hope he'll be all right. Give him a drink," I suggested.

"Definitely." Melanie took a sip of her coffee and then finished her breakfast. When she finished, I put my plate on top of hers and took the tray back to the kitchen. She was snuggled back underneath the covers when I came back. I crawled on the bed and straddled her.

"It's time to get ready for work," I said. "It's seven."

"I can't even go in late?" she asked me like I was her employer and signed her payroll check.

"Birthday girl, stop pouting. Let's get you up."

"Why are you rushing me?" she whined. She patted the area in front of her. "Lay with me for a few more minutes."

I got under the sheet and encircled my body with hers. Mentally I reviewed my schedule for the day. Once I got Melanie out of the house it was my plan to work a few hours from home. In the afternoon I needed to pick up the dress I had purchased with Jillian the weekend before. After waltzing in and out of various boutiques over a two-hour time span I had settled on a boho tube dress with a bold geometric print in deep orange, dark brown, and navy blue. To accompany the dress I had purchased four inch, ankle strapped high heels in a silky navy blue.

"Oh, I packed something for you to change into before the train ride," I said.

"Why? I can just wear what I already have on."

"Don't you have a meeting tonight?"

"Yeah, there's a social or something. I don't know. No one has shown me the schedule."

"Well just change so you'll be ready when you get there."

She agreed and I was glad to know that she'd come to the party dressed in a slightly flared cream colored tuxedo pant with black satin stripe and a button down silk black blouse. She was going to look hot.

Melanie and I stayed in bed another fifteen minutes before she finally rose and started to prepare for work. An hour later she was ready to leave. By that time I had made the bed, cleaned the kitchen, and was at my laptop with my cell phone in hand and was about to set up an appraisal and inspection for a client. Melanie bent down to kiss me. I kissed her back lovingly.

"Enjoy your birthday," I told her.

"It won't be the same without you." She sounded sad.

"Call me later."

"Of course." Melanie left through the kitchen rolling the small piece of luggage to her side. Through the balcony doors I watched her walk through the courtyard to the complex parking lot in the back.

Since the day Melanie and I talked about Sunday, her name hadn't come up again. We had regained the natural, easy-going essence of our relationship. Vanished were the awkward, tense moments ignited by the sly gimmicks of another. If anything, the short-lived experience involving Sunday only reaffirmed the commitment that Melanie and I shared between one another. Melanie proved that she was loyal by not caving to the advances of another woman. And I showed that despite everything that was going on, my love for Melanie had not faltered.

While viewing my e-mail account a short while later, I found several notifications of activity on the social networking site, including friendship requests and comment postings. I hadn't been onto the site since the day I met Sunday, and as far as I knew, Melanie had neglected the site as well. It's not that either of us feared it or never planned to participate in online interaction again; but I think we both had silently agreed that a short, healthy break would serve our relationship well. Although most of the cyberspace world was harmless, with a seemingly innocent enough checkerboard of honest players, the Sunday's of the web were proof that not all participants abided by the rules.

I closed my mailbox and decided to log on at another time. Melanie's birthday was my greatest priority of the day. I showered, dressed comfortably in white shorts, a pink top and white baseball cap. In my Nissan Altima I cruised over to the boutique and picked up my dress, stopped at the Macy's counter for a new shade of eyeliner, and then had an apple walnut salad at a deli a few miles from our house.

Outside on the deli's curbside seating I sat and absorbed the warm afternoon sunshine. As I finished the small salad and sipped on the last of my smoothie, I noticed a glimmer in my peripheral. Across the street to my left was a store filled with hanging glass wind chimes in unique styles and flavor. They caught my eye because Melanie and I discussed buying a colorful chime to place outside of our newly decorated and vibrant kitchen. We felt it would be pleasing to our ears on evenings we'd sit with the balcony doors open and enjoy the sounds of night.

I discarded my Styrofoam container and plastic cup, walked

over to the store and touched a few of the chimes hanging
outside the door. They created beautiful melodies. Some were
circular, resembling a downward spiral staircase. Others had
an additional decorative item on top, like a dragonfly or angel.

"That's a lovely one, isn't it?" An old, white-haired salesman
said after he came out to greet me. We admired a butterfly and
flower chime.

"Yes, it is. All of these are so wonderful."

"These here are some of our most popular from a special
designer we work with. There are more inside. Come see," he
smiled.

I followed the old man inside, just through the door to view
more that were near the front displays of the store. They spun
and shined all together and created brilliant designs through
the dim shop. I stared around, fascinated by the display.

"Pretty, right?" I could tell that he enjoyed the magical feel.

"Very," I agreed.

"Beautiful like a kaleidoscope," he said. "A bit mesmerizing
and always changing."

"They are." I browsed for several minutes and although it
hadn't been on my agenda, I selected a stained glass double
hummingbird chime. They sat atop vines of an orangered
flower with copper colored chimes beneath.

After the sweet salesman carefully wrapped it in tissue paper
and placed it inside a box, I thanked him and walked out of
the store toward my car a block away. I thought about the
comment he had made about the visual kaleidoscope effect
and recalled the decorative, kaleidoscope photo on Khamai's
profile.

When I arrived back to the condo, I hung my dress over
the closet door and retrieved the accessory items that would
accompany it. It was three o'clock and near time for me to
get ready to arrive at the restaurant by 5:30 P.M. However,
something about the elder's words continued to replay in my

mind. Before I took my second shower of the day, I opened my laptop.

Online I typed "kaleidoscope" in the search bar and read a couple of entries about how they are made and the history behind their origin. It wasn't interesting and did nothing to satisfy the nudge I felt on the inside. On impulse, next I searched under "Khamai" and fortuitously, found the answer for which I had been looking. *Khamai*, I learned, meaning ground lion, was from the Greek word *khamaileon*, or instead, chameleon, the reptile best known for its ability to change its appearance.

"I'll be damned," I said aloud and shook my head in flustered embarrassment. Not only had Sunday succeeded in antagonizing me through her profile, she had maneuvered her way into conversing with me through a false profile. It became obvious to me why there were no photos and little information about Khamai; the profile was a fictitious ploy utilized to get closer to me. What was the purpose? Would she have flirted with me and had I returned the exchange, deemed me unworthy of Melanie's love and blasted me as a disgraceful girlfriend? Or did she just want to pry her way into Melanie's life by any possible means? Regardless of the intention, I was grateful that Sunday had made a prompt exit from both of our lives. I pray that it remained that way.

My stomach was giggly and my spirit joyful while I, along with nearly fifty others, quieted behind the closed, curtain covered doors of the reserved section in the upbeat restaurant in which we had gathered. Rick had just sent a text that stated *five minutes* and it was then that I informed everyone that Melanie was on her way.

The room was splendid. I thanked Prestin repeatedly for her assistance in securing the location. Six tables for eight and one for ten decorated in dark cloth and large fresh, floral centerpieces sat about the room with an additional table of buffet style appetizers that consisted of crab stuffed mushroom, almond chicken salad spread, glazed chicken wings, and vegetable rolls. A bartender nearby greeted us with a steady stream of drinks upon request. Prestin, too, was pleased and commented that she would likely collaborate with the owners again.

I had only talked to Melanie once throughout the day and it was just before I left to her surprise party. Quietly I stood in the kitchen while she talked so that she wouldn't hear my heels tap against the floor and question my movement; she was under the assumption that I was spending the evening at home with Ali. She had told me that the guys wanted to take her for a birthday drink before boarding their train. I told her to have a great time and to call me once she arrived in Wisconsin.

Just inside the doors I stood, with Prestin, Jaye, Christina, Landon, Donna, Ivy, and Ali right behind me. Melanie's parents were present along with Ferris and Barbara, Ronan and Jillian, and my own mother who I hadn't seen in months, yet felt compelled to invite nonetheless. After an exaggerated greeting and neutral response from me, she stood near the open bar with Vincent, whose eyes danced around the room observing the open, same-sex loving couples throughout. He was fascinated.

The doorknob turned and I could see Rick take a step backward to let Melanie in. The expression on her face was an irreplaceable blend of terror and astonishment after we all yelled, "Surprise!" She took a startled step backward like one would when stepping into unfamiliar territory. Although a millisecond later she realized what was happening and her composure fell into a relaxed, appreciative state. She bent forward and rested her hands on her knees for a moment, then stood erect, walked toward me and wrapped her arms around me. She held me tightly, squeezing like I'd disappear if she let go. We held on to one another and everyone cheered.

"You're the best, Jo," she told me. "I say it all the time but I truly mean it." She released me and stared down with soft, watery eyes. "What would I do without you?"

I placed a palm to her cheek. "Leave it to me and you'll never have to find out." I stretched my neck up and she bent to kiss me lightly. Then I stepped back and allowed everyone else to greet Melanie and wish her a happy birthday. Melanie gave Jillian an extra big bear hug and thanked her for all that she had done. We all mingled about for an hour before we took our seats and were served family style dishes of chicken and fish with vegetable sides. Ali, who I thought was the only vegan in the room, was served a piece of meatless lasagna.

"Oh, I'm a vegetarian too," Mika spoke up from her table when a waiter walked by. Mika was the saleswoman at the shop where Melanie purchased the majority of her suits and had them tailored to a perfect fit for her body. Mika was an average girl, not tall and not short. She wasn't heavy or thin. She exuded a warm personality at all times and had a pleasing demeanor about her. When I invited her to the party, she was thrilled and graciously accepted. Melanie and I knew little about Mika outside of casual conversation while shopping, and I had not known she didn't fancy meat the way most of us did.

The seat next to Ali was empty. Ali had spoken little with Noni and from what I gathered in conversation with her over the phone that afternoon, it seemed their love affair had at last come to an end. Surprisingly, it was Ali who finally ended the romance. After brief deliberation, Noni had offered to Ali what had been on the plate for seven years: a non-committed, part-time relationship and Ali, suddenly aware of her self-worth and all that she deserved, declined the proposition.

"Hey, Mika, come sit with us," Melanie told her from two tables over. Mika had arrived alone and although she had been engaging in conversation with others, seemed thankful to join us. Melanie introduced her to everyone, and then Mika and Ali fell into an immediate conversation about veganism and vegetarians; was there a difference? The rest of us tuned out.

"Melanie, I spoke with Beverly today. She wanted me to tell you happy birthday," Donna said.

I tapped Melanie's thigh under the table and took a bit of food to hide my smile.

"Be sure to tell her I said thank you," Melanie told her.

"How is Beverly?" Ivy interjected. She had a cool, somewhat patronizing tone in her voice.

"She's wonderful," Donna answered, louder and more firm than I had ever heard her speak with Ivy. "Actually, I need to talk to you about that later."

Everyone took a bite of food in unison. Ivy got up and went to the bar for a drink and Donna pulled out her phone and started typing with a grin on her face.

The remainder of the evening was spent socializing and filling up on libations. I had designated a portion of time to roast Melanie, in which her coworkers, family, and friends told funny stories of Melanie that had all of us, even Melanie, in tears with laughter.

Near the end of the night, just after Prestin, Jaye and I had a conversation with the owner about the spectacular job they did with the party, Ali buzzed by me with a calm, confident look in her eyes. Mika was a few feet behind her.

"The Universe is so amazing," she whispered to me.

I smiled at her. Whether it be the Universe, God, a higher power, or whatever one chose to call the strength from which we draw, it had a way of lighting our paths in just the right direction and leading us just where we are meant to be. I smiled back at her and then at Melanie across the room.

"You're right, it sure is amazing."

Chapter Seventeen

"This is a crazy," Melanie said to me as we made our way through crowds of men and women in Piedmont Park on a Sunday afternoon just before Labor Day. The weather was sunny and inviting, and folks responded, with hundreds of people throughout the park in full celebration. We strolled the grounds for an hour, people watching and chatting with a few faces we recognized from Chicago. By this time we were ready to go and relax prior to attending a party that evening.

Melanie and I had decided to join Prestin and Jaye in Atlanta's largest annual black gay Pride celebration just after Melanie's birthday party. We hadn't been on vacation all year and figured a weeklong trip to Atlanta would serve us just fine with a healthy mix of parties to attend, restaurants to visit, shopping, sight-seeing and resting.

"Where did Prestin and Jaye go?" I asked.

She looked up and down the street. "This way," she said, and then led me to a nearby bookstore and coffee shop. The cool air inside calmed our heated skin, yet even so we ordered two hot mochas. We browsed through the aisles and scanned books while we waited for our drinks. Around one of the corners we spotted Prestin and Jaye seated comfortably in two chairs, each reading a magazine. The park had been a bit overwhelming for both of them and they departed after fifteen minutes.

After my name was called to indicate our drinks were ready, we walked back to the counter to get them. As we headed for the seating area, I saw two women sitting in the corner. One of the women had a pretty face with shoulder length hair and auburn streaks. She beamed adoringly at the woman whose back was to me. What caught my eye was the green crew neck shirt she wore with the NBA's Milwaukee Bucks team logo of a forward-facing deer. Anyone wearing Bucks attire had to have a personal connection to the team or why wear it? I led Melanie toward their table.

"Excuse me," I said. "I don't mean to interrupt but I noticed your T-shirt. You don't see many of those around." I smiled.

She looked down at her shirt and grinned. "My dad sent this shirt to me," she told me.

"Are you from Milwaukee?" I asked.

"Yes, I am," she answered.

"I have family up there," I told her.

"Oh, okay, nice. More proof that black people live in Wisconsin," she laughed. Then her expression changed as if she thought better of the comment, unsure of my heritage, and wasn't sure if she should have said it. The woman across from her smiled and shook her head. She was a stunning beauty, with long black hair, smooth dark skin and beautiful ebony eyes.

"I'm Asia." She touched the embarrassed woman's hand. "And this is Kyla."

"I'm so sorry, I'm Jovanna and this is my partner, Melanie." Melanie said hello to each of them.

"Don't worry about it," I said to put Kyla at ease. "Whenever my family travels, they get that all the time with people thinking none of us live there except the Packers."

"So where are you two from?" Asia asked.

"Chicago," Melanie told them while I took a sip of the vanilla-flavored mocha.

"Chi-town," Kyla said. "Very familiar and so close to home. Next time we visit I told Asia we'd have to spend a few days in Chicago."

"Yeah, I've never been," Asia said. "I'm a southern girl." She smiled.

"You see that woman over there?" I pointed to Jaye dressed casually in white jeans with a fitted gray top. "She's the woman behind Chicago's hottest parties. You have to go to one when you visit."

Both Kyla and Asia looked to Prestin and Jaye. "Her girl-friend?" Asia asked.

"Yes."

She raised her eyebrows. "I guess I do need to get to Chicago," she teased Kyla and they both smiled with amusement.

"Check her out online under Club Murmur. Her name is Prestin," I told them, always glad to bring business Prestin's way.

"We'll do that," Kyla said.

"Well, we'll let you two get back to what you were doing before I intruded. Nice to meet you," I told them.

"Same to you," they both replied.

Melanie nodded her head and we decided to take a seat at a nearby table and allow Prestin and Jaye the quiet they deserved.

A couple of days later Melanie and I were in our hotel room, relaxing in our pajamas after eating a room service breakfast of omelets, toast and juice when her cell phone rang.

"Should I get it?" she asked me.

"Up to you," I told her.

"Damn," she said when she looked at the caller ID and saw her work number. "This is Melanie," she answered. She listened . . . said "yes" and "sure" every few moments. "Okay, thanks, Rick. I'll see you Thursday."

"He's such a proud papa," Melanie said. "He called to tell me he just e-mailed me new pictures of the baby."

"Let me see!"

Melanie sat at the desk and logged onto the internet from

the computer in our room. In her e-mails she pulled up several photos of a red-faced, tight lipped baby wrapped in light blankets.

"He's so cute," I said after viewing all the photos, a total of ten.

Melanie continued to browse her e-mails. It was obvious she hadn't checked them in a while with the number of unread messages she had. She skimmed through them and found an e-mail from the day before sent from the networking site. It said that Kyla69Asia wanted to be friends.

"Hey, your bookstore pals sent a friendship request," she told me.

"Oh, really?" I asked, curiously.

"Want me to accept? I bet they sent one to you too."

"I'll check later," I said.

Melanie clicked on the link in the body of the e-mail to log onto the site. "I haven't been on here in forever. Look at this."

My heart fluttered as I was unsure if Sunday had attempted contact with her again.

"What's going on?"

"Just some updates and upgrades I haven't seen," she answered and I exhaled. I watched her check her requests for friendship until she found Kyla and Asia. The profile photo was a sweet picture of the two of them sitting on steps, with Asia's arms wrapped around Kyla from behind. The message sent with their request said: Found you both through Prestin's profile. Looks like a great time and we hope to connect on our next trip home. Until then, friends?

Melanie and I looked at one another.

"They seem nice enough," I said.

"What do you think?" she asked.

"I guess it couldn't hurt?" I stated, but more as a question.

We contemplated a moment. Prior to our rocky episode

with Sunday, we had not previously felt the need to carefully debate who we accepted as friends in our cyber space. However, Sunday's antics had created a quiet concern about the authenticity, genuineness, and frankly, the sanity of those we allowed to share in our world, even from afar. We had resolved to the belief that the Sunday's of our online friends represented just a small percentage of those with untrustworthy intentions. We had decided to proceed with caution and accept only those who appeared sincere. Then see if they proved righteous in our observation. If not, the delete key was always an option.

Melanie finally clicked the button to approve the request. We stared at the computer like we expected it to do something.

"Done," she said. "No flirty comments."

"No private lunches."

"What? They don't even live in Chi," she defended.

"I know. I'm just saying," I teased.

She logged off the site and we crawled back under the covers. I nestled my head in the cradle of her arms and she stroked my hair.

"Jo," Melanie said.

"Hmm?"

"I don't have any pudding."

"You ate all the pudding already?" I asked. We had purchased three cartons when we arrived and placed them in the small refrigerator in our room.

"I did."

"Greedy."

She laughed and ran her fingers over the curve of my body and down my thigh. "So what can I eat now?"

"What would you like?"

"I know something that's almost better than chocolate pudding." She kissed my neck.

"And what's that?"

She turned me over until I rested on my back. She lowered her head until it rested between my legs. She tugged at my pajama bottoms. "May I?" she asked.

"Anything for you, Mel. Anything."

ORDER FORM
URBAN BOOKS, LLC
78 E. Industry Ct
Deer Park, NY 11729

Name:(please print):_____

Address: _____

City/State: _____

Zip: _____

QTY	TITLES	PRICE
	The Cartel	$14.95
	The Cartel#2	$14.95
	The Dopeman's Wife	$14.95
	The Prada Plan	$14.95
	Gunz And Roses	$14.95
	Snow White	$14.95
	A Pimp's Life	$14.95
	Hush	$14.95
	Little Black Girl Lost 1	$14.95
	Little Black Girl Lost 2	$14.95
	Little Black Girl Lost 3	$14.95
	Little Black Girl Lost 4	$14.95

Shipping and Handling - add $3.50 for 1st book then $1.75 for each additional book.

Please send a check payable to:

Urban Books, LLC

Please allow 4 - 6 weeks for delivery

ORDER FORM
URBAN BOOKS, LLC
78 E. Industry Ct
Deer Park, NY 11729

Name:(please print):_____

Address: _____

City/State: _____

Zip: _____

QTY	TITLES	PRICE
	16 ½ On The Block	$14.95
	16 On The Block	$14.95
	Betrayal	$14.95
	Both Sides Of The Fence	$14.95
	Cheesecake And Teardrops	$14.95
	Denim Diaries	$14.95
	Happily Ever Now	$14.95
	Hell Has No Fury	$14.95
	If It Isn't love	$14.95
	Last Breath	$14.95
	Loving Dasia	$14.95
	Say It Ain't So	$14.95

Shipping and Handling - add $3.50 for 1st book then $1.75 for each additional book.
Please send a check payable to:
Urban Books, LLC
Please allow 4 - 6 weeks for delivery